Love, Honor or Stray:

New Day Divas Series Book Three

Love, Honor or Stray:

New Day Divas Series Book Three

E.N. Joy

URBAN
CHRISTIAN

www.urbanchristianonline.net

Urban Books, LLC
78 East Industry Court
Deer Park, NY 11729

Love, Honor or Stray: New Day Divas Series Book Three
Copyright © 2010 E.N. Joy

ISBN 13: 978-1-60162-866-4
ISBN 10: 1-60162-866-8

First Printing December 2010
Printed in the United States of America

10 9 8 7 6 5 4 3 2 1

*This is a work of fiction. Any references or similarities to actual
events, real people, living, or dead, or to real locales are intended
to give the novel a sense of reality. Any similarity in other names,
characters, places, and incidents is entirely coincidental.*

Distributed by Kensington Corp.
Submit Wholesale Orders to:
Kensington Publishing Corp.
C/O Penguin Group (USA) Inc.
Attention: Order Processing
405 Murray Hill Parkway
East Rutherford, NJ 07073-2316
Phone: 1-800-526-0275
Fax: 1-800-227-9604

Love, Honor or Stray

New Day Divas Series Book Three

E. N. Joy

Dedication

Giving much honor and love to my Father in Heaven.
I will not stray from His word.

Acknowledgment

For my editor, Kevin. I thank you for your keen eye and style of writing. I thank you even more for sharing it with me so that I can become a better writer with each and every book. And thank you for not chewing me out for making the same repeated mistakes book after book (the long sentences . . . I don't know why I try to write how I talk, trying to say everything in one breath). I thank you for following the dramatic lives of my characters for the past three books. I can honestly say that these women would not be the divas that they are without your input. Behind every good diva is a good man; and for the New Day Divas, that man is you, Kevin.

Other Books by this Author

Me, Myself and Him
She Who Finds a Husband
Been There, Prayed That

Chapter One

"Eleven-seventy-seven Covenant Park," Deborah said to herself as she stared down at the address on the printed e-mail.

She sat in her car parked in front of the residential address that she had assumed would be an office building of some sort. "But I'm almost certain it said to meet him at his office." Deborah shuffled around the trail of back and forth e-mails she had accumulated with Mr. Born, a.k.a. Born2Write@writersworld.com.

Since returning from her three-month sabbatical a couple of weeks ago, it seemed as though Deborah had done nothing but sit in front of her computer checking e-mails. She'd spent Christmas and New Year's checking e-mails. And when she wasn't checking e-mails, she was checking voice mail messages. While away, she hadn't used her cell phone or e-mail. She had cut off all communication with everybody; that is with the exception of God. Her pastor of New Day Temple of Faith was the only person who knew how to get in touch with her in case of an emergency. There had been no emergencies.

Upon returning home, she was greeted with a cell phone with a full voice mail box. Even though the voice mail greeting informed callers that she would be unavailable until December, many had opted to leave messages anyway. Then there were the gazillion e-mails that needed her attention. She had no idea that many messages could be stored. AOL wasn't playing when they said "unlimited e-mail storage."

The Deborah three months ago, along with the average person, would have lost her mind had she had to deal with such a tedious task. But the new refreshed, cleansed, and restored Deborah wasn't fazed by the workload that awaited her. In order to clear out her voice mail box, she had given her voice mail messages her immediate attention. With a notepad in hand, she'd listened to every single message, writing down the caller's name, subject matter of their message, and return contact info. She then went down the list and returned each call that required feedback. This had taken her almost a week alone. The e-mails were another story. She was still working on those, although she'd managed to acknowledge a good chunk of them. Mr. Born was among the chunk.

After several e-mails back and forth, it typically taking Deborah a day or two to respond to him, they'd decided to meet up. Mr. Born was interested in Deborah doing some literary consultation with him and several people he knew who were interested in self-publishing. He'd written in one of his e-mails that he, along with three others in an online writing group he belonged to, decided that they wanted to self-publish their books. They'd concluded that with the economy not being on the up and up, and major publishers not giving out book deals like they used to, self-publishing might be the better route for them to go for now. Deborah's name and Web site had been posted to the group as someone who could possibly assist them. After doing their research and choosing Mr. Born as the ring leader, Deborah was contacted.

As the owner and only employee of Everything Literary,

Deborah loved the different hats she wore. For the four years her own literary agency had been in existence, out of editing, literary consulting, and agenting, Deborah adored consulting the most. She loved taking her clients step by step, from just being a writer to being a published author. She, too, had started off wanting to be a published author. She'd written the book and everything; but God had other plans for her. Still, she wasn't giving up completely on the idea of maybe one day being published herself. Who knows? Maybe God still had plans for that two hundred and seventy page manuscript of hers. For now, her mission was to help others reach that status, and it included Mr. Born. Through Mr. Born's e-mails, she could feel the same drive, passion, and determination she'd started out with after penning her novel. She couldn't wait to use him as her muse.

The plan was that since Mr. Born and his friends were scattered about the map, with him being local, she'd do some one on one consulting with Mr. Born, who would then pass on the information to the others. They'd all do some conference calls and online chats here and there, but the majority of the instructions would be between Deborah and Mr. Born.

"Yep, there it is," Deborah said, finally finding the e-mail in which the two had initially set up their meeting. "We can meet at my office. . . ." She read Mr. Born's reply after she suggested they meet instead of sending e-mails back and forth. She'd printed off the contract she had customized to fit him and his fellow writers' specific needs. If all was agreed upon, they'd sign the contract, she'd receive half down for her services, and they'd be in business.

She looked up at the quaint little house that sat about twenty-five feet from the curb. A stone walkway traveled right up the middle of the yard to the front door. Deborah contemplated for a moment before opening the car door. She stood up to look for any signs of life inside. The sun had just started to go down, so she wasn't surprised not to notice any lights beaming from any of the house's windows.

She contemplated a few more seconds before grabbing her messenger bag and purse, all the while keeping her eyes glued on the house. She closed the car door and set the alarm with the remote. The clickety-clack of the heels of her leather winter boots sounded eerie as she headed up the walkway. For a moment there, fear tried to rear its ugly head. "Lord, you have not given me the spirit of fear"—she spoke out loud in an effort to chase away the unwelcome spirit—"but of love and power and . . . and . . . something else, only I'm too scared to remember it right now."

Finally reaching the door, Deborah admired the heavy, oak double doors and the lovely Christmas wreath hanging on them. What she noticed, though, was that one of the doors was slightly cracked. "And a sound mind," she said, recalling the final line of the scripture she'd been confessing." Being that God had given her a sound mind, she knew that what she should have done was turn around and hightail it back to her car. Of course, she didn't. The curiosity of it all had too much of a stronghold on her to allow her to do that.

Slowly, Deborah placed her hand on the gold door knob and pushed on the door just a little. She had fussed out many leading women in thriller movies for doing this exact same thing. Knowing what had become of those leading ladies, she still proceeded to push the door open.

I can't let fear get to me, Deborah told herself. *Mr. Born could be inside hurt or something.* Deborah continued to try to convince herself that perhaps God had brought her there to that place at that specific time to intervene in what could possibly be a tragedy. Perhaps Mr. Born had fallen and couldn't get up. After all, she didn't know his age. He could be some eighty-year-old man lying helpless on the floor. She'd never forgive herself if that were the case; if she let fear prevent her from doing God's will. Yep, all those were things she told herself just to keep from facing the truth: that she was more curious than she was a Good Samaritan.

Taking a deep breath, Deborah pushed the door all the way open, simultaneously calling out Mr. Born's name. Not hearing a response, she stepped inside the foyer while calling out his name again. "Mr. Born. Mr. Born, it's me, Deborah Lewis." Although she didn't hear him reply, she did hear some soft music coming from what sounded like the next room. She couldn't see inside the room, but she could see the opening. It appeared dark with the exception of a very dim light.

"Mr. Born, are you in there?" Deborah called out. When she didn't get a response, she slowly took steps toward the room from which the music was coming. She stopped in her tracks when something flickered. "Mr. Born?" She knew calling out his name would probably be in vain; still, she did it anyway.

She looked behind her at the door she'd left open. She could turn around now and leave if she wanted to. She could turn all five feet, seven and a half inches and one hundred thirty-five pounds around and get the heck out of there. She turned and faced the room again, wondering if Mr. Born was in there injured. Murdered, even. Now she looked back behind her, this time focusing on the door knob. *If I leave now and Mr. Born is in there, victim of a murder, perhaps a robbery gone bad, my prints are all over the door knob.*

A stinging sensation ran through Deborah's veins when she thought there was a chance that this was all a setup: that she'd been set up to take the fall for a murder. She shook the thought out of her head before saying, "The devil is a liar and I have to stop watching all of those prime time crime shows."

With that final thought, Deborah held her head up high, straightened her shoulders, took a deep breath, and walked into that room like she owned the place.

"Oh my God!" With her hand over her mouth in complete shock, Deborah wasn't prepared for the sight before her eyes.

Chapter Two

"I still can't get over what a beautiful wedding you and Blake had," Mrs. Robinson said to her daughter through the phone receiver. "And I couldn't believe how beautiful your dark chocolate skin looked in that snow white gown."

"What I can't believe is that I got this size sixteen body in that size fourteen dress." Paige laughed, revealing her deep dimples even more, dimples that were apparent whether she was smiling or not. "I'd planned on losing weight by next April, which was our original wedding date, of course, but when Blake and I decided we couldn't wait that long to become husband and wife, well . . ." She batted her thick, long eyelashes.

"Girl, you know you just big boned like your mama and all your aunties," Mrs. Robinson reasoned, although she herself wasn't very big at all. "But you're still beautiful, and for once I got to see your hair in something besides that slicked-back ponytail you always wear."

"That style makes my face look thinner," Paige said as she rubbed her cheek. "Not that I'm trying to look like something I ain't, because thin I'm not. But that's all right, because I found me a man who likes all two-hundred-plus pounds of this big-boned woman." No longer able to contain her excitement of being a bride all of a week, she shouted, "Ma, I's married now!"

The mother and daughter both chuckled at the line from the Oscar-slighted movie, *The Color Purple*.

Mrs. Robinson got her laughter under control then sighed. "But it's a shame you two had to postpone your honeymoon."

"Yeah, I know, but this was Blake's golden opportunity on his job to prove himself. So, when his boss told him how important it was that he be at the closing, Blake knew it was now or never. It was really never up for debate between the two of us."

"Let me tell you, that man is just lucky he married such an understanding wife. Some women might have seen it as the man putting his career before his family. After all, you two did have to cancel a honeymoon in Jamaica."

"Actually, we didn't cancel it; we just postponed it. Had we gone, Blake's mind would have been back here in Ohio in his company's boardroom anyway. Blake had been trying to get a meeting with some big shot for months. It just so happened that the day he gets it would have been the third day of our honeymoon."

"And you're not the least bit upset?" Mrs. Robinson sounded slightly doubtful.

"Disappointed maybe, but not upset. Disappointed that I couldn't be like Angela Bassett in *How Stella Got Her Groove Back*, running on the beach, minus the tight-bod," She chuckled. "But elated that his company is going to reimburse us for any loss we had to take, plus pay for the honeymoon once we do take it."

"Well, you sound convincing."

"Ma, I'm not trying to be convincing. Blake proving himself to his company means a higher position, which ultimately means more money, which means I'll be able to get that dream house I want built from the ground up. I've been visualizing it so that it will manifest just like it says to do in that book *The Secret.*"

"Girl, what secret? It ain't no secret. It's God! The Bible been done let that cat out the bag. You being a Christian should know that. What they teaching y'all up there in New Day Temple of Faith anyway?" Mrs. Robinson was using playful sarcasm with her only daughter.

"You know what I mean, Ma. Stop playing. But anyway, when it comes to Blake and his job, I'm straight."

"Child, you are going on thirty years old and are somebody's wife; talking about you straight. You better leave that talk for the hip hoppers and talk like you have the education you do. Is that how you're going to be talking at the dinner parties Blake takes you to and introduces you as his wife?"

"No, Mother dear." Paige rolled her eyes up in her head. "There is a time and a place for that kind of talk. You raised me well, and considering you raised me, you should know that I'm only twenty-eight, thank you very much."

"Twenty-eight, thirty . . . same difference."

"Anyway, to kinda sorta make things up to me, Blake is going to take me out to dinner tonight. We're going to that fondue place where you have to have reservations in advance. His assistant's husband made reservations for them a while ago, but with their child being sick with that swine flu he caught on their trip to Mexico, they can't make it. So, she gave her reservation to Blake."

"That sounds nice. It's no Jamaica, but nice nonetheless."

"I've never been, so I think—" Just then Paige's other line clicked. She looked down at the face of the phone. Blake's office number appeared on the screen. "Ma, that's my husband. I'll call you later." She blushed. "Husband. That's my husband."

Now it was Mrs. Robinson who rolled her eyes. "Go on and talk to your *husband*. And tell that son-in-law of mine that his father-in-law is still waiting to show him around the construction business, for real this time."

Paige recalled the visit she and Blake had made to her parents' house. The visit was when Blake was supposed to spend the afternoon with her father, checking out the family construction business. Instead, Blake had just used that as an excuse to get her father alone so that he could ask him for his daughter's hand in marriage. "Okay, Ma. I'll be sure to tell him. I love you. Kiss Daddy for me. Bye."

Paige ended the call with her mother and clicked over to the other line. "Hello, my handsome, butter-complexion, six-feet-tall hunk of a husband, who I can't wait to run my fingers through your soft, wavy hair and then kiss you in places that—"

"Whoa, hold up. I think I better stop you there before my wife gets jealous," was the reply that made Paige blush.

"Oh, I'm sure she won't mind me borrowing you for an hour or two. As a matter of fact, I'm pretty cool with your wife," Paige played along, "so if you really want to get down and dirty, I'm sure the three of us—"

"Please, Mrs. Dickenson, my wife really would get jealous."

That's when Paige realized that the voice on the other end of the phone was just an octave lower than Blake's. "Blake?" Paige held her breath.

"Uh, sorry, Mrs. Dickenson, it's Klyde." He was Blake's best friend and partner in crime at the commercial real estate agency they worked at. "Blake is in a meeting that is running way over, so he sent me a text and asked me to call you."

Paige smiled. Her husband knew her well—well enough to know that she did not do the texting thing on her cell phone. She felt that phones were meant to talk on and computers were meant to type on. Besides that, she could never figure out how to use it anyway, which is why texting wasn't part of her cell phone plan.

"Apparently the meeting is going to run into the dinner hour and he's not going to be able to go to dinner with you tonight," Klyde explained on his friend's behalf.

Paige's smile quickly faded.

"He says to tell you that he's very—" Klyde paused before saying, "Oh, here he is now. He can tell you himself."

Just then Paige heard her husband's voice, for real this time, come through the phone.

"Hi, honey. I only have a second. We broke from the meeting for just a minute. I'm so sorry about tonight." Blake's voice was rushed. "I know taking you to dinner was supposed to be my gratitude for you being so understanding about having to delay the honeymoon and everything, but I am so close to closing this deal that I just know a Bang Bang shrimp appetizer from Bone Fish will do the trick." Bone Fish was the restaurant Blake's company always took their clients to. It had an elegant five star atmosphere and menu choices. The amazing thing about it, though, was that it had next-to-fast-food-restaurant prices.

"But, babe, I didn't eat a single thing all day. I've been saving my appetite and calories for tonight," Paige whined. "I guess we can just cancel and go some other time . . . like with our honeymoon." She let out a deep, pitiful, exaggerated sigh.

"I'd hate for those reservations to go to waste after my assistant was so kind as to pass them on to us. On top of that, I'd hate for you to starve. Maybe you can get Tamarra or someone else to go with you. "

"It won't be the same," Paige pouted. "Plus, I remember Tamarra saying that she and Maeyl are taking his daughter to see *Sesame Street on Ice*, so she's not available. I can always call Sister Deborah up, but she's not too long from being back from her sabbatical. She's been saying how she's been working into the wee hours of the night trying to catch up. I don't know anyone—"

"I've got an idea." He cut off his wife. "See if Norman would like to go with you," Blake suggested.

Paige thought for a moment. "Hmm, I guess I would have never thought of that. Well, okay. He's off work at eight o'clock and the dinner reservation is for nine. I'm sure he'd loved to if he doesn't already have a hot date. But then again, Norman has toned it down quite a bit since he started visiting New Day."

"Great, honey, but look, I gotta go. The meeting is rejoining. Give Norman a call, and tell him to take good care of my wife for me. Okay? And I promise I'll make it up to you. Saturday I'll take you to lunch or something while we get your check engine light on your car looked at, okay?"

"All right, honey, I love—" The click in Paige's ear halted her words. She looked down at the phone. "You." She finished her sentence then hung up the phone.

Although he was the last person she would have imagined having dinner with tonight, Paige picked up the phone again and called Norman. While she invited him out to dinner and he gladly accepted, never once did Paige think about what it might look like to an outsider, the two of them sharing an evening dinner. As she hung up the phone to a growling belly, she didn't care.

Chapter Three

As Maeyl sat at the stoplight, he couldn't help but peep over his shoulder at his snoring little girl. Sakaya was as snug as a bug in a rug in the backseat. Looking at her, he regretted not being in her life for the first three years. In just the last few months, she'd brought him so much joy; he could only imagine all that he'd missed out on. A tinge of guilt tried to creep in, but Maeyl quickly declared the devil that was trying to influence his thoughts a liar. After all, it had not been his fault, nor his decision, not to be a part of his child's life.

Although he could have easily turned guilt into blame, blaming Sasha, the child's mother, he chose not to. Sakaya had been the product of a one night stand between a stripper and a tipper. Just as easily as Maeyl had slipped into Sasha's bed on the same night they'd met, he'd slipped away, not even leaving his contact information. Unbeknownst to him, he'd left behind something far greater than that.

Ashamed at how the child was conceived? Yes, he was. Ashamed of the child? Not in a million years. Fatherhood was becoming to Maeyl. It was becoming to Tamarra also: becoming a pain in the butt.

"Isn't she just the sweetest little girl you've ever known?" Maeyl asked Tamarra, who sat in the passenger seat. His eyes remained glued on his little girl.

"Oh, yes," Tamarra replied in a singsong voice. "She's something, all right." Tamarra looked back at the little girl and tried to muster up the same joy Maeyl was so obviously filled with. But she couldn't. She couldn't to save her life.

"Just think, it won't be long before she becomes your little girl too." Maeyl looked over to his fiancée. "You're about to become a mommy. Aren't you excited?"

Tamarra remained silent as she turned back around to face the road. That's when she realized that Maeyl's question hadn't been rhetorical. He was looking at her . . . waiting on her to tell him just how absolutely beside herself she was to inherit a stepdaughter. God had truly brought her through so much. Did she repay Him now by allowing a lie to roll off of her tongue and then repent later? Or did she tell her husband-to-be the honest to God truth that the last thing she ever wanted in life was to deal with a man with a baby? Which meant, of course, there was a baby's momma to go along with it, and baby's momma drama to top it all off.

God had been too good for her to become a slave to the father of sin by worshipping Satan with a lie. When she accepted Maeyl's proposal to marry him, she knew it was a package deal; she would have to accept his daughter as well. Eventually, she figured, she could, but in the meantime, she had come up with the ol' "fake it until you make it" master plan. Seeing as how drama class had not been one of her electives in high school, she didn't know how believably she could play the role, so before she was found out, she might as well come clean now. And if Maeyl chose not to go forth with the marriage, then so be it. Besides, going into a marriage based on a lie was not a good foundation to build upon.

"You're so excited about becoming Sakaya's other mommy that you're speechless, huh?" Maeyl asked Tamarra.

"Maeyl," Tamarra started, her head down, eyes locked on her fumbling fingers. "About Sakaya and becoming her step-mother and all, I—"

Beep! Beep! Beep!

The blaring horn from the car behind them interrupted their conversation.

"Oh, shoot!" Maeyl looked up in front of him. "Green light." He drove off. "Speaking of green light, Sasha said that Sakaya's doctor gave her the green light to go ahead and enroll into regular pre-school. No special educational needs classes or anything. Just regular schooling with regular kids." Maeyl beamed. "I wish I could find that woman who laid hands on Sakaya and prayed for her after the doctor diagnosed her with symptoms of autism. Her obedience to what the Lord told her to do changed my little girl's life. That woman laid healing hands on my child and changed the course of her life. It's a miracle. My Sakaya is a miracle, and I wouldn't trade her for anything in the world."

"Not even me?" Tamarra thought the color would drain from her oak-with-gloss-finish complexion. It was times like these she wished she wore makeup in order to add a little color to her face. She nervously ran her fingers through her short, natural hair that she'd started growing out.

"Excuse me?" Maeyl wasn't sure if he'd actually heard the words come out of Tamarra's mouth.

Tamarra couldn't believe the words had actually come out. She'd only meant to think the words, not speak them out loud. She looked over to see Maeyl give her a quick glare. He looked at her as if she were a stranger. She felt awful. She wanted to tell Maeyl the truth about how she felt about his newfound daughter, but not this way. Not so crude and blunt.

She looked up and silently said to God, *Forgive me, Lord, for I know exactly what I'm about to do.* She then looked to Maeyl. "I said 'Not even me.' Not even myself . . . Not even I would trade Sakaya for anything in the world." Then came the fake laugh. "Ahe-he."

Maeyl exhaled. "Sweetie, you don't know how good it makes me feel to hear you say that." He leaned over, keeping his eyes on the road, twisted his lips, and planted a kiss on Tamarra's cheek. "That's why you're one of my favorite girls." He then happily drove up the road.

Tamarra turned her head in disgust. Already she'd gone from being Maeyl's favorite girl to just one of his favorite girls. Now she couldn't help but wonder who ranked the highest. Who was Maeyl's most favorite: her or Punky Brewster back there?

Tamarra shook her head in shame. She was a grown woman. She couldn't believe she was comparing herself to a little girl who was just a month shy of turning four. But what was even worse, she knew that if she kept living this lie, she'd spend the next fourteen years competing with this child as well. She wouldn't have peace and security in her and Maeyl's relationship until the child turned eighteen and headed off to college.

The entire situation was driving her stir crazy. She should have gotten out of this relationship when she could, before Maeyl proposed and she accepted. That day she met him at the park with the intentions of breaking things off, she should have just told him. But before she knew it, he'd proposed, she'd accepted, and he'd slipped that beautiful ring on her finger.

Tamarra looked down at the two carat diamond engagement ring. On the day he'd given it to her, the bling on it had her caught like a deer in headlights. It was so beautiful. She'd never had a ring that beautiful. Not even that low down, cheating, having a baby on the side ex-husband of hers had invested in such a gem.

I wonder if I break off the engagement if I'd have to give the ring back. Tamarra flushed that gold-digging thought out of her head quick, fast, and in a hurry, not even knowing where it had come from. She'd never had that type of mindset before when it came to men, so what was going on inside that head of hers now?

She might not have known what was going on inside her head, but she definitely knew what was going on inside of her heart. Too bad her head and her heart just couldn't get on one accord. Why couldn't her heart feel the same way about Maeyl's little girl as it did for the man himself? Perhaps she could just fast and pray, asking God to work on her heart so that eventually it would.

With their wedding date set for late spring/early summer, she knew she only had a few months to get it together. Was that enough time to fall in love with Maeyl's daughter just as easily as she had fallen in love with him?

Chapter Four

"I didn't mean to scare you," the familiar voice spoke over the soft music. "I know you are probably more than surprised to see me right about now." He gave Deborah a mischievous look. "But you didn't think I'd give up that easily, did you?"

Deborah stood in what she now knew to be the dining room in the house. Her mouth hung wide, the opening for words to march out. But none came. Not a single one. Then finally, she was able to speak. "I . . . I can't believe this. Wha . . . what have you done?"

He looked down and helped himself to one of the roses that sat in a vase in the middle of the dining room table. "Isn't it obvious?" He slowly walked toward Deborah while smelling the rose. "I've fallen in love." He extended the rose to her.

At first she just stood there staring down at the rose, still in awe at the sight before her. There were roses, dozens of them, in vases all around the room. There were flickering candles, scented ones. Deborah inhaled: vanilla candles. A bottle of sparkling cider sat in an ice bucket next to the roses on the dining room table. There was a place setting for two. It looked to be fine china and silverware. The flutes at each setting waited to be drenched with the non-alcoholic chilled beverage. The laced table cloth, a slightly dingy white, looked as though it might have belonged to his grandmother, probably the china too.

She met her hand with his, momentarily taken in by the delightful ambiance. Deborah quickly snapped out of her vanilla-scented trance. She demanded her hand take its rightful place by her side without the likes of the rose.

"Still up to your same old tricks again, huh, Mr. Chase?" Deborah asked with a glare, shaking her head. "First your little stunt at Family Café and now this."

"Deborah—"

"Miss Lewis," she corrected him.

He relented with a smile. "Okay, Miss Lewis. I'm not sure what you mean by my little stunt at Family Café. I remember you rambling something about me arranging a bogus meeting. I didn't know what you were talking about then, and I don't know what you are talking about now."

He wasn't lying. He had no idea what she was talking about because he hadn't been involved in setting up any bogus meeting. Right before she'd left for her sabbatical, Deborah thought he'd gotten someone to pretend to be a prospective client just so she would agree to a meeting. With every intention of meeting this so-called prospective client at Family Café, Deborah was shocked when Lynox showed up. Initially, she thought he'd tricked her. When she later learned at Mother Doreen's going away potluck dinner that there really had been a real client, that the meeting was legitimate, she had to admit that she had been wrong. But still, him just happening to be there, as if he'd been stalking her, was considered a stunt in her book.

"If I were going to set up some bogus meeting with you, Miss Lewis, trust me, it wouldn't have been at the Family Café. It would have more like . . ." He looked around, impressed by his own handiwork. "Something more like this."

She'd known from the first time she met him that Mr. Ly-nox Chase was persistent, but she was certain she'd seen the last of him that day in Family Café when she'd spit her lemon water all over him. Not only that, but she'd snapped at him and practically threw his manuscript he'd wanted her to shop as his agent back at him. What man in his right mind would still want to deal with a woman capable of all that?

That's it! Deborah had figured it out. This man standing before her had to be out of his mind.

"You're out of your mind, Mr. Chase, to think that I would fall for this . . . this . . . this whatever it is you're trying to do," she told him. "I am a child of the Most High. God is not go-ing to allow me to be ignorant of the enemy's devices."

"Good, because I'm not the enemy. If I were, then why would God have allowed you to even come here in the first place, let alone come inside? I mean, what woman besides those crazies in those horror movies would have actually come into a stranger's dark house? Are you kidding me?"

Deborah had to admit that he had a point, a good one. Why had God allowed her to come here? If it was a trick of the enemy, why had she fallen for it? Why hadn't she gotten one single suspicion about the entire Mr. Born thing? She didn't have the answers, but for now she had the solution, and that was to get out of there.

"Whatever, Mr. Chase. If I've told you once, I'm telling you again, I don't have time for games. I hope you enjoy your evening." On that note, Deborah turned on her heels and headed back toward the front door.

"But wait!" Lynox called out. Deborah stopped, but didn't turn back around to face him, to face the brown-skinned, me-dium height, sculptured figure. He took a couple of steps in her direction and turned on the light.

"I didn't know what else to do. You wouldn't take my phone calls, you blocked my e-mail address." He paused before continuing. "I had gone to eat at Family Café at least a dozen times before God showed me favor and you finally showed up." He took another step toward her. "And I promise you on everything, before I'd walked into that restaurant, I'd said a prayer to God. I had told him, 'Lord, if this is meant to be, then let it be, because this is my last time coming here.' And I'd meant it. If you didn't show up, I was going to let things go . . . let you go. But you did show up, and now I can't . . . I can't let you go."

Deborah's heart almost melted like the candle wax. She slowly turned to face him. She noticed his fresh haircut, a nice, tight fade. She blushed within at the thought he'd gotten a fresh cut just for her.

"I'd heard Family Café was the town restaurant that everyone went to, so I knew sooner or later you would too." He grabbed his stomach. "I only wish it had been sooner. You have no idea what those twelve bowls of chili did to my digestive system."

Deborah chuckled.

"Ah ha! The lady laughs." Lynox pointed at Deborah, happy to finally see some emotion other than anger displayed. "Anyway, I'm sorry . . . about everything. Will you forgive me?" Once again, Lynox extended the rose to Deborah that he still held in his hand.

And once again, she stared down at the rose. After a few seconds of contemplation, she accepted it. "Because I am a woman of God, I must obey Jesus and forgive you."

Lynox cheered up. "Great." He rubbed his hands together. "Does that mean you'll stay? I made a wonderful chicken parmesan dinner."

Deborah looked around at the romantic surroundings. Not even recalling the last time she'd had an evening appetizer with a man, let alone a romantic dinner, she knew if she stayed, there was a chance she'd end up being dessert—or the brown-skinned hunk of a man standing before her would be hers. That was a chance she didn't want to take. Well, she wanted to—her flesh did, anyway—but she couldn't. She wouldn't. For His name's sake.

"Sorry, Mr. Chase, but it's a no." She turned around and walked away before she could even consider changing her mind. She swooped a couple of her sister-locks out of her face before exiting his front door.

"You haven't seen the last of me, Miss Lewis," Lynox said with a smile as he watched her walk to her car.

Deborah got into her car and started it up, thinking, *I hope not, Mr. Chase. I hope not.* After inhaling the sweet fragrance of the rose, she pulled away from Lynox's home, but not his heart.

Chapter Five

"I cannot believe what a wonderful time I had," Paige told Norman as they exited the fondue restaurant. "And you know you a fool, right?" Paige laughed. "Sitting up in there with a bib on like you're a toddler or something." She looked him up and down. "With your big ol', grown self."

"Laugh all you want." Norman popped the collar of his multi-colored, expensive dress shirt as he walked Paige to her car. "But it's not like I can afford another Versace shirt on my salary. I wasn't about to drip any of that fondue stuff on me, especially the chocolate from the dipped strawberries." Norman closed his eyes and licked his lips in remembrance. He opened them again and looked down at his shirt, double checking that he hadn't spilled any chocolate on it. "I wouldn't even have this one if what's-her-name hadn't bought it for me while we were in Vegas."

"Who's what's-her-name?"

Norman thought for a minute. "Hmm . . . I don't recall. I guess it's really true what they say: What happens in Vegas stays in Vegas."

"Yeah, Norman, but I don't think they meant the names of people you go with, especially people who buy you expensive gifts." Paige stopped and rubbed the soft fabric of Norman's shirt. "Hmm, nice." She made the final few steps to her car.

"Well, you know how I do it." He smiled and ran his hands down his gelled, dirty blonde hair.

With a grin on her face, Paige asked, "What is it with all the white guys wearing their hair like that boy in *Twilight*? To me it looks like he has a *Something About Mary* thing going on." She quickly looked to Norman, hoping she hadn't offended him. "But not you, of course. Yours looks good on you." She patted his hair playfully. "Oh, wow, and it's soft." She looked down at her hand. "I expected it to cut me. Seems like it would be hard and spiky."

"Where have you been? The days of Dippity-do hair gel and Aqua Net spray are long gone. There is stuff on the market now to make it stiff but keep it soft."

There was awkward silence. Paige cleared her throat. "I'll leave that one alone."

"As you should, you being a Christian and all. But I really wasn't trying to be funny or—" Norman seriously began apologizing before Paige cut him off.

"I know, I know." She put her hands up to let him know it was okay.

Back before she got saved, Norman would have deliberately made a comment like that to Paige. She and Norman would have taken the comment and run a mile with it, as most of their conversations had involved the adventures of single-hood, dating, and mating. But not now that Paige had been saved for well over two years.

Only a few months ago Norman would have those same conversations with Paige, but they would be one-sided. Eventually, Paige got frustrated that Norman wouldn't respect the fact that she was a Christian and continued to talk to her as if she were still in the world. That all changed a few months ago when she invited him to a church service at New Day. He got to experience firsthand a move of the God Paige now served. After that, not only did he respect God, but he respected Paige's walk with God.

"Anyway, I can't thank you enough for inviting me to dinner with you tonight. Blake is going to be sorry he missed it. But his loss is my gain."

"Thank you for coming. I can't think of a better date—besides my husband, of course. And thanks for walking me to my car."

"Well, you said that Blake said for me to take good care of you. If you know anything about me, it's that I know how to take care of a woman."

Paige pursed her lips, tilted her head, and with furrowed eyebrows, shot Norman a glare.

"Oh, my bad." He forced a grin. "Some old habits are hard to break."

Paige smiled. "Not to worry, my friend. Keep coming back to New Day, and between Pastor's preaching, the Holy Ghost's conviction, and a miracle from God Himself, you'll be delivered and all those old habits will be forgotten . . . like what's-her-name in Vegas." Paige winked.

"You know something? You really are cool, boss," Norman complimented. "And I think I will come visit New Day again. It's been a couple of months. Lord only knows how much sinning I've done in those months that call for repenting."

"You know we always love to see you there. And don't feel bad; I'm there pretty much every Sunday, and I still find myself having to repent on occasion."

"Like your pastor preached that one time: We have to die daily to ourselves."

"So you do be listening?" Paige joked. "Yes, my brother, we are all a work in progress."

"Speaking of work, tomorrow's Saturday. Early morning, long day."

"You're right," Paige agreed, unlocking her car door. "Thanks again for being my date tonight."

Norman gave her a hug. "The pleasure was all mine." He went to give her a friendly kiss on the cheek, but she turned quickly, preparing to make one final comment. With her mouth open, Norman's lips landed on hers. Realizing that it wasn't her cheek his lips were pressed against, Norman quickly pulled away. Okay, not quickly, but eventually he pulled away.

"I'm sorry," they both said simultaneously. "No, I'm sorry." Again, simultaneously. "I was trying to—" Simultaneously. "Good night." Simultaneously.

Paige watched as Norman scurried off to his car. She pressed her index and middle finger against her lips, still in disbelief that the lips of a man other than her husband had just been there. She put her entire hand over her mouth, trying to cover the smile that for some reason she couldn't stop from forming. She chuckled like a school girl, and then laughed even harder as she said to herself, "Well, Norman, looks like you ended up getting a little bit of chocolate on you anyway."

Chapter Six

"You won't be sorry that you hired me, Sister Tamarra. I promise you," Unique said as she tied the apron around her waist. For the past two weeks, she had helped Tamarra set up a catering affair or two, but today would be her first time actually serving. Having this job meant the world to Unique. After a conversation she'd had with Lorain, the Singles' Ministry leader, she'd considered doing something with herself besides sitting on welfare. Lorain had made a valid point to Unique. She'd informed her that sitting on welfare wasn't paying into social security, and that if anything, God forbid, was to happen to Unique, where would money come from to take care of her children? Unique's three boys meant the world to her.

Tamarra had been contemplating hiring some extra hands for her catering business for a while now. In spite of all the turmoil her personal life seemed to be caught up in, her business was booming. Word of mouth had nearly doubled Tamarra's clientele in the last six months or so. Just two weeks ago she'd invested in a new catering van and two new employees, one of them being Unique, her New Day sister in Christ.

Unique's position doing setup and serving only called for a few hours a week, but that was all the time she could spare as a single mother of three young sons. Tamarra knew that eight dollars an hour for a less than part-time position wasn't big money, but she knew Unique would appreciate the opportunity.

"I know I won't be sorry I hired you, Unique." Tamarra smiled, grateful to see such determination and excitement in the twenty-three-year-old mother.

Tamarra didn't know a whole lot about Unique. She'd only really started getting to know her since Unique had taken over the position of co-leader of the New Day Singles' Ministry. For the past month or so, with Lorain being on a sabbatical, Unique had been serving as the interim leader. She'd been handling both her duties well as she now stood in a party house with Tamarra about to serve food to more than seventy-five women of all ages.

The women were members of a national book club with various chapters throughout the country. Every other year one of the chapters hosted an annual book club meeting with a featured author. This year the Columbus chapter was hosting and the guest author was someone named Tysha. Tamarra had never heard of the author, but Unique seemed to know exactly who the young lady was.

"Not only do I have a job, a real paying job, no under the table flim-flam stuff, but I am about to serve food to an *Essence* magazine bestselling author." Unique clapped her hands together. "God is good." She noticed that Tamarra wasn't as excited. "You do know who Tysha is, right?"

"With the way you're acting, I guess I should, but sad to say, I don't. Does she write Christian fiction?"

"Oh, no, far from it. She writes that street lit stuff—hood books—and I love 'em."

"Then that explains it. I try to stick to Christian fiction and some clean chick lit."

"I feel you," Unique said, putting on some plastic gloves.

Tamarra smiled. The girl had listened when she'd explained to her how important it was to wear gloves when handling food.

"Street lit probably would be a bit much for someone your age." Unique looked Tamarra up and down. "No offense. I can just tell that you're not the typical street lit following."

"'Scuse me," Tamarra said playfully, hands on hips. "I'll have you know that I own and have read every Donald Goines and Iceberg Slim book ever written. Now, you wanna talk some real gangsta lit . . . boom!" Tamarra sucked her teeth, snapped her neck, and rolled her eyes. Both women burst out laughing. Forty-something or not, Tamarra could be hip when need be.

"Okay, all right, Sister Tamarra. I see you, boo," Unique said. "I had you pegged wrong. My bad. You do know a little somethin'-somethin' 'bout that gangsta stuff."

"Know a little somethin'-somethin' about it? Girl, back in high school you might as well have called me *gangstress*." Tamarra gave a snap around the world.

"Okay, Sister Tamarra, now you're exaggerating just a little too much." Unique chuckled.

"Hmm . . ." Tamarra slouched her shoulders and stared off as if reminiscing. "I wish I was, Sister Unique." She shook her head at some of the things she had done back in her hoodlum stage of high school, back when she was rebelling against her parents, and God, for all the bad things they'd allowed to happen to her.

She had been suspended and assigned to Saturday school more times than she could count. As a freshman in high school, she missed more classes than she attended, always cutting to hang out with some upperclassmen boy. She got a reputation by doing so, but not a good one. Still, by the time she was a junior, deep inside, a part of all the girls wanted to be just like her. She was their alter ego, that chick who wasn't afraid to do whatever she wanted whenever she wanted to do it.

Tamarra's mother missed so much work having to take off and go up to the school that she lost more than one job throughout Tamarra's high school years. Just once, Tamarra wanted her father to come all the way from Maryland and show up at one of the meetings. She just wanted him to show that he cared. She wanted him to love her more than he loved protecting her brother, the brother that had raped her as a child and stolen her innocence. She wanted the charade to be over. He never came. So, Tamarra would always top off her last incident with something worse, hoping eventually her father would come. Still, he never came.

Thankful for Tamarra, though, in her senior year, Missy Swanson, the new girl, did come. Missy, too, was a girl who did whatever she wanted whenever she wanted. She was a rebel, but she was a rebel for the Lord. When told she had to do a book report of some sort, Missy did it on a book in the Bible, reading her Bible during study hall and free time in class. During lunch, she'd hold her own little Bible study, a big no-no since, like Mary's little lamb, Missy's lamb, Jesus Christ, wasn't really allowed in school either. Missy and her lamb were kicked out, from the cafeteria anyway, but that didn't stop her. She and her growing group would pack their lunches and hold their Bible study outside.

"Jesus is the answer," were the four words Missy said to Tamarra one day in passing. It was those four words that planted the seed that ultimately led Tamarra to her salvation. It was also the beginning of a friendship for the two girls.

For some reason, Tamarra was led to tell Missy of the things she had endured in her young life. She shared with her the details of her brother raping her and how her parents dealt with it. Well, she didn't outright tell Missy that the things had happened to her; she told Missy that they'd happened to a friend of hers. But Missy knew, and Missy never judged her; she only prayed for her. Not once during that school year did anything that Tamarra ever said to Missy get back to her.

Missy was an army brat, so before the school year was even over, she and her family were off to another state. She and Tamarra never even vowed to exchange phone numbers and addresses to keep in touch. It was unsaid, but they both knew that God had placed them in each other's lives for a mere season, and for that they were grateful.

A smile now covered Tamarra's lips as she stood in the party house thinking back to who she used to be, just like it was yesterday. She couldn't help but thank God that she was no longer that person.

"The author has arrived," the Columbus chapter president said, sticking her head in the kitchen. "You ladies can begin serving now." She smiled, then quickly disappeared again.

"You all set?" Tamarra asked Unique.

"All set," she confirmed, then picked up a tray of barbeque meatballs and exited the kitchen.

"I'm right behind you," Tamarra told her.

After Unique was out of sight, Tamarra took a long, deep breath. Thoughts of the past about high school and Missy had momentarily taken her back to a place she wished she could completely forget. She knew, though, that no matter how hard she tried, those memories would always be embedded deep in her heart.

She picked up a relish tray and held her head high before exiting the kitchen. With the turn of events that were about to take place in her life, how long she'd be able to keep her head held high was yet to be determined.

Chapter Seven

"Are you sure your business in Kentucky isn't over with yet?" Deborah asked Mother Doreen over the phone. "You sure you don't want to come back to New Day and run the Singles' Ministry?"

"Is that the only reason why you want me back there? To work me?" Mother Doreen teased. "And I thought you really missed me."

"Now, Mother Doreen, you know I miss you something awful, but somehow I got dragged back into working with the Singles' Ministry."

"Why? What happened? Sister Lorain didn't work out?" Mother Doreen sounded concerned.

"No, she worked out just fine, but she's on a sabbatical. You know she had some type of accident. Fell and hit her head, lost part of her memory, and came back to church thinking Sister Unique was her daughter."

"Lord, have mercy. I didn't hear about that. I haven't really been staying in touch with my New Day family like I should," Mother Doreen confessed. "Things here in Kentucky were just more than I thought I could bear, but God saw me through."

"He always does."

"Amen," Mother Doreen agreed. "But go back to Sister Lorain thinking that Sister Unique was her daughter."

"Oh, yes. Apparently Pastor had assigned Sister Unique to help assist Sister Lorain with the Singles' Ministry. The two had obviously grown close in working together; so close that after Sister Lorain's accident and her coming back to church, she saw Sister Unique and thought she was her daughter. Everybody laughed it off, but I don't know, Mother Doreen. My spirit tells me that there's something more to it."

"Well, I'll tell you what: you better get your master's degree in *Kneeology*. Stay on your knees praying and stay on your face in the Lord to make sure you're hearing clearly from Him," Mother Doreen warned. "Don't let Satan try to infiltrate your thoughts like I almost let him do while here in Kentucky. Had I not started to hear clearly from God when I did, I might have jeopardized my relationship with a good man of G–" Mother Doreen cut off her own words. She'd said too much. Way too much.

There was a moment of silence while Deborah waited on Mother Doreen to finish. Mother Doreen had no intention of finishing. The cat's tail was already wagging out of the bag; she didn't need the whole feline creeping out.

"Go on. You were saying, Mother Doreen," Deborah pressed.

Mother Doreen thought for a second, trying to find a way out of the hole she'd dug for herself. There was only one way out. "Oh, well, I might as well tell you. I met someone. A man. A man of God."

"My, my, my, so that's what's keeping you in Kentucky," Deborah teased. "And here I thought you were down there on assignment."

"I was on assignment. I am on assignment. I mean I–Oh, girl, you got me all flustered and twisted up."

"And I bet beads of sweat are dancing all over your forehead too." Deborah chuckled. "But don't blame me. My spirit also tells me that it ain't me who's got you all flustered and twisted up."

"Sounds like to me, child, you better get that spirit of yours in check before it gets you in trouble. It might need a tune-up or something."

"Mm-hmm, whatever, Mother Doreen. I'm going to let you slide for now, but don't think you're off the hook."

"Now, wait a minute. Who's the elder here?" Mother Doreen reminded Deborah that she was a couple of decades her senior.

"No disrespect, Mother Doreen, but I gotta watch out for you. Black don't crack. You lookin' good for your age. I'm going to have to come pay you a visit in Kentucky and regulate. Let those male callers down there know who they are dealing with: a child of the King on assignment doing Kingdom work." Deborah decided to throw in a little playful sarcasm. "And from the sounds of it, your work is never done. You're putting in overtime."

"Oh, child," Mother Doreen lightheartedly scolded, "you done came back from that sabbatical fresh and brand new. Humph! And if I remember correctly from my younger days, besides turning your life over to Christ, only one other thing makes you feel that way."

"Oh yeah?" Deborah baited.

" Yeah. L-O-V-E. Love."

"Then I guess you would know."

"Listen, baby, I have to go. My nephew's baby momma is getting an ultrasound today to find out the sex of their baby."

"Baby?"

"Child, like I said: we got a lot of catching up to do. You wouldn't believe half the stuff that happened for those three months you were away. Just pray for us."

"I will."

"And we'll talk again. Send everyone at New Day my love."

"I will, considering you've got lots of love to go around." Deborah threw in one last comment in reference to Mother Doreen's male interest. "As Sister Unique's generation would say, don't hate, celebrate. Or even better, participate."

"Oh, Lord, help her." Mother Doreen laughed.

"Talk to you later." Deborah ended the call with laughter on her tongue. "That Mother Doreen is something else," she said out loud to herself as her computer beeped, signaling she had an e-mail. She almost forgot she had been sitting at her desk replying to e-mails before Mother Doreen called.

Deborah looked at her computer screen to see that the new e-mail was from Born2Write, whom she now knew to be Lynox. She shook her head, smiling at his refusal to give up his pursuit of her.

For a minute she thought to just delete the e-mail, but for some reason, that curious spirit had been guiding her decision-making process. A part of her knew that if she cracked open that e-mail, she was as good as cracking open an icky, sticky can of worms. But with that final thought, she opened and read the e-mail anyway. After doing so, she typed a reply. The reply sat on her computer screen for ten minutes before she built up her nerve to hit the send button.

She'd done it. She'd taken one of the worms from the opened can; she'd baited her hook and cast her pole. Now she sat back in anticipation, waiting on a bite.

"What am I getting myself into?"

Chapter Eight

"You did what?" Tamarra shouted as she and Paige sat on Paige's living room sofa.

They'd had many talks on that sofa in the past couple of years. Even though the couch now sat in Blake's premarital home instead of Paige's, nothing had changed. They still enjoyed their sista-girlfriend talks all the same.

Paige and Blake had decided to get rid of Paige's premarital dwelling and reside at his since it was bigger. But this was just temporary until they could get their dream house built. That was one of the reasons Blake was working exceptionally hard. He wanted to make sure that they could afford the house they desired. He didn't want to end up like so many couples who had bitten off more house than they could afford. The two agreed that they wanted to enjoy their residence and not be so burdened by paying the note on it that they couldn't appreciate it. Blake, especially, had been adamant about that.

As a very small child, after his father was seriously injured on the job and confined to a wheelchair, his mother grew weary of taking care of him. She grew weary and tired of taking care of them—her husband and her only son. As quiet as it was kept, she'd grown weary of taking care of her only daughter too; but because she was a female, Blake had supposed, his mother felt forced to continue to care for her. So, that's what she did: one day while his father was in the television room and little Blake was napping, his mother scooped up his sister and left. Before doing so, she'd served his father a tuna sandwich, potato chips, applesauce, and grape Kool-Aid. She'd left Blake's in the refrigerator; then she vanished as if she'd never been there.

Blake's father never tried to locate her, and he never divorced her. To this day, Blake hadn't tried to find her either. He'd been only three years old when she left. He only vaguely remembered her or his slightly older sister. He didn't miss what he never recalled having—or so he had convinced himself.

He and his father lived off of his dad's social security benefits for a while. Then eventually, after years of fighting in court, a jury finally awarded his father a huge settlement from the job in which he'd been injured. With that money, his father moved them from their house into a nice little, affordable condo. Nurses and home health aides came in weekly to assist them, but Blake had learned to care for his father and insisted on doing the bulk of the care.

By the time Blake was eighteen, he'd been awarded a partial scholarship to Bowling Green College. His father paid all of his remaining expenses, including room and board. Despite the many challenges Blake's father had suffered in his life, he saw to it that he and his son had the best they could possibly have. They never lived above their means, but always had enough and then some. Blake was truly inspired by his father, who died shortly after Blake graduated college. Blake vowed that he'd walk in his father's footsteps and persevere in life. His dedication and perseverance were just some of the things Paige admired about Blake.

The couch was one of the few things he'd allowed her to keep, vowing their new life together called for new things, including furniture. After a week of going back and forth, the couch stayed. Blake had only given in because it had been a gift to Paige from her parents.

Paige hugged one of the throw pillows on the couch. "I kissed Norman," she confessed again to Tamarra. She sat giggling and looking all starry-eyed like she didn't have the sense that the good Lord had given her. "Well, actually he kissed me. Come to think of it, we kinda sorta kissed each other. On second thought—"

"Blah, blah, blah," Tamarra interrupted. "All I want to know is, was there a kiss?"

Paige paused and then screeched, "Yes." She buried her face in the pillow in giddy embarrassment. "But it was an accident. All he really meant to do was kiss me on the cheek, but then I turned to say something to him and our lips just met."

Tamarra sat back and relaxed. "Oh, thank God." She let out a deep breath. "I thought you were talking about a real kiss. Girl, you had my heart racing." She playfully swatted Paige's hand, but then got serious, sitting up straight. "But do you mind me asking why you seem to be all in La-La Land about this?"

"I'm not really in La-La Land," Paige said. "I just thought it was cute. I mean, it was like a scene out of a movie. I mean, who would have thought it? Me, attracting a white boy?"

"What are you talking about? You said you've dated a couple of Caucasian men before."

"I know, but it's different with Norman. In all the years I've known him, he's never once showed the slightest interest in me. Besides that, he usually goes for the small, model type girls." Paige chuckled and observed her body. "And trust me, I'm nobody's model."

Tamarra sat staring at Paige for a moment.

"What?" Paige asked when Tamarra didn't speak, but only stared at her.

Tamarra was wondering if Paige was for real, if she'd been for real all this time about who she was—about being happy with her size. Was she always making it a point to mention her weight, make light of it or express how confident she was in the skin she was in because she really meant it? Was she doing it because she wanted to believe it herself? Tamarra had always been led to believe that Paige was cool with being a member of the "Big Girls' Club." Everyone around her had. She never gave them a reason to believe otherwise. But now, at this very moment, Tamarra thought she was starting to see a crack in Paige's exterior, allowing her real feelings to seep through. She wanted to speak on it, but the Holy Spirit had seasoned her lips, silencing her.

"I can tell you're thinking something," Paige told Tamarra. "Come on. What gives?"

Tamarra thought about going against that voice inside of her. "Oh, nothing," she replied, opting for obedience.

"Like I was saying, because you know me, I'm not only a member of the 'Big Girls' Club,' I'm the president, honey." Paige stood up and did a peacock walk. "And proud of it."

"Are you really?" Those words slipped out of both Tamarra's thoughts and mouth.

Paige stopped in her tracks. "And what do you mean by that?"

"Nothing," Tamarra perked up with a jolly tone. "I just meant are you really serious about . . . you know . . . this whole Norman thing." What a nice save.

"Oh, girl, I'm just messing with you." Paige swooshed her hand and flopped back down on the couch, grabbing the throw pillow she'd been toying with. "I just thought it was . . . cute, that's all. But anyway—" Before Paige could finish her sentence, her cell phone rang. She retrieved it and looked down at the caller ID. "Hmm, speak of the devil." She smiled before answering it.

"And the devil appears," Tamarra whispered under her breath, knowing that something serious was brewing. But who was she kidding? She had her own fires to put out, and with the inferno she envisioned about to consume Paige's life, she didn't know if there was enough water to go around.

Chapter Nine

"Mother, I don't know what kind of game you and Raymond are playing, but I promise you, you won't win," Tamarra spat through the phone. She sat on her bed, pointing with each word she said as if her mother could see her.

Her mother had barely gotten out the word "hello" when she'd answered the phone before Tamarra dug into her tough. For the past two days, Tamarra had been trying to get a hold of her mother, ever since the book club event she and Unique had catered. Her phone calls to her mother had gone unanswered, and her voice messages had gone unreturned. It didn't feel good being on the other end of the stick, being the one getting ignored. Now that she had finally gotten her mother on the line by blocking her phone number, she could no longer contain her composure.

"Hello to you too, daughter," Mrs. Evans replied. She silently snapped her finger, upset that she'd gotten caught off guard by her daughter's call. She'd been deliberately avoiding Tamarra the last couple of days in an attempt to get her words in order. "What's got you so uptight?" As if she didn't already know.

"Please don't act like you didn't foresee this call coming, Mother," Tamarra seethed. "I just can't believe it. You've done it again. How many times do I have to tell you that I don't want any parts of that man?"

"She's your blood, for crying out loud," Mrs. Evans countered, making it clear to Tamarra that her mother knew the exact reason behind her phone call.

"Humph, so I see you know exactly what I'm talking about." Tamarra shook her head. "And see, initially, I had the nerve to give you the benefit of the doubt. That's why I didn't even mention her to you last month when I talked to you. And here you've known all along."

"Yes, I have known, but believe me when I say that I had nothing, absolutely nothing to do with it. It was her very own decision to come there. I neither encouraged her nor discouraged her. She just felt that it was time."

"Why is it that I make one little baby step and forgive you, and now you think that I'm able to take giant leaps? I'm barely crawling my way through this forgiveness thing and you think I'm capable of a marathon. I just don't get you, Mom."

"Please, Tamarra. Really, now. Do you think that after all we've just been through with me trying to make you deal with your brother that I would play a part in having you deal with your brother's daughter? I know I'm only a babe in Christ, but I know how to get out of God's way, that's for sure." Mrs. Evans sounded highly offended. Yes, she knew that her granddaughter had planned on visiting Tamarra in an attempt to ignite a relationship between the two, but she hadn't influenced her in any way. She'd asked God to keep her out of His way, but in His will. And that's just what He'd done. Even when her granddaughter called her crying after the initial ice cold encounter she'd had with Tamarra, all God had permitted her to do was to soothe the girl with comforting words. She'd been proud of herself for her obedience. And even though the Bible said that obedience was better than sacrifice, she hoped she hadn't sacrificed an opportunity to play a role in mending her family

Even with her mother almost sounding convincing, Tamarra couldn't be too sure. "Mother, do you swear you didn't put that girl up to coming here to Ohio and trying to make a connection with me?"

"I don't swear, but I'll promise you. I promise I had nothing to do with Raygene coming to Ohio. It's something she wanted to do."

"Well, you raised the child. Didn't you teach her to call first before she shows up at someone's house?"

"You wouldn't talk to her father, so she knew you wouldn't talk to her. She thought that maybe if she just showed up—you seeing her in the flesh and all—that things would turn out better. And I promise you, I didn't put her up to it."

Tamarra was convinced, but she still wasn't letting her mother off the hook. "But you knew about it, and you didn't warn me."

"Well, I tried to warn you, both your brother and I tried. But remember, you didn't want to talk to him, and you didn't want me to talk about anything that had to do with him. That was the whole reason why he had been trying to talk to you on the three-way. Raygene had been speaking more and more about you, about wanting to get closer to you and possibly bringing the family together."

"That's why you should have never told her," Tamarra stated. "I begged you not to tell her."

"She deserved to know, Tamarra. She deserved to know why you don't want anything to do with her. Besides, what's done is done. Raymond knew it was only a matter of time before Raygene made the attempt to see you. I mean, with her moving to Ohio and all to go to school, he knew it wasn't something she'd be able to leave alone. Not with you that close by to her."

Mrs. Evans paused then continued. "Raymond just wanted you to welcome his little girl with open arms and not hold against her what he did to you." Mrs. Evans sounded more sincere than ever. "He just wanted to make sure that Raygene doesn't have to pay for her father's sins, is all. From the sound of things, she's paying, all right."

Tamarra rubbed the hand that wasn't gripped around the phone down her face. She was tired of the entire situation regarding her brother, which is why she'd killed him in her mind so many years ago. It was in her mind where she battled daily not to wish that he was dead in real life.

"The girl just wants a relationship with you." Her mother spoke to the sighs and breathing coming from Tamarra's end of the phone.

"Well, I don't want a relationship with that girl," Tamarra was quick to reply. She heard her own voice. It sounded so sharp and cold. "Not now," she lied, just so her mother wouldn't think she was a total monster. What she was really thinking was *Not ever!*

"Is that what you told her?"

"No, but I wish I had. Then maybe she'd get the clue and quit stalking me."

"Stalking you?" Mrs. Evans was confused.

"Yes, stalking me," Tamarra confirmed. "I thought I'd seen the last of her when she showed up at my place unannounced last month, but then just a couple of days ago, I'm all set to serve some women at a book club event, and lo and behold, when I enter the room, there she is amongst the women. I guess it didn't take her long to make friends here in Ohio."

"Oh my, that had to be a shocker," her mother empathized.

"You're telling me. My knees buckled. I had to grab a hold of my new hire to try to keep from falling."

"You didn't fall, did you?"

"No, but my relish tray did. How come every time I receive the shock of my life, a tray of food has to suffer for it?"

"Dear, I'm sure it was just a coincidence, her being there. It had to be."

"I don't know. I didn't stick around long enough to find out. I had my worker finish up, and I went back to help clean up after it was over."

"Tamarra, honey, I really wish you would just give you and Raygene a cha—"

"Mom, I can't. I can't do it." Tamarra got choked up. "I'm still healing. After all these years, I'm still healing."

"Dear, that's because you've been running all these years instead of just stopping to face things and deal with them. I know your father and I made a great mistake by making you believe that running was the right thing to do. And I can't say I'm sorry enough. But I've forgiven myself. I've received your forgiveness, and I've received God's. I've been set free. I feel like a massive weight has been lifted, and my only regret is that it didn't happen sooner. But for so many years I ran from it; I ran from the truth, thinking it was what held me captive. All the while it was the one thing that could set me free." Mrs. Evans paused for a moment. "Baby, isn't it about time you get set free too?"

Tamarra didn't reply.

"Stop running. Just turn around and face it; not just one thing at a time, but everything at one time."

"It sounds good, Mother, but I have to take this thing one step at a time."

"Is that what God told you to do, or is that just how you want to do it?"

Tamarra had never really stopped and asked God exactly what He wanted her to do. She didn't ask just in case she didn't like His reply. She was giving new meaning to the term 'Don't Ask, Don't Tell.' If she didn't ask God about her situation, then maybe He wouldn't tell her.

"Look, Mother, I have to go. I'm sorry I snapped at you and all."

"It's okay. I know this is hard for you, dear. Seems like you get over one bridge and another is waiting. But we'll get through it. With God's help, we'll get through it."

"Thanks, Mom. I love you." Tamarra ended the call then said to herself, "I don't want to get through it. If at all possible, I'd prefer to go around it."

Chapter Ten

EverythingLiterary: To answer your question, Mr. Born, if I were to write the greatest love story ever told, my ideal leading man would be, first and foremost, believable. The tall, dark, and handsome thing is played out. How about a tithing, delivered, and holy man? What about you, Mr. Born?

Born2Write: Well, I'm two out of three.

EverythingLiterary: LOL. That's not what I meant. I meant what about you as far as if you were to write the greatest love story ever told, what would your ideal leading woman be?

Born2Write: Hmmm. Well, like your leading man, she'd have to be believable. I can't do the fake thing. Like God, she'd have to be the same tomorrow as she was yesterday and today.

EverythingLiterary: Are you saying she has to be perfect like God? No woman could meet those standards without being fake.

Born2Write: No, I'm saying that I want her to be herself whether she is at home, at church, with her friends, with her momma and daddy, with her man, or without her man. Some women have a different face and personality for every place they are or for the different people they are with.

EverythingLiterary: Sounds like you speak from experience.

Born2Write: I do. I've met women before who are absolutely nothing like the people they presented themselves to be the first month I met them. By month two, I feel like I'm with a stranger, or auditioning for the remake of *Fatal Attraction*.

EverythingLiterary: Had your share of crazies, huh?

Born2Write: Don't get me started. What about you? I'm sure a woman like yourself has had her share of relationships gone bad.

EverythingLiterary: Wait a minute . . . I thought we were talking fiction here. How did we go from make believe characters to ourselves?

Born2Write: And what's so wrong with that? Getting to know a little bit about each other? You never know; the two of us just may have a lot in common. For example, I like to write; you like to write. Maybe we can get together sometime and brain storm. Who knows? Between the two of us, we may just get that greatest love story ever told written ourselves.

EverythingLiterary: Sorry, Mr. Born, but I'm not in the habit of meeting up with guys I meet over the Internet.

Born2Write: So you've NEVER met up with a guy you've met over the Internet before???

EverythingLiterary: Well, only for business.

Born2Write: Who said it would be about anything other than business? The last I checked, we were talking about writing. That is your business, right?

EverythingLiterary: To some degree, but something tells me, Mr. Born, that your idea of business and mine might not be the same. And just like my two main characters, if I were to write the greatest love story ever told, they'd have to be equally yoked.

Born2Write: What makes you think that we aren't—I mean, that they aren't?

EverythingLiterary: You ever heard of something called spirit of discernment?

Born2Write: I might have heard of it a time or two. What about it?

EverythingLiterary: Mine tells me that I like my eggs boiled until the yoke is that greenish color. It tells me that you like your eggs over easy.

Born2Write: Actually, I like mine scrambled with cheese.

EverythingLiterary: See, you don't get my point, Mr. Born. And, unfortunately, I'm really busy today. Still have a lot of catching up to do.

Born2Write: I see. Well, thank you for taking time from your busy schedule to chit chat with a wretch like me.

EverythingLiterary: Cute.

Born2Write: Thank you. I think it's the new haircut. I got my Rick Fox thing going on.

EverythingLiterary: I meant your comment was cute, not you.

Born2Write: Wow. That hurt. That was a . . . What would you call it? An un-Christlike thing to say.

EverythingLiterary: LOL. I didn't mean it like that. I apologize. But I hardly believe your feelings are the least bit hurt. You don't need me validating how handsome you are. I'm sure every day when you look into the mirror-mirror on the wall and pose your question, it gives you the reply you long to hear.

Born2Write: Are you calling me vain?

EverythingLiterary: Your words, not mine.

Born2Write: Ouch.

EverythingLiterary: Put a Band-Aid on it, Mr. Born. I'm sure it will be okay.

Born2Write: You're relentless.

EverythingLiterary: Says the pot calling the kettle black.

Born2Write: Okay, I bow out gracefully. You're the champ.

EverythingLiterary: Nobody likes a quitter, Mr. Born.

Born2Write: Trust me, I'll keep that in mind. Good day. Hope you get caught up.

"OMG, what am I doing?" Deborah laughed out loud as she spun around in her home office chair.

For the past few days, she and Lynox, a.k.a. Mr. Born, had been sending e-mails back and forth. Even now that it was out in the open that Lynox was the infamous Mr. Born, the two, in an unspoken agreement, decided not to make mention of it. They continued the charade, sticking to literary topics of discussion. They'd managed to talk about everything from the increase in African American *New York Times* bestselling authors over the last few years to the untimely deaths of some of the more popular African American authors such as Octavia Butler, BeBe Moore Campbell, and E. Lynn Harris.

Today was the first time they had ever come this close to veering off course into personal matters. "Maybe I should just nip this in the bud now before it goes too far and he starts getting the wrong idea," Deborah told herself as she stood up and slowly paced the floor. But she really couldn't see the harm in just a little fun on the Internet. Besides, she had to admit that she had never really given Lynox an honest chance to woo her, and he must have really found her to be someone he could see himself being with, considering nothing she did or said convinced him to give up on her. "Just like you, God," she thought out loud. "The same way, in spite of myself, you have never given up on me, neither has Lynox."

Perhaps that was a sign from God that maybe she was supposed to give Lynox a chance at love. She plopped back down at her computer to check her other e-mails, secretly hoping that the next one to pop up would be from Born2Write. After all, as she saw it, she had nothing to lose and only a possible future soul mate to gain.

Chapter Eleven

Paige had to admit that she'd been thinking about the accidental kiss she and Norman shared ever since he laid it on her. She'd been thinking about it a lot. She was thinking about it now. When she should have been thinking about her husband's show of affection, she was lying on the living room couch thinking about Norman's. Perhaps if her husband had been showing her any signs of affection lately, that wouldn't be the case.

She hadn't even realized her mind had wandered off in that direction as she replayed the scene in her mind over and over. Like she was directing the scene from a movie, she added parts: a few more seconds to the kiss, a slow parting of Norman's lips, the two of them staring in each other's eyes, Norman confessing his secret love for her. Once her thoughts had gone that far, she shook her head and sat upright on the couch.

"Too much time on my hands," was the vocal excuse Paige made for her inappropriate daydreams.

Only minutes before, her thoughts had been consumed with checking the clock every ten minutes. She'd stopped checking the pot roast more than an hour ago, once she realized its original heat could not be restored, especially after she'd removed it from the warming oven for fear it might dry out. It was now freezing cold as it sat in the middle of the dining room table. The Corningware could keep it warm but so long. It had already been sitting on the table close to two hours.

Two hours ago was when Paige had expected her new husband to walk through the door, but now here he was, walking through it two hours later with a bundle of "I'm Sorry" flowers he'd picked up from some twenty-four hour grocery store on his way home.

Well, Paige was sorry too. Sorry she'd spent the entire afternoon shopping for all the ingredients her mother had told her she needed to prepare the meal. Sorry she'd wasted $69.95 on a new lounging outfit in her husband's favorite color of crimson. Thank God she hadn't splurged for the matching clear house pumps with fur lining at the top. She was also sorry she'd spent the entire evening on the phone following her mother's instructions on preparing the pot roast. But what she was most sorry for was that she'd waited up this long for her husband to join her for dinner—her husband who hadn't even had the decency to call and tell her he would be late.

"I told you that you didn't have to wait up for me, honey." Blake glanced behind Paige and into the dining area after closing the door behind him and setting down his briefcase. He could see the spread on the table and the place settings. "Did you eat already?"

"Did I eat already?" Paige was trying her best not to get indignant. "I've been waiting for you . . ." She looked at the clock on the wall. "For two hours now."

A puzzled look raced across his face. "But didn't you get my message?"

"What message? I checked my cell phone repeatedly to see

if I missed your call or something. There was no call and there was no message."

"Well, maybe next time you might try checking the home phone." He nodded toward the cordless phone that sat on the couch next to her. She'd kept it close just in case he had tried to call. He hadn't—at least not to her knowledge. "I called earlier. You didn't pick up, so I left a message."

Paige picked up the phone and turned it on. Placing it to her ear, sure enough it made the beeping sound that it makes when someone has left a voice message. "But I've been home. I don't know how or when I could have missed . . ." Her words trailed off when she thought about the couple of times she'd put the phone down while talking to her mother in order to retrieve an ingredient. The other line must have beeped then without her knowing.

"I think your other line was clicking when you had me on hold," she recalled her mother saying. She'd forgotten all about it by the time they'd hung up, so she didn't think to see if the missed caller had left a message.

"Anyway," Blake continued, "I'm sorry, honey. And it looks as though you really went out of your way with tonight's meal."

"Well, I had the day off, so I wanted to spend it doing something for you."

Blake felt bad. Paige could tell by the look on his face.

When her stomach grumbled, she said, "I suppose we could still have dinner. It probably won't taste as good nuked, but I'm sure it will be appetizing nonetheless. It's an old family recipe."

Blake hesitated for a minute. "Actually, I already ate. That's what I was telling you in my message. We had dinner with a client, Klyde and I."

"Oh." Now Paige was even more disappointed, but she didn't want to show it. She didn't want to be the angry black woman. Not yet. It was far too early in the marriage. But if Blake thought she was going to sit back and allow him to take her for granted, he had another thing coming.

"But hey, I can keep you company while you eat," Blake suggested right before yawning and looking down at his watch. It was ten o'clock.

Trying to keep it together, Paige took a deep breath, then walked over and kissed her husband on the cheek. "That's okay, honey. You've worked long and hard today. Go ahead and get your shower and go to bed. We'll have it tomorrow. I'm sure it will still be just as tasty as leftovers."

Blake smiled and moved in close to his wife. "That's why I married you. You are so considerate and selfless. I love you, Mrs. Dickenson."

Paige closed her eyes and leaned in to close the minute gap that was between her and her husband. She puckered her lips just as Blake puckered his. She waited to feel his soft lips touch her lips. Instead, they touched her forehead.

"See you upstairs, sweetheart," Blake said before climbing the steps, headed for their bedroom, no doubt.

Paige stood there dumbfounded and confused. "What the heck just happened here?" she questioned herself, feeling slighted. She looked down at herself, donned in her new lounging outfit. Heading toward the dining room to put away the food, she covered as much of her upper body as she could with her arms. She hugged herself until she realized that if she was going to put away the food, she needed the use of her arms.

Slowly, Paige picked up her main dish and proceeded to

put the food away. As she did, she almost subconsciously engaged in picking and eating away at the dinner. A hunk of pot roast. A potato. A roll. Another hunk of pot roast. Another roll, this time dipped in the roast's gravy. A handful of carrots. More roast. Another handful of carrots with a couple of peas mixed in. Yes, that's right, she was pecking away at the food with her hands while putting it away. She was gnawing away at the food the same way her husband's neglect was gnawing away at her.

"Looks like leftovers will be out of the question," Paige told herself as she turned off the kitchen lights. She belched and then headed for the stairs. Making her way up the steps, a part of her still felt that the night might not be a total bust. And she had a receipt for $69.95 plus tax that agreed with her.

Reaching the top landing of her steps, she adjusted her outfit and then entered her bedroom. The scent of Blake's after shower smell-good lingered in the air. She felt her way through the dark room until she reached her bed. She climbed in and scooted close to Blake, prepared to consummate the marriage . . . again. Just as she went to whisper his name and put her arm around him, a loud snore almost scared her half to death.

She shook her head in pure disbelief. This night had turned out nothing like the way she had planned.

She flopped down on her side of the bed, her lips poked out. The pot roast may have gotten cold, but it seemed as though their bed had gotten even colder. If Blake kept this up, among all the other things she'd been sorry for that night, he'd better hope she wouldn't be sorry she'd married him.

Paige pulled the covers up to her neck then let out another belch. Her husband may not have filled her up, but at least the pot roast had.

Chapter Twelve

"Happy birthday to you. Happy birthday to you. Happy birthday dear Sakaya. Happy birthday to you!" Everyone clapped as Sakaya stood in a chair over the cake that was lit with four candles.

Sakaya closed her eyes tightly to keep the wish inside her head. After a few seconds, she opened her eyes and blew out all the candles in two breaths. "Yay!" she shouted and clapped for herself along with the other guests in attendance at her fourth birthday celebration.

Maeyl snapped a picture of his little girl gleaming over the Black Barbie cake. Her mother stood beside her, helping her to balance.

"Let me get another one," Maeyl stated while aiming the camera at mother and daughter.

"Let's at least let her cut the cake," Sasha said as she held Sakaya by the waist.

"Just one more," Maeyl insisted. "I want to make sure I get a picture with the cake in it this time."

"Okay, Daddy, just one more," Sakaya said with a pointed finger. "But you get in the picture this time. Me, you, and Mommy."

"Yeah, you get in one this time," Sasha agreed. She then looked over at Tamarra. "Would you mind?" Sasha took the camera from Maeyl and handed it to Tamarra.

"Uh, no, not at all." Tamarra, appearing quite uncomfortable with the task at hand, walked over and took Maeyl's spot as he went and stood next to Sasha and his daughter.

"Get in close," Sasha said as she released one of her hands from around Sakaya's waist and put it around Maeyl's.

Tamarra peered through the camera lens at what looked to be a perfect, happy family. She couldn't help but visualize her head attached to Sasha's neck, thinking it should be her in that type of picture instead. How she longed to be the one and only matriarch of such a happy family: mother, father, and child—birthday celebrations, proms, and graduations—but she'd been robbed of that thanks to her brother.

The more Tamarra thought about it, maybe deep inside she had forgiven her brother for raping her. Perhaps it was the fact that his actions robbed her of the ability to bear children for her husband and be that happy family that she couldn't forgive him. And looking through that lens only reminded her of it more. She didn't even realize several seconds had passed, her hand was trembling, and she'd yet to snap the picture.

God, help me, Tamarra thought. And He did; He sent help her way.

"Here, let me take the picture," Zelda insisted as she walked up and relieved Tamarra of the duty.

"Oh, no. I can do it!" Tamarra insisted after taking note of the look Zelda had shot her. She couldn't distinguish whether or not it was an I-told-you-so look, or an I-can't-believe-you-are-going-to-go-ahead-with-this-charade look. Either way, it was a look, and it was one Tamarra wasn't too pleased with. She and Zelda had had a private conversation about how Tamarra truly felt about Maeyl's situation with his daughter. For some reason, she felt as though Zelda was reminding her of the conversation. She didn't need reminding. She'd made up her mind, and now she had to follow through. She took the camera back from Zelda.

"Actually, I don't think you can do it," Zelda expressed, hoping that Tamarra could read between the lines. She took the camera from Tamarra again.

Tamarra felt as though she and Zelda were having the conversation all over again, only this time, in front of everyone else. Could everyone read between the lines? Zelda was the only one Tamarra had told how she really felt about marrying a man with a child, with a baby momma. Actually, Tamarra didn't have to tell her. Zelda had seen right through Tamarra by her actions. Could everyone else?

"Trust me, Zelda, I can do it." Tamarra took back the camera. "After all, you've done enough by allowing us to have Sakaya's birthday party here at Family Café."

Zelda paused for a minute. "Okay, so maybe you can do it, but do you want to do it? I mean, *really* want to do it, Tamarra?"

Tamarra thought for a moment as she took in Zelda's words. Zelda kindly took the camera again as she did so.

"Can somebody take the picture already? I want cake," the now pouting four-year-old stated.

"Yes," Sasha chimed in. "Are we missing something here?" She looked back and forth from Tamarra to Zelda.

"Uh, no, not at all. Isn't that right, Zelda?" This time Tamarra snatched the camera from Zelda.

"If you say so, Tamarra. If you say so." Before shooting Tamarra a glaring look and walking off, Zelda stated, "You folks let me know if you need anything else over here." She glared at Tamarra the entire time.

Maeyl cleared his throat. "So, honey, you gonna take that picture or what?"

Unique's oldest son blessed the cake before they all dug in. Sasha and Maeyl had invited a couple of people from the church to help celebrate their daughter's birthday. Unique and her three boys were included on the list.

A few other people from the church showed up to lend their support as well. Some attended just to be nosy, to see if anything happened that they could run and talk about. "The Love Triangle" was the title given by the rumor and gossip mill at New Day to the situation between Tamarra, Maeyl, and Sasha. It was obvious it was titled by those who didn't know all the facts. Had they known the facts, they would have realized just how improper the title was. After all, there was no love triangle. Maeyl loved Tamarra and only Tamarra. He didn't even have love for Sasha based on GP that she was his baby's momma. At least Tamarra didn't feel that he did. He'd never told her such. But then again, she'd never asked. She had only assumed that the mother of his child didn't somehow hold a piece of his heart.

The only connection her man and that woman had was their daughter, Sakaya, so if there was any love triangle, it would be between Tamarra, Maeyl, and Sakaya. But who was Tamarra kidding? She knew that even then the love didn't go three ways. She just couldn't force herself to warm up to the child like she knew she should. She couldn't grasp the idea of a ready-made family, a child already made by another woman with her man.

"Tamarra, you haven't gotten a picture with Sakaya yet,"

Maeyl realized. "Why don't you go stand by her with that cute little doll you bought her and let me get a shot of the two of you?"

"Okay," Tamarra agreed. She could do this. It was just a little ol' picture. "Is that okay with you, sweetie?" Tamarra turned and asked Sakaya.

"Sure!" Sakaya, being the little ham she was, was happy to oblige. "Let me just find Mommy."

"Uh, baby," Maeyl told his daughter, "I kind of just wanted to get a picture of you and Tamarra."

"But I thought you said you wanted me to take it with the Barbie Miss Tamarra bought me."

"I do, sweet—"

"Well, I named her Mommy. Mommy is my new Barbie's name." Sakaya grabbed the doll that donned a beautiful wedding gown, went and stood by Tamarra, then posed. "I named her Mommy because when my real mommy gets married, this is the kind of wedding dress she is going to wear."

"Oh, okay, I see," Maeyl said, relieved he didn't have to boot Sasha out of a picture and risk hurting her feelings. He really did just want one of his daughter and his future wife for his scrapbook. Ever since he went to that single scrapbooking session one of New Day's members held at the church, he'd been hooked. Tamarra had claimed the hobby was far too tedious and time consuming to take on. Ironically, she was the one who had talked Maeyl into going. She had also catered the event with some finger sandwiches, cheese and veggie trays, and refreshments.

"Oh, no! Wait, Daddy," Sakaya yelled. "Mommy's shoe is missing." The little girl looked down at her doll's feet, bearing only one shoe. She frantically looked around.

"I found it!" Tamarra shouted, picking the shoe up off the table and then walking it over to Sakaya. "Here, let me put it on for you." Tamarra went to slip the shoe on the Barbie's foot until Sakaya stopped her.

"No! Daddy has to do it! Daddy has to do it!" she shouted as her eyes welled with tears. She drew so much attention that everyone gathered around to see what was the matter.

"Just relax, honey. Calm down," Maeyl coaxed her.

"What's wrong? What's going on?" Sasha asked, breaking through the crowd.

"I need Daddy to put her shoe on." Sakaya held up her doll to show her mother.

"Tamarra was going to put it on, honey," Maeyl told his daughter. "It's okay."

"No, it's not okay," Sakaya replied to her father. "You have to slip the missing shoe on Mommy just like the prince did in Cinderella when he finally found her. He slipped the shoe on her and then they got married and lived happily ever after . . . just like you and Mommy."

For some reason, Tamarra didn't think the child was referring to her doll anymore. Something told her that she was referencing her real mommy. *Embarrassment, humiliation, awkwardness, mortified:* those were just a few words to describe the way Tamarra was feeling at that very moment.

Both Maeyl and Sasha were speechless as their daughter now stood before them bawling. They decided to pull her to the side and whisper, but loud enough for everybody to hear.

"Now, sweetie, remember Daddy told you that he's marrying Miss Tamarra?" Sasha said. "Not me, sweetie. Mommy and Daddy are not getting married." Sasha tried to assure her daughter.

"But . . ." Sakaya looked to Maeyl. She wanted him to tell her that her mother was wrong.

"There is no but, pumpkin. I'm marrying Miss Tamarra. You're going to have two mommies." Maeyl backed Sasha up.

Sakaya now cried even harder.

"Sweetie, when I explained all this to you, you said that you liked Miss Tamarra," Maeyl reminded her.

"I do, and I'd want Miss Tamarra to be my mommy too. Only she doesn't want to be my mommy."

Both Maeyl and Sasha let out a sigh of relief. They were relieved to know that they weren't going to have to deal with rebellious stepdaughter syndrome. All they had to do was to explain to her that Tamarra did want to be her other mommy.

"Oh, honey." Maeyl pulled Sakaya close to him, "Miss Tamarra wants nothing more than to be your mommy too."

"No, she doesn't," Sakaya told her father.

"Well, how do you know?" Now Sasha was curious. "Has someone said something to you?

"Yes," Sakaya responded matter-of-factly.

"Who?" both Maeyl and Sasha were quick to ask.

And once again, matter-of-factly, Sakaya replied, "God."

Chapter Thirteen

"Child, what you are doing is nothing short of cybersex," Mother Doreen spat with the aftertaste of disgust still on her tongue. Remnants of it made its way through the phone receiver and into Deborah's ear.

"Come on now, Mother Doreen. I wouldn't go that far as to say all that," Deborah said, downplaying her and Lynox's back and forth e-mails.

"'I wouldn't go that far,' said the stripper before she turned her first trick."

"Mother Doreen!" Deborah's nervous laughter was from both shock and amusement at her elder friend's comment. "I hope you are not pairing me with the likes of a stripper. Because if you are, I resent that remark."

"Humph. Sounds to me like you resemble that remark." From the gasp she heard on the other end of the line, Mother Doreen knew that she just might have gone too far. "I'm sorry, Sister Deborah. I don't know; maybe I'm just too old school for today's technology, but I ain't never heard of no man courting a woman via Internet."

"Well, he's not really courting me, but I guess I prefer that term over *cybersex*. Geesh. Besides, I suppose even if we were involved in cybersex, which we are not, it's the safest sex I know."

"I beg to differ. The safest sex is no sex."

Deborah really didn't want to debate about it with Mother Doreen. She knew eventually Mother Doreen would start quoting scriptures, and although Deborah was pleased with the amount of biblical knowledge she had, she couldn't go toe to toe with New Day's former church mother. If it came down to it, Deborah felt Mother Doreen wouldn't be able to give her Bible as to whether what she and Lynox were engaging in was sinful. "There's no sin in what Lynox and I are doing. It's not like we're actually—"

"Oh, don't take me there, because I might not be able to find my way back," Mother Doreen pleaded, cutting Deborah off before she could say what Mother Doreen suspected she was going to say.

Deborah couldn't help but chuckle at how offended Mother Doreen was acting. Here she had been excited to share with someone about the little tit for a tat via Internet she'd been having with Lynox. When she decided to call up Mother Doreen and share it with her, she had no idea the woman would make it seem so dirty.

"It's like I said back when New Day had that issue with those pictures of Sister Tamarra and Brother Maeyl being posted to the church Web site. The Internet is supposed to be a source to do Kingdom work, to spread the gospel, but man has tainted it. Don't let Satan use you, child, to be one of those people who taint it."

Deborah shook her head. "I promise, Mother Doreen, I am a woman of God. I know not to cross the line."

"Well, if you ask me, if you trying to stay saved, then you shouldn't even be walking the line."

"All right, Mother Doreen," Deborah said, preparing to

end the call, seeing that she was not going to change Mother Doreen's opinion regarding Internet chatting. "I better get back to work. I'm editing a manuscript that I have to have back to the author by the end of this week."

"Okay, child, I'll be praying for you. By the way, how's the Singles' Ministry, especially now that it has some men folk?"

"Same old New Day Divas. It doesn't matter whether men are members or not; some of them are just set on holding on to the hurt, pain, and failure of past relationships. There's so much of it that there isn't any room for them to love someone new. Half those women aren't ready for God to send them a husband. And there are some wonderful and blessed brothers up in New Day, too. It's unfortunate that too many of us wouldn't know our God-sent husband if God Himself placed him in front of us."

"Does that include you as well?" Mother Doreen decided not to put her friend on the spot like that and wait for an answer, so she said her farewells and they ended the call.

Deborah sat there for a minute pondering the unanswered question Mother Doreen had posed. Would she know the husband God had for her when she saw him? Had she truly been delivered and cleansed from her past? Surely she had. Ever since she got her spiritual breakthrough and went on her sabbatical, she didn't feel the same. She felt a hundred pounds lighter. That's how much baggage she'd been towing around in a hefty bag over her shoulder: garbage that had an embarrassing stench.

But just in case, she decided to say a prayer to God. One could never be too sure about something unless they prayed about it and waited on God to answer.

With her eyes closed and head bowed, Deborah, at first,

prayed out loud, but then she reverted to praying silently in her mind. She didn't want to speak it out loud for fear Satan might try to intercept her prayer. She'd learned on her sabbatical about spiritual warfare. Part of the teaching was about the three heavens: the heaven God resides in, the second heaven Satan resides in, and the heaven on Earth where man resides.

Satan resides in the second heaven in between Earth and the Heavenly of Heavens. He makes it his business to try to keep man's prayers from reaching God. Deborah was not about to play pitty-pat and ping pong with the devil, so as not to take any chances, she spoke her prayer in her head. The devil has powers, but only God knows man's heart. The devil can influence the mind, but he can't read it, she resolved.

Heavenly Father, I come to you repenting for my sins, forgiving those who have hurt me, and asking for forgiveness for those who I have hurt. Father, if there is someone who I have truly not forgiven in my heart, that maybe I've even forgotten about, please reveal them to me, bring them to my remembrance so that I may do so. Lord, as you know, Lynox has been persistent in his pursuit of me. No matter what I do or say, he's there.

A smile crossed Deborah's lips as she continued.

I can't help but wonder if that's because you have placed him in my life, Lord. If he is maybe . . . perhaps . . . you know . . . the man you have for me, my Boaz. God, you know more than anyone that I love what I do, my writing, my career. I love New Day and the ministries. But, God, I sometimes hide behind those things. Well, in the past I have. But I don't want to hide anymore. I want to be found . . . by him . . . by the man you have seeking me as his wife. So, Lord, I just want clarity in the matter, and ask that you do all things I've requested in this prayer. In the name of your son and my savior, Jesus Christ, amen.

Deborah felt a flush rush over her. It was like a waterfall was cleansing her. "Oh thank you, God. I love you, Holy Spirit!" She had no pretenses about verbalizing her praise out loud, though. She hoped of all things, Satan heard her praises to God loud and clear. "I love you, Lord. Thank you, Jesus. Hallelujah. Glory to your name. You are so awesome. Thank you, God. Thank you in advance as I feel you moving now regarding my prayers. I only want to please your heart, Lord. Give me the guidance I need to please you. I don't want to do anything that would offend you or your people," Deborah said as she thought about what Mother Doreen had to say about her going back and forth with Lynox on the Internet.

"Rah, tah, sa, bay yah, row tou, hey sah . . ." Her rambling tongues continued for about twenty minutes. She couldn't seem to stop. Obviously, her spirit had a lot to say and was going to get it out in spite of her time frame on finishing up the manuscript.

"Thank you, Lord," Deborah said as she paused, giving God a moment to reply to her spirit. After a few more minutes, she opened her eyes and closed out her conversation with God.

"Whew! That's what I'm talking about," Deborah said, feeling as though she'd just had a makeover.

She walked over to her computer and logged on. Lo and behold, there was a message from Lynox. Deborah paused, took a deep breath, and then clicked it open. Deborah's jaw dropped as she read his e-mail.

Born2Write: I've really enjoyed my e-mails back and forth with you for the past couple of weeks. It's been entertaining and has allowed me to get to know you. But after this e-mail, I won't be sending you any more. Why? Because I want to get to know you better and I can't do that by Internet. Besides, if I'm being honest, it's kind of creepy, you know, using made-up characters from a made-up book when we can just keep it real . . . be real . . . be ourselves and not just some online personalities. My only prayer is that you feel the same way. I still have your number, so I'm going to take a risk and call you. If you want to get to know me better as well, then I'd really like that. If not, if this was just something to keep you entertained, to break the monotony of the real work-related e-mails I'm sure you have to sort through daily, then just hang up in my ear. I hope you won't choose the latter.

Deborah finished reading the e-mail, stood up, extended her arms toward the heaven and then shouted out another praise. "God, like that one book title says, you don't play!" She clapped her hands and did a little dance. Just that quickly God had given her a sign that He was answering her prayers. Right before Deborah went to delete the e-mail, her cell phone rang. She picked it up and noticed that the call was private. Back when Lynox had first contacted her, he'd called her from a private number.

Still ecstatic, she regained her composure and answered the phone. "Everything Literary. How may I help you?"

"Deb, it's me. I hope you got my e-mail. I know you probably weren't expecting me to call so soon. I just couldn't wa—"

Before the gentleman caller could finish his sentence, Deborah slammed the phone down in his ear. She looked up and yelled, "God, what kind of dirty trick is this?"

Chapter Fourteen

"Uh, so, uh, how're things going?" Paige asked as she walked into the ticket booth of the movie theatre. She'd been at work for three hours and had managed to dodge Norman by doing busy work in her office and assisting at the concession counter.

She hadn't seen him since their accidental kiss. Being the boss had its perks in needed situations, and in this situation, it was making sure she arranged the work schedule so that she and Norman didn't work the same days or hours. It had worked up until now. An employee had called off, and Norman was the only one available to come in and cover.

Paige had made up her mind that she would avoid Norman at all costs, but doing so was driving her crazy. She felt as though everyone could sense that something was going on with her. As a matter of fact, she knew that they knew something was going on with her.

"Are you okay, Mrs. Dickenson?" the young female concession stand worker had asked Paige after she'd insisted on preparing the next batch of popcorn.

Yes, pitifully enough, Paige's attempt at busy work had resulted in her insisting that she load the popcorn popper in preparation of a fresh batch. The young worker didn't want to appear as though she couldn't do her job and needed her manager to go behind her, so she countered Paige by insisting that she load the machine. The two tugged the poor bag back and forth until it split in half and icky, sticky popcorn cornels went flying in the air. They'd given new meaning to making it rain.

"Uh, yes, Morgan, I'm fine," Paige said as she looked down at the mess on her hands. "I'm sorry. Perhaps I should let you do your job." As Paige walked away to go wash her hands, she could feel the eyes of the girl and the other crew members burning a hole in her back with their puzzled glares.

As she dried her washed hands with a paper towel, she knew that if she was ever going to be productive on the job, she needed to just go ahead and get it over with, talking to Norman. After all, she was probably making more out of the kiss than there really was. Norman most likely hadn't thought twice about it since.

"Get yourself together, diva," Paige pepped herself as she threw away the paper towel and headed for the ticket booth.

She'd walked in with so much confidence, but now that she was standing there next to Norman trying to speak to him, her words lacked that same confidence.

"Things are going great," Norman replied. "A little slow, but you know how Wednesdays are."

"Yeah, I know." *Whew.* Paige exhaled. Everything was good. Norman seemed to be his regular old self, not the hot mess Paige was. And here she'd been worried and acting crazy for almost two weeks for nothing.

"Haven't seen you in a minute. I've kissed you—I mean *missed* you." Freudian slip.

Paige had exhaled much too soon. She needed that breath back, because now she couldn't breathe. The big ol' fat, pink-with-purple-striped elephant that was stuffed inside the ticket booth with them seemed to be consuming all the air.

Swallowing hard, Paige replied, "I kissed you too—I mean I *missed* you too." She was blowing it big time.

There was an awkward moment of silence, as neither of them knew what to say next. Well, they knew what to say, but were afraid to say it, as nothing seemed to be coming out of either of their mouths the right way. The mood was saved when an elderly couple approached the ticket window to purchase tickets.

Thank God for retired senior citizens who can come catch a movie in the middle of the day, Paige thought, relieved at the break the couple provided. As Paige watched the two accept their tickets and walk off hand in hand toward the movie theater, she couldn't help but smile. She imagined her and Blake growing old together and catching movies in the middle of the day and walking around the mall in the mornings before the stores actually opened. She pictured their days in retirement long lived, but then that's when the daydream ended. It just didn't seem like a fantasy that could come true due to the fact that Blake lived and breathed work. Paige felt that retirement was something he would never fathom. Just when he'd close the huge deal he'd been working on, another one would just so happen to come along, and then another, and then another. It was a never-ending cycle.

Paige was convinced that her husband, simply put, truly loved what he did for a living. It fueled him. Unfortunately for her, though, by the time he made it home and into their bed, his tank would be on empty.

"Well, I better go. I think they need my help at the concession counter." Paige let out a nervous chuckle.

"Thanks again for the other night," Norman told her. "The dinner." He wanted to be sure she knew what he meant.

"Oh, no problem." Paige shrugged and smiled.

"And be sure to tell that husband of yours I said thank you as well," Norman added. "How is the married life anyway?" He was treading.

"You know, it's good." Paige sounded doubtful. "I just wish Blake didn't work so much. We haven't really gotten to . . . you know . . . enjoy the married life as much as I imagined we would."

"Oh, is that so?" Norman was treading again. "Sounds like Blake is a good provider."

"Yeah, so I guess it's not too bad." Now Paige was comfortable. It was as if the elephant had disappeared and now she was just talking to her friend again, the same friend she used to spend hours chatting it up with back in the day. She didn't realize until now how much she'd missed that as she sat down in the empty chair next to Norman.

"But I know it must be hard being newlyweds and not really being able to take advantage of the newness of the relationship"—Norman winked—"and its perks." He caught himself about to slip into his old ways of talking with Paige, the days before she got saved.

Paige didn't even catch that. She was just glad to have a sounding board at the moment. Norman had been her sounding board once upon a time, and she, his. Maybe now that he respected her Christianity they could go back to those days of conversation that made the work days go by fast.

The saying must be true that time flies when you're having fun, because before she knew it, an entire hour had passed with her sitting in the ticket booth talking to Norman. Paige felt good. Norman had given her some male insight that she couldn't get from her conversations with her best friend, although she loved talking with Tamarra and heeded most of her advice. Glad she and Norman were able to put the entire kissing thing to bed and rest, Paige didn't realize that something else between them was awakening.

Chapter Fifteen

Tamarra hadn't even heard the last comment the little girl had declared to her parents inside Family Café. She'd crept out of the restaurant without anyone noticing. She could tell where the whole thing was going with the doll shoe anyway.

She'd been standing in her living room the past twenty minutes or so, pacing back and forth. Seems like pacing was the only exercise she'd gotten in the last year or so. Her phone had been ringing: Maeyl calling to see where she'd run off to, more than likely, but she wasn't ready to talk yet.

"Who am I kidding?" Tamarra asked herself as she slumped down on the couch. She looked up. "Surely not you, God."

And she was right. The Word of God said that He knew his children's hearts. That meant that He knew hers, and she couldn't fool Him with the façade she was putting on for the folks at New Day and the rest of Malvonia. God wasn't the only one she couldn't fool, either.

The doorbell caused Tamarra to stand to her feet. She slowly walked over to the door, hoping that it wasn't Maeyl. She'd have some explaining to do, for sure, if it was. Like why she got up and walked out on the middle of his daughter's birthday party.

She shrugged her shoulders uncaringly. "Heck, the party was almost over anyway." She then walked over and opened the door. She wasn't expecting the person on the other side.

"Hmm, looks like that child didn't know what she was talking about. You're the real Cinderella. What happened? Your Jeep was about to turn back into a pumpkin or something? I could have given you a ride home." Zelda stood on Tamarra's doorstep being just as sarcastic as she knew how to be.

"Come in, Zelda," was all Tamarra said.

Zelda stepped inside and Tamarra closed the door behind her. "Nice place you got here," she complimented after eyeballing what she could see of the place.

Zelda and Tamarra had never really been friends. Of course, they used to fellowship at New Day together back when Zelda was a member, but that was as far as it went. Like some church folks' relationships, theirs never left the four walls of the church building.

"Thank you," Tamarra replied as the two just stood there in a glass fish bowl of silence. It was only a matter of time before Zelda shattered the glass.

"So, you thought you'd made a clean getaway, huh? Thought you'd creep up on out of there without anybody missing you?" Zelda shook her head and sat down on Tamarra's couch without being offered a seat. "Who do you think you're fooling, girlfriend, and how long do you think you're going to get away with it? You can't possibly think that I'm the only one with eyes."

"Who am I fooling?" Tamarra repeated the question, sitting down in the chair across from Zelda. "Funny, I was just asking myself that question before you rang my bell."

"Well, what was the answer?" Zelda leaned in, waiting on a reply.

Tamarra felt as though she was on the hot seat as she scrambled through her mind for a reply. She couldn't come up with one. She became frustrated at the fact that Zelda was even there pressing her. "Zelda, what are you doing here anyway, showing up on people's doorsteps unannounced?"

"You're not answering your phone."

"How would you know? You didn't call. You don't even have my phone number." Tamarra was sure she'd never given it to her.

"Because I knew you wouldn't. I know your kind. Maeyl's probably called you about fifty times by now. At least I assumed it was you he was calling as I watched him dial repeatedly on his cell phone, then slam it closed without holding a conversation. And you know he ain't gon' drive over here and leave his little girl on her birthday. But see, I ain't Maeyl," Zelda reminded her. "I got nothing to lose by coming over here and telling you about yourself. But see, Maeyl is afraid he might lose you."

Tamarra lowered her head.

"Like I said, that man ain't no fool, and if he's got eyes, which we know he does, he sees what I see. Only he doesn't want to say anything, because he knows that if he puts it out there, it will be choosing time."

Tamarra just listened.

"So, you still don't have anything to say?" Tamarra was still silent. "Humph. Well, let me give you some food for thought. Do you know what that little girl told her parents after you left? She told them that you didn't want to be her second mother. She told them that God told her that."

Tamarra's eyes bucked.

"Yep, you heard me right. She stood right there and told them that God told her that you don't really want to be her stepmother."

Tamarra's eyes watered.

Zelda knew she'd said enough to penetrate Tamarra's heart and thoughts. She stood, preparing to leave. "So, I guess now you only have to ask yourself one question."

Tamarra remained silent, but her eyes pleaded for Zelda to tell her what the question was.

Obliging her, Zelda said, "What is God telling you?" On that note, Zelda made her way to the door. Tamarra followed to close it behind her. "Oh yeah, I almost forgot about the real reason I came by." Zelda reached down into her huge purse and pulled out something wrapped in foil. "Here. You left your piece of birthday cake. Guess you can have your cake and eat it too."

Chapter Sixteen

StillBallin: Hey, Deb, it's me, Elton. I know it's been forever, but you've been in my spirit here lately. I ended up taking a chance at googling your name and, Voila! Your literary website popped up. I'm glad you had a contact page with your e-mail address, otherwise I'd have had to hire a private investigator to find you (just joking). Anyway. I'm back in the States for good. So much has changed since I've been gone. You know I've only been back a couple/three times since I left to play ball almost six years ago. There is one thing that hasn't changed, though, and that's the way I feel about you. I really don't want to get into things by e-mail, so I think I'm just going to reach out to you on the phone number that's on the contact page. I'll give you a minute to digest this e-mail first, or even reply back to me. Talk to you soon, Little Debbie.

How dare he! How dare he send Deborah this blind e-mail! How dare he end it with the pet name he'd so affectionately given her! And how dare he call her up like they were the best of friends . . . even just plain old friends, for that matter!

Elton. It had been Elton on the phone. Elton, Deborah's

would-have-been baby's daddy had she not elected to terminate the pregnancy.

So many emotions ran through Deborah's body as she
stood up from her computer after reading the e-mail Elton
had sent her. Had she continued reading her e-mails after the
one Lynox had sent her, she would have found Elton's right
underneath it. Maybe then his phone call wouldn't have been
so devastating. Okay, it still would have been as devastating,
but at least she would have seen it coming. Maybe. Okay, no
she wouldn't have, because she would have replied to the e-
mail telling him to not even think about using his bony, evil
fingers to dial her number.

"No way, God. This can't be happening," Deborah said,
shaking her head while her face was buried in her hands. Not
only was her face buried, but so were her feelings and all the
remnants that had haunted her after that day in the abortion
clinic. This was a bone that she didn't need some dog sniffing
around trying to dig up, and that's just what she feared Elton
was about to do.

"The devil is a liar, a doggone liar!" she shouted and
stomped her feet as if all of the devil's heads were underneath
them. "I have the victory," she reminded herself. "I've come
too far . . ." She looked upward. "Lord, you have brought me
too far to leave me here. I'm going to get through this thing,
all the way through it. Not stuck in the middle, not almost
out, but all the way through, all the way out. I will not allow
Satan to continue to beat me over the head with my past.
God, you have forgiven me and I have forgiven myself," Deborah declared in a victorious tone.

*What about the baby you killed? What about Elton? Have they
forgiven you as well? Yeah, perhaps Elton portrayed himself as wanting you to have an abortion, but what if he really hadn't? What if*

all of that had been a test—a test that you failed miserably? the devil shot back at Deborah.

Before the devil had stamped his time card and gone to work on Deborah's mind, she had never even considered those things, seeking forgiveness from the others involved in her sinful deed, the two people who really had no say in what she did. Yes, Elton had suggested she terminate the pregnancy, but that didn't mean she had to do it. Ultimately it had been her decision to make with her body. And in hindsight, it hadn't even been her body to make the decision for. It was God's body, something she was supposed to present to Him holy and acceptable. She'd committed a sin against her body, His temple.

Thank God the Lord had finally forgiven her for it, though, after she'd sought such forgiveness. It had never dawned on her that the matter involved more than just her and the Lord.

Deborah was starting to get weak in the knees and queasy and lightheaded. What did Elton really want? What did he really want from her? Whatever it was, she had no intention of finding out any time soon. No, she had some praying to do. She had some fasting to do. She needed to be clear on whether Elton was coming in the name of Jesus or to stir up some mess.

Her phone began ringing. She looked down at the caller ID. It read PRIVATE again. Could it have been Elton calling her back? Perhaps it really was Lynox calling this time. On one hand Deborah didn't want to answer the call, just in case it was Elton. She wasn't ready to talk to him. Not yet. On the other hand, she wanted to answer it, just in case it was Lynox. She didn't want to play Lynox to the left one time too many by dodging his calls and risk ruining anything that coulda, woulda, shoulda. But what if that relationship wasn't supposed to be either? What if that was Elton's purpose for all of a sudden popping back up in her life again, to keep her from making a mistake with Lynox? Was God using Elton to block any mistake she might be making with Lynox?

"Lord Jesus, help me!" she cried out in frustration as she held the ringing phone in her hand. "Take a deep breath and get it together," she instructed herself. "I've run for too many years. I'm done running, so, Holy Spirit, whoever is on the other end of this line, please give me the very words that I need to speak, in Jesus' name." After inhaling a deep breath, Deborah answered the phone just before it went to voice mail. "Hello," she answered, and after hearing the voice on the other end of the line, she exhaled.

It was Lynox. *Thank you, Jesus*, she said to herself. "Lynox, it is sooo good to hear your voice."

"Oh, wow." He sounded relieved. "And here I was as nervous as all get out before calling you."

"Why? It's not like it's the first time you've ever talked to me."

"It's the first time I'm ever talking to you with my intentions laid out on the table."

Deborah thought for a minute. "This is true."

"And if you don't mind me cutting to the chase, what are yours?"

Deborah was flabbergasted. She hadn't been prepared for that at all.

"I hope I'm not being too forward. It's just that I'm forty-three years old. I'm not interested in having 'just friends.' I'm not interested in dating 'women.' I'm interested in a courtship with *a* woman. And not just any woman, but you, Deborah Lewis, if I'm being absolutely honest. I haven't even been able to hold a conversation with another woman since the day I met you. You've been in my system. You've been in my spirit. So, as corny as this might sound, I feel like I'm so close to you."

Deborah said nothing. She just listened.

"I don't want to scare you off by sharing too much with you, but I feel it would benefit the both of us if you know exactly where I'm coming from and exactly where I want to go. I don't expect for you to feel the same way about me, not just yet, but I expect you to give us a chance, knowing what I desire the final destination to be. If you notice your feelings going down a different path than mine, then I trust you'll be honest and let me know. That way neither of our time is wasted and no one gets hurt." He let out a deep breath. "There, I said it."

"And boy, oh boy, did you say it." Deborah chuckled. "Wow . . . I . . . I don't know what to say."

"Then don't say anything. When you don't know what to say, don't say anything. That way you don't risk saying the wrong thing. I don't mind doing all the talking for now. I want you to get to know me. But do know I expect some reciprocity at some point. So, where do you want me to start?"

And there it was: the beginning of Deborah getting to know everything there was to possibly know about the man she'd been dodging for months and months. She'd never lied to herself by denying an interest in Lynox, even an attraction, but she wasn't ready back then. She needed some fixing, some deliverance. There was a healing that needed to take place within her before she could even think about sharing herself, any part of herself, with a man. But after her breakthrough that started in the New Day sanctuary and completed in her very own living room, and after the sabbatical, she was ready. She was delivered and healed and ready to walk in it. And who better to walk with her than a fine, sculptured specimen of a man like Lynox?

Even if it turned out that Lynox wasn't the one for her, for now, he would serve as the perfect distraction from Elton.

Chapter Seventeen

"I'm so sorry, honey. I know you were really looking forward to driving up to Cleveland to watch the game, but I can't miss this cocktail party. A bunch of big wigs are going to be there. Three years ago, at this very same party, a coworker landed a deal that sends him, his wife, and kids to the Mediterranean every year to their vacation home. Just imagine that," Blake said, trying to convince Paige that in the long run it would be worth canceling their plans tonight.

"It's hard for me to imagine you ever even finding time to make our honeymoon happen, let along going on vacation every year," Paige whined. "I miss you, Blake. You're always working." She sat down on the queen bench at the foot of their bed and watched him loosen his tie.

"I miss you too, sweetheart, but like I said, I'd love for you to go with me." Blake took off his tie, followed by his light blue dress shirt.

Paige ran her hands down her body. "Look at me. Do I look like I'm dressed for a cocktail party?"

Blake admired his wife's jersey and nice fitting jeans that she dressed up with a pair of wine-colored stilettos. "Just change into something else real quick while I'm in the shower," he suggested as he took off his pants, preparing for a shower.

"I don't want to change into something all fancy schmancy. I need more notice if I'm going to represent as your wife."

"Babe, you represent me well no matter what you're wearing." He looked down at her feet. "Even if you were just wearing nothing but those pumps." He winked a mischievous grin. "Especially if you were wearing nothing but just those pumps."

Paige matched her husband's mischievous grin with one of her own as she stood up and moved in closer to Blake. "Then why don't we say the heck with both the game and the cocktail party and I show you just how well I can represent in nothing but a pair of four-inch wine-colored stilettos?" She went to kiss him, but he backed into the bathroom to turn on the shower.

"Honey, I can't. Klyde will be here in a few minutes. I'm going to follow him because I don't know exactly where I'm going."

Paige was determined—or desperate. "Let him wait," she said, putting her arms around Blake as he adjusted the shower water. She planted kisses up and down his back.

"Come on now, honey." Blake gently removed Paige's hands from his body as he turned around and faced her. "I don't want to have that man waiting." He kissed her on the forehead and then got into the shower, closing the door in her face.

"Oh, so you'd rather keep me waiting?" she pouted.

"You know it's not like that." As Blake lathered himself up, he peeked out of the shower door. "Why don't you . . ." He thought for a moment and then a light bulb went off in his head. "Why don't you ask Norman to go with you? You seem to enjoy his company better now that he's been visiting church and gets the whole Christian thing." He went back in the shower.

"He's been to New Day about as much as you have lately," Paige mumbled under her breath. She was referencing the fact that for the past month, Blake had worked himself so sick throughout the week, right down to Saturday evenings, that come Sunday morning he'd be too worn out to attend church with her. He'd ordered her to grab a twenty out of his wallet for offering, promising to write a check for his tithes the following week. But the next week would only be a repeat.

"Did you say something?" Blake asked from inside the shower.

"I'll call Norman up, but it's too short notice. I'm sure he won't be able to drop everything. I'll just hang out here alone." She turned to walk out of the bathroom.

"The offer still stands for you to come with me. Matter of fact, I think Klyde's wife is joining us."

"Nah. I'll be okay." Paige moped out of the bathroom, and although she felt it was a useless effort, she called up Norman and asked if he was free to join her for a little trip to Cleveland. "I'll drive. We'll come back tonight. It'll be fun," she persuaded him.

Surprisingly, Norman agreed to go. She left the house before Blake even did in order to go pick up Norman. They made the two hour and some change drive and arrived at the game by the end of first quarter. The two had an absolute blast. The tickets were excellent, as they practically had courtside seats.

During one of the time-outs, a song was played and the camera roamed around trying to catch people performing the song. When it landed on Norman and Paige, the two put on the best twenty-second Karaoke act they could. They ended up being the crowd favorite, and were given coupons for free souvenirs and team gear.

When a team mascot shot rolled up T-shirts into the crowd,

both Norman and Paige reached for one that was coming in their direction. At the same time, both their hands landed on it. They each gripped it and just stood there looking at each other.

"You can have it," Norman told her.

"No, you take it," Paige insisted, "as a thank you for coming with me."

"You sure?" Norman asked as the two stood there holding the shirt.

"Positive. It's the least I can do. This is the second time I didn't have to be alone because of you."

"But I feel like I'm the one who should be thanking you. I mean, a free dinner at an amazing restaurant, courtside seats to an NBA game. I should have started hanging out with you a long time ago, Paige Robinson."

"Dickenson. It's Dickenson now." She reminded both Norman and herself of the new last name she held now that she was a married woman. And on that note, she released the shirt, relinquishing it to Norman.

After that, the two smashed hot dogs, popcorn, cotton candy, and sodas. They cheered, clapped, and rooted for the home team, and they booed the away team. Paige couldn't imagine having a better time even if she had been with Blake. She knew she wouldn't have been able to have a tenth of this kind of fun at some boring old cocktail party. Norman had been the perfect person to go with. She had no idea he could be so much fun. And even more so, she had no idea that the two of them would end up in a hotel room together that night either.

Chapter Eighteen

"Are you feeling one hundred percent back to your old self again?" Maeyl asked Tamarra as the two stood and talked in the sound booth after Sunday church service. Tamarra had just entered after giving three people hugs and telling them she loved them, per Pastor's request after church was dismissed.

"Huh?" Tamarra had the most confused look possible on her face.

"I said are you feeling better? Are you over the flu bug? You know, the bug that bit you and chased you up out of Sakaya's birthday party?"

"Oh, that bug." Tamarra feigned a cough. She'd forgotten all about the excuse she'd used when Maeyl had finally gotten in touch with her and asked her why she'd left the party so abruptly. She'd told him that all of a sudden she'd became sick to her stomach and weak at the knees, and she threw in the loose bowels for good measure too. "Oh, I'm feeling much better. Not quite one hundred percent." She coughed again. "But close." She smiled.

"Good, because I can't have my girl sick. We have a wedding to plan."

And that's when she noticed it, the way Maeyl was looking at her. The way he had been looking at her almost every time he made a comment and then waited on her to respond to it. It was as if he were trying to read her, to see if her words, her voice, her tone, and her gesture matched the expression on her face.

"Yes, wedding." She swallowed.

"And about our wedding, I was thinking maybe we shouldn't wait. Maybe we should just do it."

Okay, now it was getting hard for Tamarra to keep her expressions together, but she was doing it nonetheless. "Just do it? You sound like it's a Nike commercial or something. This is the beginning of the rest of our lives together." Tamarra's palms became sweaty. Just how soon was this man talking? She needed time, much more time.

"I don't mean it like that. It's just that I love you, you love me . . . and you love Sakaya." He was doing it again; looking at her.

The lie almost got stuck in her throat, but she managed to force it through. "Yes, and I can't wait to be your wife and Sakaya's mother." She looked down at her nose with crossed eyes. She knew it was just a fairy tale, but she couldn't help but wonder if her nose was growing anything at all like that wooden kid named Pinocchio.

"So let's not put it off any longer." He stopped what he was doing and grabbed her hands. "It's not like we were going to have some big ol' wedding anyway. We have plenty of time to throw something together by next month."

"Next month?" Tamarra hadn't meant to shout, but shout she had. The few congregation members who were still hanging around directed their attention to the sound booth.

Too embarrassed to look and apologize for her outburst, Tamarra cast her eyes downward and stared at her hands intertwined with Maeyl's.

"Hold on a second," he told her as he wrapped things up in the sound booth and then proceeded to lead her out of the church. "I don't want you to feel as though I'm rushing you or anything. It's just that I'm ready to start living our life together. I'm ready to give up my place and live with you as man and wife, coming home to you after work, me cooking dinner for you every once in a while." He brushed his finger across her nose as they made their way through the sanctuary. She smiled as he continued. "Us sitting up watching the game one night, then a *Lifetime* movie the next night." She knew he didn't mean that last thing, but Tamarra smiled nonetheless. "And us putting Sakaya to bed together with a bedtime story when she comes to visit on the weekends."

That was it. The needle had been ripped across the record, leaving traces of peeling vinyl. Tamarra's smile was gone. When she noticed that Maeyl was doing it again, looking at her, she tried to muster one up real quick.

"Is there something wrong? Not feeling well all of a sudden again?" Maeyl asked her in a tone that she could have sworn was condescending.

She stopped in her tracks just as they made it to the church foyer, right outside Pastor's waiting lobby. "As a matter of fact . . ." Tamarra grabbed her stomach. Sweat poured from every part of her body. She turned a pale color.

"You don't look too good," Maeyl stated as he lent his fiancée support in standing. "Want to go in here and sit down?" he suggested, nodding toward Pastor's waiting area.

"No! No," Tamarra quickly shot out. "I . . . just . . . need to . . . get some air is all," she managed to get out.

"You sure, babe? I think you might need to sit down in here for a min—"

"I said no!" Tamarra repeated, not embarrassed at all about her loud tone like she'd been in the sound booth.

Maeyl was embarrassed, but his concern for Tamarra overshadowed his embarrassment by a couple of points or so, so he did as she asked. He led her outside, where she inhaled and exhaled deep breaths of God's air once she hit the doors. "Feel better?"

After a few seconds, Tamarra was starting to feel better, but then she looked up. With Maeyl supporting her outside of Pastor's office, where nothing separated them but a huge window, she saw the window blinds open; then she saw Pastor offer the other occupant in the office a seat.

"This can't be happening," Tamarra said under her breath and started taking deep breaths again. But it was happening.

"Maybe we should get you to the doctor's. The ER, or urgent care, at least," Maeyl suggested, followed by that all too familiar knowing look.

If Maeyl thought she was faking, Tamarra had news for him. She thought Maeyl might have been on to her cover-up, but this was no cover-up. She was truly having what medical professionals might describe as a panic attack. She'd heard of them, but had never had one before.

"Is everything okay with Sister Tamarra?" the church secretary asked Maeyl as she approached them.

"She's just a little—" Before Maeyl could finish his answer, what was left of last night's dinner tumbled up out of Tamarra's mouth and onto the secretary's patent leather pumps.

"That's it." Maeyl pulled a handkerchief out of his suit pocket and handed it to Tamarra as he led her to his car. "We're going to get you checked out, baby," were the last words he said before putting Tamarra into the car and driving her to the emergency room. "Everything is going to be all right once I get you to the emergency room."

Maeyl had said it with a reassuring tone, but unless Jesus Himself was waiting for her in His scrubs, she knew nothing was going to be all right. Nothing at all.

Chapter Nineteen

"I honestly can't believe that I'm sitting here across from you, on a real date. No trying to get you to agent my manuscript, no pretending to be some make believe client, and no cyber space in between us." Lynox gloated as if he were on cloud nine.

Deborah had no idea this man, who had initially come off so cocky and strong almost to the point of conceit, was showing his vulnerability. On purpose. It wasn't wimpy like the character of Kenny on the series of *Soul Food* sometimes came across. There was just enough sensitivity and flattery to let a woman know that he was still the man.

"I'm glad we could start fresh," Deborah stated. She figured she could let her guard down a little too, as she didn't want to come across as Terry from *Soul Food*; although she was indeed guilty of having several of the character's traits.

"Are you guys ready for me to take your orders now?" the waiter asked as he set Lynox's strawberry lemonade in front of him and Deborah's water with lemon wedges in front of her.

Neither Deborah nor Lynox had looked at the menus yet.

"Can we have a couple more minutes?" Lynox asked on their behalf as the waiter granted it to them then walked away.

It was as though the couple had come full circle as they sat in Max and Erma's, the restaurant where they'd first met in person. Only this time, they sat smack dead in the center of the restaurant.

"And I'm glad we're not hidden back in the cut in some booth like the last time," Deborah teased.

"Hey, I'm sorry if I just happen to favor booths . . . and more privacy. I promise that day I wasn't trying to be low key so that one of my many girlfriends wouldn't catch me dining with you. Like I told you then, it had been a while since I'd dated—really dated."

"Oh, don't try to clean it up now. So, you admit you had many girlfriends," Deborah pressed with a raised eyebrow. She was teasing, but still awaited his reply.

He nodded with some reluctance. "In complete honesty, I might have dated a woman or two in my time, trying to find that perfect one. It was difficult, focusing on the writing of my book and all, but like I said, when I met you, I knew I'd found her. I've never been this serious about anyone, especially not . . ." His words trailed off. He didn't know if it was safe to mention the name that had halted his speech. He remembered Deborah's reaction the last time he'd mentioned the woman's name. It was like Kryptonite: it got Deborah all rattled up.

"Especially not Helen?" Deborah finished his sentence. Not only could she now stand to hear the name, she could say it herself without her blood boiling or nerves getting out of control. She'd forgiven Helen for taunting her with the fact that she was there at the abortion clinic the day Deborah had terminated her pregnancy. Never mind the fact that Helen had gotten one of her own, but because Deborah had been late term and visibly pregnant, Helen had made Deborah feel as though her act was ten times worse.

But that was all water under the bridge. The two women had moved on. Deborah was back to helping out with the New Day Singles' Ministry, and praying and fasting to see what else God would have her do in His Kingdom. Helen was helping out in the New Day Children's Church. The two women had come to a crossroads and had forgiven where forgiveness was due, but most importantly, God had forgiven them both.

"I wasn't sure if it was safe to say her name," Lynox noted.

Deborah smiled. "I know, but everything is good. Matter of fact, I owe you an apology for the way I acted about you and Helen. It wasn't about you; it was about some history she and I had. But like I said, everything is good between us now. We're not BFF's or anything like that," Deborah made clear.

"I hear you, because I hope you don't mind me saying, but that woman was a nut case." He chuckled. "I only went out with her a couple of times. It had been months since I'd last seen her that day she showed up at the restaurant acting like a complete luna—"

"No offense, Lynox"—Deborah held up her hand—"and I know you're probably just trying to make me feel secure about the whole 'you and Helen' thing, but I don't care for you to talk about her negatively. No, we're not BFF's or anything, but she is still my sister in Christ, and I don't take too kindly to folks talking about my family."

Lynox wasn't offended, not the least bit. He was impressed, now more attracted to the woman who sat before him than ever. "I'm not offended at all." He smiled. "And I apologize. It won't happen again. I won't monopolize our time together bad mouthing someone else. This is about us." He reached over and grabbed her hands. He was just about to kiss them when he felt a presence at their table. He sighed, thinking about the waiter's bad timing.

Instead of sending him away once again, knowing the man would keep coming back like a roach in the projects, he quickly picked up his menu and rambled off his order. He surmised that the quicker they gave their order, the quicker they could get back to their alone time. Deborah followed suit by picking up her own menu.

"I'll have the Erma burger with fries," Lynox ordered. After scanning the menu, Deborah ordered the same.

Lynox took the menu from her hand to turn over to the waiter as Deborah took a sip of her drink.

"Well, that sounds like a delicious meal. Perhaps I should relay that to your waiter."

Just then Deborah lifted her light brown, slanted eyes to the person standing at their table. Before she could control it, the liquid in her mouth squirted across the table onto Lynox's shirt.

"Not again." Lynox sighed as he picked up his napkin and wiped himself down, wondering to whom they owed the pleasure of interrupting their meal this time around.

Every time Deborah's phone had rung, she'd been on pins and needles wondering if it was going to be Elton. For a moment she had considered just e-mailing him back in order to get her first communication with him in five years out of the way. But that was her flesh telling her to do that. God had not spoken yet concerning the matter.

It appeared as though Elton was a little quicker on his feet than God, because now, as Elton stood over her and Lynox on their date at Max and Erma's, she wished she'd just gone ahead and talked to him. Now really wasn't the time or the place for them to have their first encounter after all of this time . . . after all they'd been through. Well, at least all she'd been through.

Deborah cleared her throat. "Elton, uh, how are, uh . . . what are you . . . I'm surprised to see you here." She couldn't get her words together, so she cleared her throat once again and tried it all over, trying her best to sound cordial. "What a coincidence for you to be dining at the same exact restaurant that I'm at." Her smile and forced cheery voice almost hit the sarcasm bull's eye.

"Oh, it was no coincidence," Elton assured her matter-of-factly. "I followed you here." He stood there with this stupid grin on his face, daring Lynox to challenge the actions to which he'd just confessed.

Deborah didn't give Lynox the chance. "Followed me? Elton, are you serious?"

"Very." His confidence and surety matched Lynox's to some degree, as well as his appearance. With his cocoa brown complexion and standing six feet, seven inches tall, the man was dapper. He had a swagger that was running a tight race to P. Diddy. The parts in his hair separating his cornrows were as straight as arrows. There wasn't a loose hair coming from either of the dozen or so rows that looked as though they had been sculptured onto his head. The diamond Gucci watch: Bling. The basketball championship ring: Bling. The diamond earrings that adorned his ears: Bling. Oh, he was flashy, but it was just enough, not too much.

"But . . ." Deborah didn't know what to say. She hadn't expected the man to admit to stalking.

"You left me no choice. You never replied to my e-mail. You slammed the phone down in my ear. I knew there was only one way I would ever get to talk to you, and that was face to face."

"But how did you know—"

"I have my ways." Elton smiled. There was even bling in his mouth: one tooth, the second one to his left front tooth. Deborah had remembered him chipping that tooth in a basketball game. He'd initially repaired it with a basic cap that was covered by his insurance plan. Looked like he'd upgraded both his dental plan and his cap.

Lynox was now the one clearing his throat. He felt the need to remind Deborah that he was there, that he was the one she'd gone out on the date with. Not LeBron James here.

"Oh, uh, Lynox, this is—" Deborah started to introduce.

"I'm Elton Culiver." He extended his hand.

"And I'm—" Lynox extended his hand and started before Elton cut him off as well.

"Lynox Chase," Elton stated as he shook his hand.

Both Lynox and Deborah were shocked to see that Elton knew who Lynox was. Seeing the shock on their faces, Elton decided to answer their unasked question.

"Once again, I have my ways." Elton winked, and both Lynox and Deborah had surmised by now that Elton had used the change he had left over from all that bling to hire a private investigator. Either that, or he'd met up with New Day's church secretary, who even knew what time the ants in Malvonia ate dinner.

"I suppose, then, that the pleasure is all mine," Lynox stated. There was a brief moment of silence, as it looked as though Elton wasn't about to go anywhere any time soon. "Honey, should we invite Mr. Culiver here to join us?" Lynox asked Deborah.

"Honey?" Elton chuckled, but neither Deborah nor Lynox could find the humor; although Deborah did wonder why Lynox was using that term of endearment with her. Had it just slipped out, or was he trying to mark his territory in front of Elton? "Oh, pardon me," Elton said as his laughter ceased.

"Well, Elton, it was good to see you after all these years. Take care of yourself." Deborah dismissed Elton just like that. Or at least she tried to.

"Oh, so it's like that? You're going to just get rid of me like yesterday's trash?" Elton asked.

"I thought that was how we do it, Elton: get rid of things we don't want in our lives like it was just yesterday's trash." Deborah glared at Elton, and for the first time since he'd arrived at their table, she'd shut him down.

"Uh, look. In hindsight, maybe this was a bad idea," Elton admitted. "Sorry I interrupted your dinner, player," he said to Lynox before turning his attention back to Deborah. "It was, uh, good seeing you too. Take care, Little Debbie." As he walked away, his head was practically between his legs and his tail lagging behind him.

What surprised Deborah was that she felt bad for him . . . and she couldn't understand it. Maybe it had been that look in his eyes when she'd alluded to her aborting their baby, getting rid of it like trash. For all these years, she'd been in so much pain about her decision, her loss, but not once did she ever think about the pain he might have been in too. Just as he'd never bothered to find out how the abortion had affected her, she had never bothered to find out how it had affected him. Something inside told her that she was about to find out

Chapter Twenty

"You spent the night with Norman? What did Blake say? Oh my God, Paige, what were you thinking?" Tamarra couldn't believe her ears. "You guys have only been married a couple of months and already you're sleeping with another man?"

"Slow down. It's not what you think," Paige told Tamarra as she handed her a cup of juice. "I said I spent the night in a hotel room with the man. I didn't say I slept with him."

"Come again?" Tamarra accepted the juice and took a sip of it. She then curled her trouser sock–covered feet up under her as she listened to Paige explain herself.

"Because of the basketball game, the hotel was booked. They only had one room left. It was late, too late for Norman and I to be driving around Cleveland lost, looking for a hotel that had two separate rooms left."

"Okay, and why was it, again, you two needed to be looking for a hotel room in the first place?" Tamarra adjusted her bottom on Paige's couch.

With a smile on her face, Paige sat down and told Tamarra how after she and Norman left the game and made it to the parking lot, Paige's car wouldn't start. They tried getting a jump, but that didn't do the trick either. She realized it must have been something serious, and then she remembered the fact that Blake had never gotten around to getting her check engine light looked at.

"Well, what did Blake say when you called him and told him you were stranded in Cleveland?"

"Oh, he felt awful. He was so upset with himself for not getting around to getting my car looked at like he'd promised. The day he promised he'd get it checked out he was suppose to take me to lunch as well. But you know Blake, always looking at the cup half full. He felt some sense of security knowing that Norman was with me and that I wasn't out there stranded alone."

"Hmm, I suppose one might say that was the lesser of two evils." Tamarra sounded skeptical.

"And what's that supposed to mean?" Paige set her own cup of juice down on the table. "Are you trying to insinuate something here?"

"No, Paige . . ." Tamarra's words trailed off as she tried to find the right ones. "Well . . ."

"Just spit it out, friend." Paige waited patiently for Tamarra to get her words together.

"It's just not a good look is all," Tamarra finally said. "I know firsthand how important it is to avoid even the mere appearance of evil. Trust me; I learned that enough times early in Maeyl's and my relationship."

Paige stared at Tamarra as if she certainly had a point she was trying to make, because the one she was teetering with, Paige wasn't trying to hear.

"All I'm saying is be mindful of what things might look like with you and Norman. I mean, first he's at a fancy restaurant with you, then he's out in the parking lot with you, accidentally kissing you. Next he's courtside at a basketball game with you, and then he's spending the night in a hotel room with you." Just hearing it brought on a reality check for Tamarra.

"Seriously, girl, do you hear how all that sounds? So, imagine how it might look. And poor Blake—"

"Poor Blake?" Paige snapped, her once relaxed body stiffening. "Don't you mean poor me? I'm the one who has to keep finding a seat-filler for my own husband. And ironically enough, he's the one who told me to call Norman in the first place."

"I'm not accusing you of anything, Paige," Tamarra confirmed after hearing just a hint of an accusatory tone in her voice. "All I'm saying is just imagine what all this would look like to your husband. You don't want to disrespect him in any way."

Still feeling as though she was the victim, Paige retaliated. "Well, if he doesn't like what it looks like, then maybe he should think about that the next time he chooses work over his wife!" Paige spat, and that's when Tamarra realized what was going on here.

"Oh, I get it now." Tamarra nodded. "The hubby isn't spending as much time with wifey as she'd like, huh?"

Paige didn't answer, not verbally anyway, but the slight twitch of her neck and rolling of her eyes told it all.

"I understand all that. When my ex and I first got married, he was the same way. And then when he did set a day aside for leisure time, it was to hang out with his boys. Well, instead of me finding someone else to hang out with, I managed to get Edward to spend some of that time with me."

"But Blake won't take any time off period."

"Then call up his assistant or whoever and schedule an appointment with him. Plan a nice intimate moment for you two."

"Intimate moment. Tah. Yeah, right." Paige sucked her

teeth and rolled her eyes. Hard. "File that under 'N' for Never."

"Why do you say that?"

Paige's eyes cast downward as if she was embarrassed.

"Come on, Paige. What is it? You know you can tell me."

Paige looked up into her friend's eyes and knew that she could. "I'm almost embarrassed to admit that we haven't even made love since the weekend we got married," Paige confessed.

Tamarra was flabbergasted. "Are you serious? You haven't made love to your husband since your wedding night?"

"No," Paige corrected her, "since the weekend of our wedding. You saw him on our wedding night. He was loaded. He'd had one too many toasts of champagne."

"Yeah." Tamarra recalled their wedding night with a smile. "He was pretty buzzed."

"And with it being my first time having sex, I didn't want no drunken lovemaking."

"So you mean your new husband couldn't minister to you in the bed on your wedding night?"

"Now I know firsthand why Pastor says that even though drinking is not a sin, why risk being under the influence if God calls you to be used? The last thing a saint should want is for Jesus to call on them when He needs them most and He can't even use them like He wants to because they are under the influence of alcohol . . . even if it's just a little bit. All God wants is for them to be filled with the Holy Spirit, not liquid spirit."

Paige sighed. "I needed my husband to minister to me that night and he couldn't. I'd waited years for that very moment, the infamous wedding night where the bride who has been saving herself loses her virginity. So much for fairy tales."

"Well, I think you and I both know that life is no fairy tale," Tamarra said. Paige shrugged in halfhearted agreement. "But things have gotten a little better, right? I mean, he's not a drinker, so surely he's more prepared to . . . you know . . . minister in bed."

"I wish, but by the time he puts in all those hours at work, he's too tired to . . . minister."

Tamarra shot Paige a pitiful look. Paige shifted in her seat, trying to shift away the embarrassment.

"Anyway, enough about me. How are you feeling after your little spell yesterday?"

"Oh yeah, that." Now Tamarra was the one who was embarrassed. She couldn't believe she'd almost fallen out at church. "The doctors said it was just something similar to an anxiety attack, or a minor anxiety attack or something. . . . I don't know." Tamarra downplayed it.

"Girl, anxiety attack? Black people don't have those, do they?"

"More than you know, according to what the doctor told me," Tamarra said. "We just don't realize that's what we are experiencing. We like to dress it up with the word 'overwhelmed.' Anyway, it was a first for me. I've got it all under control, though."

"Did the doctor prescribe you something?"

"No, he tried to, but I'm going to try prayer and God."

"I hear that, girlfriend." Paige gave Tamarra a high-five. "God is still in the healing business. If you truly believe, try Him and you will see. He can fix anything." This time Paige picked up her glass and clinked it with Tamarra's, thinking the entire time, *Now if only God can fix my marriage.*

Chapter Twenty-one

"A baby? They're saying I have a baby?" All of a sudden, Tamarra felt nauseated, as if she could be experiencing morning sickness. Where, when, why had that rumor started? She tried to control her breathing, a technique she'd just learned from the emergency room doctor who had treated her after her spell on Sunday.

"That you are having a baby, or something crazy like that." Unique told Tamarra of the latest New Day gossip as they drove to their catering affair. "You know ain't nobody started that rumor but the old busybody church secretary. She planted the seed anyway, talking about you had morning sickness or something, and that Brother Maeyl had to take you to the urgent care place or to visit your doctor after church on Sunday. I don't know. I half pay attention to that stuff. I was just in the women's bathroom trying to pee is all."

Tamarra was disgusted, both at the fact that Unique had just given her too much information regarding her bathroom business, and at the talk that was going on in the bathroom while she was trying to do her business. Nonetheless, though, she relaxed a little more. Knowing that the source of the rumor was the New Day Temple of Faith church secretary, she knew that many would take her word with a grain of salt, not really looking into it, or taking what she said at face value.

There would be a couple, three or four people who did their part in spreading the rumor to some degree. Tamarra was confident, though, that still, it would be taken with a grain of salt, considering how much the church secretary loved to talk and draw her own conclusions. And even though this served as some sort of comfort to Tamarra, allowing her to fight off another near panic attack, she was still a little ticked off.

"You know, enough is enough already. It's about time somebody shut that old woman down. She's been stirring up mess at New Day since I can remember," Tamarra fussed. "I bet if Pastor knew, that secretary would be replaced in a heartbeat. Every pastor needs someone on their team they can trust, otherwise members won't feel comfortable talking with their pastor if they know it's going to make its way to the grapevine."

"So, you gonna turn snitch?" Unique asked nonchalantly as she nibbled on the Pop Tart she'd brought along with her.

"Huh?" Tamarra asked, confused, keeping her eyes on traffic as she drove.

"You gon' rat on her? You know, run and tell Pastor?" Unique chewed, unmoved one way or the other as to Tamarra's answer.

"Well, uh, I wouldn't call it snitching or being a rat or anything."

"No, you wouldn't, but in the streets where I come from, we would." Unique finished chewing, swallowed, then broke it down for Tamarra. "See, where I grew up, if we had a problem with someone, we didn't go running to their mommy and daddy first. We stepped to them first, gave them the opportunity to explain what's what. If we didn't like what they had to say, or if they wanted to get all froggy and try to jump bad, then we'd go to their mommy and daddy." Unique took another bite of her breakfast treat and then with a mouthful added, "Or beat 'em down . . . one of the two."

"So, you're saying I should go to the source, the root of all this matter of evil first?"

"I'm not saying it. God is saying it."

That same confused expression from earlier returned to Tamarra's face. "Come again."

"It's in God's word in Matthew eighteen, which states: *If your brother wrongs you, go and show him his fault, between you and him privately.*"

A look of surprise came across Tamarra's face as Unique, someone she'd categorized as a little ghetto girl she was helping to make a dollar out of fifteen cents, had given her Bible for her situation.

Unique noticed the look. "I know. Folks are always shocked when I give 'em Bible." She turned her attention back to her Pop Tart and looked out the window without any hurt feelings.

Tamarra, on the other hand, was convicted immediately for prejudging the girl. "I . . . um . . . I'm sorry, Unique," she started.

Unique held her hand up. "Unh-unh. No need to apologize. I actually like that folks can't figure me out. I like being the sheep in wolf's clothing, if you know what I mean." She smiled and winked. Tamarra returned the smile and they enjoyed the rest of their ride together. Although they didn't talk about the church secretary spreading rumors anymore, the thoughts of whether to approach the woman still played around in Tamarra's mind.

***

"God is good, all the time, and all the time, God is good," Tamarra sang as she danced around the house while cleaning. Although she had the CD of the song she was singing, it wasn't playing on her stereo. She created the music in her head. In life, she'd found herself in situations where she didn't have music around to move her and ignite a praise, like in the ER this past Sunday. She had to be able to give God some praise about her situation without all the musicians and singers lighting up a fire up under her. At some point, if everything really was going to be all right, she had to call on Jesus Himself to make it so. She had to ignite her own fire, and it needed to rise up out of her belly.

That's just what had happened on her way to the hospital this past Sunday as Maeyl drove her. The two of them prayed together and called out the name of Jesus the entire drive there. They requested that God prepare the way for Tamarra's visit to the hospital; that He'd touch the minds and hands of the doctors and nurses so that they would be effective and in their sound minds; that His healing powers would fall down on Tamarra and that she, too, would be and remain in her sound mind. Together, those two did more than ignite a fire; they set a blaze. And that same feeling, a feeling of thanks and gratefulness, was exactly what Tamarra was experiencing now. She was on fire for the Lord.

It started off with just her head being on fire, angry at the church secretary's actions. This hadn't been the first time the woman had started a rumor about Tamarra. It was she who had spread the rumor around New Day last year that Tamarra had spent the night at Maeyl's place. The more Tamarra thought about the church secretary and her ways, the angrier she got. She'd even found herself shouting the words she'd confront the woman with. But then, after not being able to withstand anymore, she felt the Holy Spirit rise up like an internal flame and burn her flesh down to a crisp. The fire still burned, but now it was a burning in her belly, a yearning to give God praise. Soon her shouting toward the church secretary turned into shouts of praises unto God. Just the touch, the presence of a part of God within her, made her so grateful that she couldn't do anything but shout. She was shouting so loudly that she almost didn't hear the doorbell ring.

"Oh, Lord have mercy," Tamarra said to herself, catching her breath. She hoped it wasn't one of the neighbors at the door with two men in white coats coming after her. With all the hollering and praising she'd been doing, they probably thought she was over there going crazy.

Tamarra straightened herself up as best she could, considering she was wearing a gray fleece jogging suit. She peeked out the window and saw a UPS truck parked directly in front of her house. She gladly opened the door, figuring the serving products she'd ordered online had finally arrived.

As she swung the door open, the UPS truck was pulling off. Parked across the street from the house was a sporty little red Honda that was now in her view. It was a car she'd only seen once, but clearly recognized. Its owner stood on her doorstop, next to the package the UPS man had left.

The girl picked up the package, offering it to Tamarra, who stood behind the closed screen door. The girl had pleading eyes, as if she were begging Tamarra to please accept the package, to please accept the girl herself.

Tamarra started to get all twisted up inside as she stared into the girl's eyes. They were eyes that tugged at every emotional string within Tamarra's body. But they were also eyes like her brother's, reminding her of the monster he was. And with this child being his offspring, no matter how sweet and innocent she might have appeared to be, Tamarra assumed there had to be some kind of monster buried in her as well.

Everything in Tamarra wanted to slam the door closed in the girl's face and pretend as though she'd never been there. Then there was that side of her that wanted to know why she'd been at her church on Sunday, going into her pastor's office. It was a vision that landed Tamarra in the emergency room with a near panic attack. She couldn't deal with this anymore: this girl popping up whenever and wherever. She knew she had to deal with it now, and what better place than the privacy of her own home. Because if she didn't, she had a feeling her brother's daughter wasn't going to give up until she got what she'd come for.

Bravely, Tamarra inhaled then exhaled, opening her front screen. The girl handed Tamarra the package. She accepted it, then nodded, gesturing for the girl to come in. As the girl entered her house, Tamarra knew the remaining skeleton bones of her past were about to exit her closet.

Chapter Twenty-two

"Thank you for agreeing to meet with me." Elton stood and greeted Deborah as she approached the table.

She'd just arrived at Family Café for her meeting with Elton, the man who had been the love of her life. He was the man she thought someday would make her a member of the millionaire wives club, thanks to his lucrative basketball contract overseas in Chile. And thanks to their above-well-to-do status, she'd be able to spend her days doing volunteer ministry work, like visiting homeless shelters and nursing homes. She would visit children in the hospital who were suffering from life-threatening illnesses, in addition to taking care of her own children, dog, and cat. And on some evenings, after a hard day of her husband playing basketball and her doing ministry, the children would be cared for by their live-in nanny, while they'd sit down to dinner at a nice, quiet, fancy restaurant, exchanging details of their day's activities.

None of that had happened, and now they were sitting in a restaurant, all right, about to share the details of their activities of years past. Years they'd spent without each other. Years that had passed without them exchanging anything but abortion money. They weren't in some fancy restaurant, either. They were in Family Café, a Malvonia diner where all the locals ate. It was a place where she was sure to see several familiar faces, perhaps one or two New Day members. And that's just the way she wanted it.

Not sure of how she might respond to being alone with Elton after all of these years, she wanted folks that could be around to hold her accountable for her actions. She didn't know whether hate from her flesh would rise up against him, or the love of God. Maybe even the lust of her flesh. After all, Elton had been her first love, and she had to admit, he'd been looking pretty dapper at Max and Erma's, and he'd even topped himself today with his perfectly fitting Nike sweat suit and fresh kicks. Deborah sniffed, because the fragrance of the man lingered just enough to tease her.

Now the moment was here, when she was actually face to face with Elton. She was ready to have a discussion that should have taken place years ago. For Deborah, it felt surreal. For some reason, she'd always felt that she'd never see Elton again for as long as she lived. She hadn't planned on it, anyway, so she was still not quite sure whether she should have agreed to meet with him. But back at Max and Erma's, she'd let that puppy dog face of his get to her so bad that she initiated contact with him again, in the form of an e-mail. It was the e-mail she'd sent him after arriving home from the restaurant:

EverythingLiterary: Elton, the way things ended at the restaurant today wasn't closure at all. It was more like opening up a half-opened can of worms all the way. We need to talk.

Short and sweet and to the point was her e-mail, nothing like the e-mails she'd sent to Lynox. She'd typed the one to Elton quickly, and had quickly hit the send button before she could change her mind. It was one of those moments when she wished the e-mail had come back undeliverable. But it hadn't. It had made it safe and sound into Elton's e-mail box, and just as quickly as she'd sent it, he'd replied:

StillBallin: My ear is still ringing from the sound of you slamming the phone down when I called you the other day. My head is spinning from how quickly you turned me away at the restaurant. I had figured I'd give you a minute to digest it all, my contacting you out of the blue and my being back home, but I couldn't help it. Sorry for intruding on you and that suit's dinner, but I'd really like to see you again. Let me take you to dinner. The place of your choice. You name the date and the time. I hope you'll accept. I'd really like to see you again . . . to talk to you . . . to apologize in person.

Being a Christian woman, Deborah really didn't have to ponder the e-mail too long. Elton wanted to apologize; so did she. Perhaps this was the one moment when she could fully be set free, leaving no room for Satan to come back and try to attack her mind with this situation. And in the process, she could set Elton free. She could forgive him for the role he played in her late term abortion. So, she replied to his request with:

EverythingLiterary: Okay. Family Café. Tomorrow at 7:00 P.M.

His response had been immediate, like he'd been sitting by the computer holding his breath awaiting her reply.

StillBallin: Great. Thank you so much. See you tomorrow.

Last evening, after reading his last e-mail and logging off her computer, Deborah had tossed and turned all night. She heard the clock ticking, even though her clock was digital. She was anticipating the next day like kids on Christmas Eve waiting to see what Santa had left them. Tomorrow was now here, but Elton was no Santa.

"Please, have a seat." Elton slightly rose to his feet while extending his hand for her to sit down.

Deborah could see that he still exercised chivalry, just as always. "Thank you," she replied without looking in his eyes. She was afraid to, for fear she'd be looking into the eyes of the child she'd aborted, who she was sure would have had eyes like his daddy . . . or her daddy. Although she'd been far enough along for the doctors to determine the sex of the baby, she hadn't wanted to find out. She'd wanted to be surprised. Well, surprise, surprise.

The two sat across from each other like strangers on a blind date. Elton took the liberty of breaking the ice.

"I ordered your water with lemon wedges," Elton told her with a smile. His lips were smiling, not his eyes. They were taking a journey across Deborah's face, a place they hadn't visited in more than five years. "And your open-faced roast beef."

Water with lemon wedges and open-faced roast beef were the words Deborah digested. He remembered. She couldn't believe he'd actually remembered her favorite Family Café meal. She wondered what else he remembered. "Thank you."

"No problem." He cleared his throat. "You look good."

"Thank you." Deborah took a sip of her lemon water, still avoiding eye contact.

"You're welcome." Elton thought for a moment before saying, "Your, uh, Web site . . . it looks great."

"Thank you."

"Everything Literary; nice catchy name."

"Thank you."

Elton sighed. "Are those the only two words you're going to say to me?"

Now Deborah stared him straight in the eyes. "I've got two more words for you if those won't do."

He chuckled. "My Little Debbie. I see you still have quite a sense of humor. Good one."

"Thank you." Realizing she really was starting to sound ridiculous, she chuckled as well. They both chuckled until it turned into all-out laughter. They laughed so hard their eyes watered.

"Mind letting me in on the joke? I want to laugh too," Zelda stated as she walked over to the table with her hands on her hips.

"Oh, hi, Sister Zelda," Deborah greeted.

"Hey there, Miss Deborah."

"Please, Zelda, drop the Miss."

"I know, I know. You Northern folks don't like that. Says it makes you feel old. I try. It's just hard for a girl whose family has Southern roots."

"Well, Zelda," Elton chimed in, "I must say that I'm glad to hear you still calling her *Miss*." He was looking at Deborah with telling eyes when he said it.

Shocked at his bluntness—and in front of company, too—Deborah lowered her head, trying as hard as she could not to blush.

All of a sudden, Zelda felt like a third wheel. "Uh, why don't I go check on your meals? I'll be back with your orders in a minute." Zelda rushed away from the awkwardness like it was a cloud of secondhand smoke.

Deborah gathered the nerve to look up at him. "Look, Elton, before we go any further, I'm only here because you said you wanted to apologize, and as a matter of fact, I'd like to do some apologizing too."

Elton looked puzzled. "You apologize for what?"

"For my role in the—" Deborah lowered her tone. "You know . . . the procedure." She took her napkin and wiped away what wasn't on her mouth, at the same time looking around to make sure no one was in their business.

"I'm the one who owes you an apology. You didn't want to do it. I left you with no other option. I worked on your mind. I let the devil use me to get to you. Then I left and went on with my life knowing I had destroyed a part of yours." He reached across the table and grabbed Deborah's hands and caressed them in his. "A part of *our* life."

Deborah closed her eyes and allowed his apology to saturate her heart. Was it sincere? She wondered. She sniffed, a habit she thought she'd gotten rid of when it came to men. She thought she'd grown enough to trust God to protect her from the hurt and pain a man could sometimes bring along.

"I mean it, Little Debbie," Elton continued. "I know you may think that I've just been off playing pro ball and living the life, but believe me when I tell you . . . it . . ." His words trailed off as he got choked up. "Our baby, the choices we made, has been haunting me something fierce."

Never one to get all emotional, at this moment Deborah couldn't hold back the tears that formed in her eyes. What was it about Elton Culiver that just made her turn to mush? That just made her putty in that man's hands, willing to do whatever, whenever for this man? Now, all these years later, he still had that same way about him that was responsible for her making the choice to sleep with him on her visit to Chile. That same way about him that was responsible for her making the choice to terminate her pregnancy, even though she'd been well into her second trimester. She'd heard of women being so in love that they'd commit murder for the man they loved, but she never thought she'd be weak enough to be one of them, until she found herself in the clinic that day.

"That's why I had to see you," Elton said, pulling his hands away from hers in order to wipe the tears before they could fall from his eyes. "I'm sorry. I'm so sorry, Deborah, for going along with the whole abortion thing."

Going along with it? Deborah thought. If she recalled correctly, it was his bright idea in the first place. But still, she accepted his apology. "Apology accepted, Elton. And I'm sorry too. I was a grown woman who made a choice, a bad choice, the wrong choice . . . a couple of them, if I'm being honest. I should have never—"

Elton put his hand up, halting Deborah's words when he noticed Zelda returning to their table.

"Okay, what's really going on?" Zelda said, arriving at their table with their orders. "One minute you two are laughing like you're watching Chris Rock on *HBO*, and now you two are looking like someone died."

Deborah wiped at her eyes, making sure to get rid of all the remnants of tears. "I know you probably think we're crazy, Zelda, but you have no idea."

"And guess what? I'm still gon' pray for you. I don't need to know all the nooks and crannies to pray for you. Obviously Elton returning is bringing back a lot of emotion." She looked to Elton. "I remember when you two got engaged back when I was attending New Day. We threw that engagement party and everything. Then when the wedding never came and nobody ever asked any questions, I just figured the long distance thing had taken its toll on you two. So, it's good to see you back,

Elton. It's good to see you two together again. And from the looks of things, the town of Malvonia just might get that wedding after all."

Chapter Twenty-three

"Slumming again?" Norman asked Paige as she entered the ticket booth.

"Something like that." She smiled. "No, really, just checking to see how things are going." She sat down next to him, crossing her legs then patting down her skirt as to not show too much leg.

Norman couldn't help but notice how dressed up Paige was. She normally wore khakis and a crisp white blouse to work along with her manager's vest. He couldn't recall her ever wearing skirts to work . . . and heels . . . and—he inhaled the flowery scent that all of a sudden filled the ticket booth—and perfume.

Paige noticed the once-over Norman was giving her. "Oh . . . I . . . uh . . . have choir practice after work. Felt like giving God my best." She shrugged. "So, how is it going?" Paige asked, tilting her head to the side and smiling just enough to show a hint of her white teeth.

Once Norman could peel his eyes away from Paige's voluptuous legs that he'd barely ever seen before, or even noticed in church, he was able to speak. "Well, you know how it is." He could hardly finish his sentence after taking note that the top two buttons of Paige's crisp white blouse were undone. Not just the usual one, but two were unbuttoned, exposing cleavage he'd never even seen—or, once again, never noticed—back when she was in the world. Either way it went, it was no easy feat to tear his eyes away from the peek-a-boo game her breasts were playing with him. "Mondays are, uh, even slower than Wednesdays," he finished. "I bet there's no more than a handful of people in each showing. Some days it doesn't seem worth opening the doors to this place."

"Yeah, well, we still get a paycheck, so that's really all that matters."

"You're right about that," Norman said, catching his eyes wandering back down to her cleavage. No matter how hard he tried, he couldn't seem to control them. When he finally looked up, Paige's eyes were locked with his. He knew that she'd caught his wandering eyes. "Nice, uh, crucifix." He pointed to the gold cross necklace that she wore around her neck. It was on an eighteen-inch chain, and sat right in the midst of her cleavage.

"Thank you," Paige replied, fondling the cross with her hand.

"So, uh, how's that car of yours running?" Norman changed the subject. He enjoyed cars as much as he did breasts, so he hoped changing the subject to a set of wheels would supersede his interest in the set of breasts before him.

"Oh, just fine now. It wasn't nothing but the favor of the Lord that the uncle of the night clerk at that hotel was a certified mechanic and was able to get my car back in shape."

"Yeah, it's amazing what a piece of Doublemint gum, a bobby pin, and a rubber band can do."

Paige nudged Norman playfully. "Cut it out." She laughed. "He used real tools and real parts. Anyway, I'm just so glad you were there with me."

"And I'm so glad that I was there with you too."

Paige thought she sensed a romantic undertone to Norman's words. It made her blush.

A couple of months ago, Paige would have been slightly uncomfortable with the direction in which she thought their conversation was going, but not now. Now she almost seemed to welcome it. It was like she needed it. But why now? That was what she couldn't comprehend. Why now when she was a newlywed? Maybe back when she was single, perhaps the validation would have been nice, but she had a husband, a man who had committed to spend the rest of his life with her, not just the rest of the night.

The irony was that now that she was a married woman, she should have been feeling more fulfilled than ever, but instead, she felt empty. There was some type of void, and a part of her couldn't deny that she felt as if she was staring at just the person who could fill it.

"Is that so?" Paige decided to tease.

"It's very much so," Norman said. Surprised that she was not only welcoming his subtle flirting, but that she was responding with a little flirting of her own, Norman moved in closer to Paige. Before he could help himself, he'd reached up and caressed her face. "I don't know what's been going on lately between you and me. I've tried to fight it, but I just can't. I don't know why, after all these years, I never saw it before. But, Paige, you are one wonderful woman, and I've gotta have you." Norman pressed his lips up against Paige's and planted one on her. This time Paige knew that it was no accident. He pulled back slightly, just to get a reaction from her. Her eyes beckoned for another, so he obliged her.

At that moment, neither of them cared that two customers were approaching the ticket window. They were in their own little world. No one else existed. For Paige, who wasn't in her God given right mind, but wrapped up in fantasy mode, had even forgotten all about her husband. That was until the alarm clock rang, waking her from her sleep, only to find her husband snoring loudly next to her.

She rubbed her dreamy eyes and shook her head, shaking loose the after-thoughts from the sunrise dream she'd just had with Norman starring as the leading man. She sat up in bed and turned off the alarm. Now the only sound that filled the room was that of Blake's snoring. She rolled her eyes up in her head at the sound. It was hard to believe that not too long ago she'd wake up and watch him sleep. The sound of his snoring was like music to her ears then. She was just in so much awe at the blessing God had bestowed upon her in the form of a husband. On this morning, her blessing felt more like a curse.

"Get up, honey," she said with an irritated nudge to Blake's back, which was facing her. "Time for you to go to work." She then mumbled under her breath, "As if anything else is new."

As Blake came out of his stupor, Paige got up and headed to the bathroom. Blake rolled over to see his wife's backside headed into the bathroom.

"What, no"—the bathroom door slammed in his face—"good morning or nothing?" He finished his query, but Paige was already on the other side of the door. He was used to Paige giving him a good morning greeting that included a peck on his lips. Neither of them minded the other's morning breath. That was a part of being married, right? Blake cupped his hand around his mouth and blew his breath into it. He inhaled only to find that his morning breath hadn't gotten any worse than it had been in days past. So what was it? What was it that was putting an end to his and Paige's morning ritual? Was the honeymoon over? That was what he asked himself, but then he remembered that it had never really begun.

Paige had taken a shower the night before, so she didn't have a logical excuse as to why she was standing in the shower this morning. Logical, maybe not, but the truth was that she didn't feel like holding a conversation with Blake. She'd already stormed off without even saying so much as "Good morning," let alone giving him the morning peck on the lips he had grown used to. She had grown used to.

Then, if truth be told, maybe she felt the need to wash away the memories of the dream from which she'd just awoken. It had felt so real that she felt the need to repent. But she couldn't control her dreams, could she? It wasn't her fault she'd had an adulterous dream.

As she stood in the shower, simply allowing the hot water to massage her body, she knew she had a part in what was going on between her and Norman—a huge part. She knew that her mind was a battlefield, and the battle had been taking place in her mind for years. But she was certain she'd won the battle after finding the perfect man—well, after him finding her—and not only that, but marrying him. For a little while it seemed as though everything was under control, but here lately she was losing it.

"I gotta get this thing under control. I just have to," she scolded herself. Closing her eyes, she began to recite, "God has given me a sound mind . . . a sound mind. Do you hear that, mind? You are sound." The frustration in her voice was evident. She wasn't convinced. It was happening again. The lust-filled daydreams and fantasies . . . about men. All kinds of men. The daydreams and fantasies she used to share with Norman in their worldly conversations. Unbeknownst to Norman, these things had actually never taken place. Well, they had taken place, but only in Paige's mind. The men had been real, but none of the romantic rendezvous had been real, just the wishful thinking of a big girl. Their interest in her had been fluffed up to the tenth power. It was all a front. She was all a front.

On the outside, Paige wanted everybody to think that she had it all together, that she was proud of who she was, confident in the skin she was in. She wanted them to believe that not only did she love herself, but that the world loved her as well, and nothing about her, especially her weight, could keep her from getting a man and the attention she deserved. The attention that any skinny little chick would get.

Once she'd gotten saved and learned how marvelous, fearfully and wonderfully made God had created her, she started to think more highly of herself than she ought. Too highly. So highly that even if a man really had taken a sincere interest in her, she'd shoot him down before he even had a chance to show it.

She tried to convince herself that she was shooting these men down because they had reminded her in one way or another of her father. For years she'd watched her mother wait on her father hand and foot, to the point where she felt she was running herself so ragged that she didn't have time to spend with Paige. But just last year, after having a long overdue conversation with her mother, Paige realized that her mother enjoyed that part of her role as a wife. It was her way of telling her father that she loved him without actually saying it. In other words, it was her mother's way of showing her father how much she loved him. So Paige's excuse and cop-out came tumbling down in a matter of minutes. But fortunately, Blake had been there to catch the fall, her fall. He wasn't a fantasy, but God had really sent her a man who loved her in spite of her thoughts. She'd been so focused and consumed with courting Blake that her mind hadn't had time to wander off to La-La Land. But now things were changing.

Paige felt as though she'd taken ten steps forward when she finally gained control over her wandering mind, but now she felt as though she'd taken eleven steps back. Tears mixed with the water as she shook her head. She covered her ears as if they were a trick passage to her mind and she was trying to protect anything foul from intruding. "Please, God, not again," she wept. But no matter how much she cried and prayed, she knew it was happening again: her mind was about to stray. She hoped she had enough strength not to follow it.

Chapter Twenty-four

"So, Raygene, can I get you anything?" Tamarra asked her niece as she waved her hand at a chair, which was the girl's invitation to sit down.

"No thanks. I'm fine," Raygene said, taking a seat. She looked around, as this was the first time she'd seen the inside of Tamarra's place. The last time she dropped by, Tamarra hadn't invited her past the driveway. "Nice place." She made standard conversation.

"Thank you." Tamarra stood, too nervous to sit down. She wanted to pace, but with her mind she had commanded her feet to stay planted. And they were planted, all right. They felt like they were planted in a tub of cement, because she wanted to run, but she couldn't. Not technically run away from Raygene, but run away from what Raygene stood for, which was a reminder of the girl's father.

"I was surprised to see you when you showed up at the book event. I had no idea you were the wonderful caterer everyone was talking about. You have quite a reputation," Raygene complimented as she sat there with her legs crossed and hands folded across her knees.

Tamarra wasn't in the mood for small talk. She wanted to know what this girl wanted. Surely it had been obvious to Raygene that Tamarra didn't want anything to do with her, that

she didn't want to strike up a relationship with her after all
of these years. So, what did she want? It must have been big,
because she was buttering her up with all these compliments
that Tamarra could care less about.

As awful as it sounded, Tamarra wanted her out, not just
out of her house, but out of her life. The quickest way to get
her out was to not beat around the bush, and get right to the
point. She needed to find out why the girl was here, in her
home and in her town. More importantly, why had she been
in her church?

"Humph, I'm sure you were surprised to see me at that
book event." Tamarra couldn't have been any more sarcastic.
"But surely not as surprised as I was to see you in my church
the other day, heading into my pastor's office."

There was silence as Raygene bowed her head. She was going to use the silence as an opportunity to think up something
to say. After careful consideration, though, she decided to cut
to the chase with the truth. "I want you to acknowledge me."
That was it, plain and simple. At least that's what Tamarra
thought, until Raygene parted her lips to speak again. "I want
you to let people know who I am. I want a relationship with
you. I want you to invite me over to dinner. I want us to cook
together." The more she spoke, the bolder her tone became,
as if Tamarra owed her these things. "I want us to go shopping together. I want you to come to my school functions: my
prom, my homecoming, soccer games . . ." Clearly the girl's
mind was going to "way back when" as she became emotional.
As a college student, prom and homecoming had come and
gone. Tears filled and then fell from her eyes as she continued. "Dance recitals, PTA meetings—"

"Hold it right there." Tamarra put up her hand. "Isn't that
a bit much?"

The girl seemed flabbergasted as she stood, but she appeared to be more hurt than anything. "Are you serious? I have friends at school with distant cousins who show them more support. I'd think after twenty-something years, and now with me living back in the same state with you, that you'd want to make up for some kind of lost time."

Tamarra's blood was boiling. Surely the girl was only running off at the mouth in hopes of piling a heap of guilt on Tamarra. It didn't make her feel guilty, though. In actuality it peeved her off. And she was about to let Miss Thang know it. "I don't care if it's been thirty-something years. You are still the child, so don't think for one minute you have any right to walk up in my house and try to read me." Tamarra was pointing her finger and her voice was different. It sounded like it did many moons ago, back before she was saved, and walked around in offense with an attitude. Looks like she was offended—highly offended.

The girl just shook her head as she wiped her eyes. "I'm sorry. I didn't mean to disrespect you." She sat back down. "It's just that I was certain once you saw me, you'd just . . ." She couldn't even finish her sentence before her shoulders were heaving up and down.

Tamarra didn't want to see the girl hurting, but she didn't want her to live in some fantasy that the two of them would ever have the type of relationship she was seeking. "Honestly, Raygene, and in no way is this meant to hurt you, but when I saw you . . ." Tamarra choked back tears of her own. "All I could see was him—your father. It took me back there, and I just can't go back there. I won't go back there. It's not your fault. I'm sure you are a good girl, but I just can't get past the circumstances."

"Then give it to God," Raygene blurted.

The girl's comment even shocked Tamarra. "Huh?"

"Then give it to God. That's what your pastor said you should do."

Tamarra dang near hit the roof. "What?" she shouted. "You told Pastor that—"

"No, I didn't," Raygene assured her. "We were just speaking in general. I wanted to see how much your pastor knew before I went into any detail, but when I realized that your pastor knew nothing—"

"And it's going to stay that way, so don't you come snooping around trying to cause confusion in my life when everything is going just perfect."

Raygene gave her a sarcastic little chuckle. "Is it now? Your life is just so perfect that there is absolutely no room for me, Miss Imperfect, Miss I Probably Wish She Was Never Born. Wow, that's nice to know because—"

"You are right; I do wish you were never born," Tamarra told her. "There are men out here who'd kill to produce a child but can't, and God lets my brother be a father. What kind of sick—"

"Do you believe in forgiveness?" Raygene shot. "Do you believe that God forgives us for our sins and wrongdoings?"

"Well, uh, of course. But don't get the wrong idea, Raygene. I'm not saying that you are a sin, that you are some evil spawn of Satan. It's just that forgiveness isn't my strong forte. But believe you me, I'm working on it. As a matter of fact, I've already done some forgiving."

"Obviously you haven't forgiven my father. If you had, then it wouldn't be so hard for you to accept me. Then when you look into my eyes, you wouldn't see his and punish me for his sins. But that's all right, because guess what? Even if you haven't forgiven him, that's okay, because God didn't sit around and wait on you to forgive him before He did. God has forgiven my father. If I didn't believe it before, I surely believe it after speaking with your pastor and the scriptures—"

"Why did you go to my pastor? There were a million and one spiritual leaders you could have gone to in order to find out whether or not your daddy had been forgiven. Why'd you go to mine?"

"I guess I just wanted confirmation. I mean, I knew in my spirit that I didn't exist in your little world. Oh, my bad, your *perfect* little world, but I guess I had to just find out firsthand. As soon as I realized your pastor didn't even know you had a brother, I knew without a doubt that your pastor had no idea that I existed. So, I just started using hypothetical situations and scenarios during our talk. But don't worry; I didn't include you in any of them."

"So, who does Pastor think you are in relation to me?"

"Your pastor just thinks I'm someone that a member evangelized to, told me about and invited me to New Day. Don't worry; I didn't blow your cover."

Tamarra exhaled. She was more than relieved. This girl's little stunt had landed her in the ER, but all was well now. Hopefully. "So, what do you want now?"

Raygene couldn't believe how cold Tamarra's voice was. She didn't know many Christians, and she hadn't been a practicing Christian herself, although she believed in God and was good people. But she was certain the Christian standing before her wasn't showing her the love of God. She wasn't showing her any love at all. Raygene felt defeated. So, with the little bit of self worth she had left, she gathered it up and stood to leave. "Nothing. I want nothing from you. Sorry I wasted your time, but more importantly, I'm sorry I was born too." Raygene walked over to the door and waited for Tamarra to unlock it so that she could leave.

A zillion-bazillion thoughts and emotions were running through Tamarra's mind right now. The emotion that surprised her most was the one that wanted to just take the girl in her arms and make up for all those years she'd missed out on her life. It was the emotion that wanted family to love so badly, but Tamarra fought it. Now wasn't the time. She prayed that one day she'd be ready, willing, and able to give Raygene what she wanted, but today wasn't the day.

Against what the more overwhelming emotions were pulling at Tamarra to do, she opened her front door and let Raygene exit.

"So, I guess this is it." Raygene was giving Tamarra one last chance to just open her arms and embrace her.

"Good-bye." Tamarra didn't seize the opportunity.

"Good-bye, *Aunt* Tamarra," Raygene said before she walked off. "And don't worry; your secret is safe with me. I'll take it to my grave. . . . All of them."

Yes, despite all the secrets Tamarra was finally facing and dealing with, there was more: one that not even her best friend knew.

Chapter Twenty-five

"Hey, I finally get to hear your voice again," Lynox said into the phone receiver. He'd been waiting to hear from Deborah ever since their ruined official first date. After Elton had finally left him and Deborah to their date, she'd explained a little bit to Lynox about her history with Elton, leaving out the sinful details, of course.

From the way Deborah spoke of Elton and the look on her face while she did so, it was apparent to Lynox that Elton's return had caused some of Deborah's feelings for Elton to resurface.

"Look, why don't I give you some time to let all of this sink in, to perhaps talk to the man? It's obvious you two could possibly have some unresolved matters that need to be addressed, discussed, or just closure period," Lynox had stated.

Deborah agreed, which was another reason she had agreed to meet with Elton. If she was going to start a relationship with Lynox, she didn't want to bring any parts of her old one into it. If by chance she and Lynox did lead into something bigger, she wanted to be able to give her entire self to him, including the piece she feared Elton still might have had.

"Oh, hi. How's it going?" Deborah replied casually into her phone as if Lynox were one of her girlfriends calling her up to shoot the breeze.

"Are you busy or something?" Lynox asked, cluing in on Deborah's tone. She had always been much more serious and focused.

"Uh, well, not really." She knew she sounded a complete mess. Her mind was a mess. He'd caught her off guard. If she recalled correctly, she was supposed to call him after she got her mind right. He wasn't supposed to have been calling her. Had she known it was him on the ringing phone, had his number not shown up as private, she never would have even answered the phone in the first place.

As she lay in her bed, she pulled the covers up to her neck. She called herself hiding from Lynox, but it was too late. He'd found her.

"I know the last time we talked, we'd agreed that you'd call me, but waiting is not my thing. Don't get me wrong; there are certain things—and people—that are very much worth waiting for."

"Oh, okay." Deborah was keeping it short.

Lynox was surprised at her reply to what he thought was a smooth Billy Dee Williams line. Maybe he hadn't made himself clear. "You're worth waiting for, Deborah, in every sense of the word."

"Mm-hmm, that's nice."

Lynox was giving this woman some of his best stuff, yet she was reacting as if he'd stolen his lines from Will Smith's character in *The Fresh Prince of Bel Air*. "So, is everything good with you?"

"Yes, very good."

"Good enough to give us another try at a date? I've got an idea, something where we can't be interrupted."

Deborah quickly sat up in her bed as if she'd just heard

something that startled her. "You know, that sounds great. Just call me back and let me know the day and time. Talk to you soon." Neither said good-bye. Deborah didn't allow the opportunity as she quickly ended the call.

"Did you say something, honey?" The bathroom door opened and Elton entered, simultaneously asking the question. His body was still wet from the shower he'd just walked out of. A towel was wrapped around his waist and he held another one, drying his head with it.

"Uh, no, well, uh, yeah. I was asking you if you wanted me to fix you something to eat," Deborah lied. She was a liar. She was a liar and a fornicator. She was a liar, a fornicator, and a sinner. She was a liar, a fornicator, a sinner, and a backslider. She looked up at Elton, who she'd just backslid with. She felt a tinge of guilt. She was a guilt-filled liar, fornicator, sinner, and a backslider. But to top it all off, Lord have mercy, the girl was whipped!

"How's your leg?" Deborah asked Elton as the two drove down the highway. They were, yet again, on their way out to eat. In just the past couple of weeks, Elton had taken Deborah to more fancy and expensive restaurants than she'd been to in her lifetime. Last week's Valentine's Day dinner was the best. Elton had reserved an entire restaurant for just the two of them. She was enjoying every minute of it.

Deborah wasn't the only one enjoying herself. Elton was acting like a kid who'd been on punishment and was just let off, instead of someone who'd been overseas playing basketball.

"Actually, the MRI results the doctor here in the States took didn't appear as bad as the ones taken over in Chile," Elton confessed. His injured knee was what had brought him back home in the first place. After dunking on an opponent, he came down on his right leg the wrong way and tore the ligament in his knee. Back in the locker room, where they carried him after peeling him off the court in the most pain he'd felt in his life, the team doctor predicted he wouldn't be able to finish the season or probably start the new one. In other words, his career was pretty much over.

"Well, then all that means is that God is still in the healing business. It's His report that matters." Deborah was trying to encourage him.

"Yeah, but even if my knee does fully heal, I just don't know if I can go back and start over. It will be time for my new contract, and I know they are going to try to play me on the money tip. I'm not starting from scratch. I'm not going backwards and have to work hard all over again to get back to where I was when I left."

Why not? Deborah thought. That's exactly what she'd have to do now. She'd managed to go backward in her Christian walk, sleeping with Elton again even after what happened the last time. Now she'd have to work hard all over again to get back to where she was before Elton had come. She couldn't help but wonder if this was some sort of payback, if Elton had come back to Malvonia to seduce her the way she'd gone to Chile and seduced him.

"But there is something I don't mind going backwards and having to work hard for all over again." He briefly took his eyes off the road and looked over at Deborah. "And that something is you." He admired her. "I missed looking into your eyes, those model-like high cheek bones"—he rubbed his index finger down her nose—"and that perfectly pointed nose."

Deborah thought she was going to melt like a bar of chocolate right there in the leather seats of Elton's Hummer he'd been leasing since arriving back in Ohio.

"But I need to know if you are willing. Are you, Deborah Lucas, willing to start over and do things right this time?"

She thought about what she and Elton had before the abortion. They'd been so in love, inseparable. There'd been no major fussing and fighting. Disagreements, yes, but no saying hurtful things to one another that they'd eventually regret. They never could stay mad at each other. Even after he dumped the abortion money on her, left the country, and took over a month to call her again, she didn't get angry with him. She just reasoned that he needed time to deal and heal, just like she did. Even after he broke off the engagement, stating that he was too consumed by the game to focus on being a husband, she didn't get angry with him. Again, she reasoned he needed more time—so much time that eventually he stopped calling her at all.

No one at New Day ever really knew what happened. They just assumed Elton had gotten caught up in the status of being a pro ball player, ended up falling into the trap set by groupies, and called off the wedding. No one asked, figuring if Deborah wanted them to know, she would have told them. She didn't, though. She never told them the wedding was off. The wedding just simply never happened.

"So, Little Debbie, are you willing to give ya boy Elton here another try?" Elton asked after exiting the highway and stopping at a red light.

Deborah, without a single doubt in her mind, replied, "Yes."

"Yes!" Elton shouted as if he'd just scored the winning point during finals. He reached over and hugged her. "Oh, Deb, you have just made me the happiest man in the world. As a matter of fact . . ." He reached into his pocket. "I know I've only been back in town a few weeks, but it has been a blessed few weeks. I honestly feel in my heart that God has allowed us to pick up where we left off. I don't know about you, but in a sense, I don't feel like we have to start completely over again. I just feel we need to do what we should have done years ago." Pulling a box out of his pocket, taking the lid off and revealing the largest diamond stone Deborah had ever seen her life, Elton did something Deborah hadn't seen coming: he proposed . . . again.

"Deborah Lucas, I have never stopped loving you, and I feel in my spirit that you've never stopped loving me. Even after all of this time, baby girl, we still have a connection. That connection is God telling us that we belong together. Let's do what's right this time. Let me make an honest woman out of you, Deborah. Marry me."

"Elton . . ." Her words trailed off as he slipped the ring onto her finger. "I don't know what to say."

"Say yes, baby. Say yes, that you will marry me."

Before Deborah could reply, the car behind them blew its horn.

"The light is green. You better go," Deborah said, stalling.

"Forget that light. The guy behind us can wait. This is more important." Looking down at the ring and then into Deborah's eyes, he asked, "Deborah Michelle Lucas, will you marry me? Will you be my wife? The wife I will love, honor, cherish, and never, ever take for granted? The wife I want to make a new home with, a new life, and to be the mother of my child— the child we should have had together five years ago?"

Could this really be happening? Could God really be giving them a chance to go back in time and erase the bad mistake they'd made? Just in case He was, Deborah didn't want to give up this chance, this opportunity to wipe her slate clean. So, without further ado, she replied, "Yes, Elton, I'll marry you."

Chapter Twenty-six

"Surprise! Honey, I'm home, and I'm all yours."

Paige could hear Blake calling out as he walked through the front door. She rolled over in bed and looked at the clock that read 5:30 P.M. What was Blake doing home at five-thirty in the evening? Though that might have been a normal time for the average red-blooded, hardworking American, it wasn't so normal for Blake. In the past few months, eight o'clock in the evening had been the earliest he'd ever made it home, unless he was dropping in to get cleaned up for a business dinner, cocktail party, or something. Even then he was right back out the door again.

Any other time, Paige would have been excited to have her man home early, and from the sounds of it, he planned on staying. But not now. It was too late. She'd slipped into her funk, the funk no one really knew about, or had ever witnessed because she'd been alone all of her life.

"Babe, get up and get dressed, I've got a surprise for you." Blake was excited enough for both of them. He sat down on the bed next to Paige, who was wearing a red plaid flannel pajama pants set. He noticed that the slicked back ponytail she usually wore wasn't so slicked back. Hair was sticking every which way out of the twisty holder. He lovingly patted her hair down.

Paige flinched when he touched her, and put her hand up as if to tell him not to touch her hair. She thought maybe he needed to check out Chris Rock's movie, *Good Hair*. Messed up or not, a woman did not like for a man to be touching all up in her hair. That was reserved for the paid stylist.

"What's the matter? You not feeling well?" Blake asked. Now he touched her forehead, checking for a fever.

"I'm fine." Paige's voice made it sound like she was fine, but her looks begged to differ. Blake had never seen her look so defeated. He was used to walking through the door and finding her at her best regardless. He'd even teased her about being a great candidate for a soap opera on the nights she'd wear light makeup to bed. She'd sleep stiff on her back so not to make a mess of the cream-colored pillow cases. But now there was a mess on the pillow, all right. The mess was her.

"Well, I'm glad you're fine, because I want you to get dressed." He looked down at his watch. "I'm gonna change out of this suit as well." He stood up and loosened his tie. "And if we hurry, we might make it before tip-off." He reached in his pocket and pulled out two tickets. "I scored another set of tickets to the game, and this time I'm taking my baby."

Paige couldn't match his excitement if she tried. "Take Klyde."

Blake's excitement was beginning to evaporate like water left in a vase too long. "I don't want to go with Klyde. I want to go with you. Besides, the reason I'm able to even go is because Klyde is sitting in on a meeting for me. He owed me."

"Then take Norman," She shrugged. "He's good company. I should know; I've been dating him ever since I got married."

Now all of Blake's excitement was completely gone. His tone was laced with concern more than anything. "And just what is that supposed to mean?"

Paige darted up in the bed. "You know exactly what it means. It means you've been pawning me off on him like I'm Dennis the Menace or something. Like I bother you so much that you can't stand to be with me."

Blake was thrown for a loop. "Wha . . . what are you talking about? Where is this coming from?" He sat back down on the bed.

"Oh, please. Don't play dumb. You've been dodging me like the plague. If you didn't want to be married, then you should have just said so."

"Are you kidding me right now? You can't be serious."

"No, you're the one who can't be serious. I've been doing everything I know how to get your attention, and now all of a sudden because you've got a moment to spare, you want to spend it with me. Well, I don't need your charity. Go to your meeting, Blake. Give Klyde the tickets; let him take his wife." Paige's eyes watered. Blake hadn't seen tears in his wife's eyes since he'd looked her in the face on their wedding day and told her that she was the woman he wanted to spend the rest of his life with.

"I guess I don't know what to say besides I'm sorry." Blake stood and ran his hand down his chin. He fiddled with the chin hairs he'd been allowing to grow for a new look. "I honestly didn't realize you felt this way. I honestly didn't realize I'd been acting this way." He thought for a moment. "I guess I have been working nonstop these past months, but I've been doing it for us, Paige. For me and you. For you especially. I just want you to have the best. I want you to have everything. And when we decide to have children, I want to already be prepared for them." Blake's jaw tightened. "I don't ever want them going without. Ever! Don't you understand that?"

Paige flinched once again, but this time it was out of fear. She'd never heard Blake raise his voice like that. She'd never seen him in an angry state. Realizing he'd frightened her, he went and sat back down on the bed and took her hands into his.

"I'm sorry, baby," Blake apologized. "I didn't mean to frighten you. It's just that . . . " He paused as his words trailed off. "Look, I love you, girl. Every vow I spoke, I meant, including until death do us part. Nothing is going to come between us, but I need you to just hang in there with me while I prepare for our future. The Bible says if you don't work, you don't eat. I just want to make sure that my family never has to worry about where their next meal is coming from. We're young. Let's sacrifice now and reap the benefits of our sacrifices later."

Blake sounded so convincing that Paige almost wanted to agree completely.

"I'm just scared," Paige confessed. "I'm scared that sooner or later you're going to divorce me and marry your job. Soon I'll just become the mistress in my own home."

Blake threw his arms around his wife and assured her, "That will never happen, baby. I promise you. Just let your man do what he needs to do to get us where we need to be, okay? I don't want to be one paycheck away from homelessness like some of the rest of the world is living. Let me provide us with that security we need."

"But you're all the security I need," Paige told him.

"And you've got me. I'm going to try to do better at showing you that. Okay?" He kissed Paige on her nose. "'Kay, sweetheart?" He kissed her again, this time on the lips.

His kiss was so warm, soft, and buttery to Paige, like having popcorn in a dark theater. He kissed her like it was a secret, like she was his secret that he didn't want to share with a single soul.

"Okay," Paige agreed, kissing him back. Then kissing him again. She reached to grab his head, to caress it, but then he pulled away.

"Now do like I said and get dressed. I don't want to miss tip-off. Maybe we can even grab a late dinner afterward."

Before she could say a word, he was floating off to the bathroom and closing the door. She pouted like a two-year-old. The heck with tip-off and dinner, she wanted to shoot right for dessert. She wanted him to be her dessert and she his, but once again he'd left her high and dry. He'd talked a good game, dang near killing her softly with his words; then he yanked the needle off the record, and just like that, things were back to how they had been only moments before he'd entered the room. Just overnight it seemed she'd gone from being made to feel like the only woman in the world by Blake to feeling like the only woman in the world . . . period.

She couldn't live like this. She wouldn't live like this. Something had to give or else she was going to give up.

Chapter Twenty-seven

"And you should have seen her, dressed up like a sunflower. It was the cutest thing I'd ever seen, I promise you," Maeyl said. He was talking about Sakaya and her role in the play at her preschool. Ever since they'd sat down at Family Café all he'd talked about was his little girl. "Me, volunteering in the CDC Head Start classroom: who would have thought it? But you know, this Daddy thing, although I was scared to death at first, just came natural. Sakaya just looks so proud when she sees her daddy walk into that classroom when I read to the kids. And you know, the other kids love to see me coming too. You can tell a lot of them don't have fathers at home. I wish there was some way to get more male involvement in the classroom. I mean, why is it that just the moms are room parents and at the PTA meetings? Seems like if more men stepped up, then we'd have less troubled boys and young men in prison, if you know what I mean. My father always taught me . . ."

Okay, now Maeyl was definitely auditioning for the role of Charlie Brown's parents. "Wha-wha-wha-wha." That was what his words started to sound like as Tamarra stared through him, lifting a spoonful of chili to her mouth like she was a robot.

"Don't you think that would be a good idea?" Maeyl asked Tamarra, who hadn't even heard the question he'd posed to her. "Tamarra, honey, don't you agree?"

"Uh-huh, yeah, Maeyl." She scooped up another bite.

"I mean, they should just save the taxpayers their money and lock all black boys up at the age of fourteen. Give 'em three to five years and let 'em just get it over with, huh?" Maeyl was being sarcastic.

"Yeah, sounds good to me."

"And I was thinking, maybe you should get married in a green wedding dress: our way of going green. And the table settings at our reception can be made of recycled newspaper. Does that sound good?"

"Yeah, sounds good to me," Tamarra replied blindly.

"Okay, what's going on here, Tamarra?" Maeyl's fist softly hit the table, enough to make it shake Tamarra out of her gaze.

"Oh, yeah, I totally agree," Tamarra rambled off.

"Woman, you haven't listened to a word I've said since we sat down."

"That's not true," Tamarra fronted. "I've heard every word you said."

"Is that so? Then when are we going shopping for your green wedding dress?"

Tamarra turned her nose up like she smelled a wet dog. "Green wedding dress?"

"Yeah, that's what you just agreed to wear."

Tamarra drew a blank.

"See, told you that you weren't listening. And I knew that before you decided all black boys should be put in jail."

Tamarra looked horrified. She'd never decide upon such a thing.

"Now, tell me what's wrong. Is it the wedding? Is planning it stressing you out? I thought that's why we decided on something small and intimate."

"No, Maeyl, it's not the wedding." Tamarra's eyes gazed downward. It definitely wasn't the wedding. She'd hardly done any planning at all, as if the wedding was just going to happen on its own—or even worse, as if the wedding wasn't going to happen at all.

"It's Sakaya, isn't it?"

Tamarra lifted her head. Was he on to her?

"You're afraid of taking on motherhood, huh? Don't worry, babe. You're going to be the perfect second mommy. You are kind, sweet, lovable . . ."

Maeyl went on and on with compliment after compliment about how wonderful a mother Tamarra would be to Sakaya. Any other woman would have been flattered—any woman who truly wanted to step into the role of motherhood to another woman's child. That woman wasn't Tamarra. Not with Sakaya, some other woman's daughter. She didn't know how much longer she could do this. She was certain that after a few movies, dinners, and trips to the ice cream parlor, she would have grown into the part by now, but with Raygene trying to force herself into Tamarra's life as well, she hadn't even gotten the chance to rehearse for the role. This was just too much. So much that Tamarra was starting to have trouble breathing.

"Tamarra, honey, you okay?" Maeyl got up and went and sat down next to Tamarra. She wasn't talking. She was taking slow, deep breaths like they taught her at the ER. "Come on. Let's go outside and get some air. Just keep breathing." So as not to make a scene, Maeyl slowly helped Tamarra to her feet and escorted her outside of the restaurant. He walked her around to the side of the building near the dumpsters and side entrance. He wanted to keep her moving so that she wouldn't be consumed with the fear of losing her breath. "Breathe, baby, breathe," he coached as they paced on the side of the building, out of customers' view.

Tamarra tried to pace her breathing as well. The last thing she wanted to do was have an attack right there at Family Café. That was giving the town and the church way too much to talk about. She was bound and determined to get this thing under control. Inhale, exhale. Inhale, exhale. She repeated this until she felt her breathing was back to normal.

"You feel better now?" Maeyl asked, now less worried than he had been only moments earlier.

"Yeah, Maeyl, I'm good. I'm good," Tamarra assured him as she stood still. "We can go back now." She started to walk away, but then he grabbed her arm to stop her.

"What?" She looked down at his hand on her arm. "Really, I'm fine. We can go back now."

"We can't go back, Tamarra. We can never go back." A sad and troubled demeanor now hovered over Maeyl. "We can't go back to how things were before." He swallowed hard as if swallowing his emotions. "We can't go back to before Sakaya came into my life. And I know that's exactly where you want to go back to."

Tamarra tried to cover the look on her face that read "Busted," but she couldn't. What would be the point? Zelda was right; she couldn't hide it.

"I've known it from the beginning, sensed it from day one, but I wanted so much for it to not be so. I could tell it's not what you wanted. You were like a fish out of water when it came to talk of Sakaya or just being around her. But I kept pushing, hoping the more I had you around her, the more she'd grow on you . . . and you know . . . you'd just . . . I don't know." Maeyl honestly didn't know what he thought would happen. All he knew was that both girls meant the world to him, but he'd have to back away from one to keep the other, or there was a chance that eventually he'd ruin his relationship with both.

Tamarra didn't know whether to feel embarrassed or be relieved that Maeyl had seen right through her all this time: relieved that she didn't have to say it herself, or embarrassed that all along he'd known she was being a fake and a phony. Either way it went, the truth was out.

"Maeyl, I'm so sorry. I tried. I really did try. I had every intention of being that perfect wife to you and the perfect stepmother to Sakaya, but—"

"Then that's where you went wrong."

"Huh?" Tamarra didn't understand Maeyl's comment.

"You set out to be perfect. Nobody's perfect, so that was never going to happen. I just wanted you to be you."

"But *me* couldn't take playing second fiddle again with my man."

"Second fiddle? Is that what you think?"

"It's what I know," Tamarra said with conviction. "Trust me; I've been chosen over a kid before."

Maeyl looked at her almost with disgust. "Woe is me. Poor me," he mocked. "Why is everything always happening to me? Why is everybody always picking on me?" Shoving his hands in his pockets to warm them up from the coolness of the late February weather, Maeyl stated, "Last call for drinks was years ago, yet you're still at the pity party. Get over it, Tamarra. Get over yourself."

Tamarra opened her mouth in shock. She'd never seen this side of Maeyl before.

"I can't believe I wanted this thing to work so badly. I mean, I've prayed and I've prayed and I've prayed that God would change your heart, allow you to receive and accept your new, ready-made family as a blessing, but you are just so selfish and so caught up in your own little world that you wouldn't stand still long enough to let God speak to your heart." He let out a *harrumph* sound. "Guess I'm not the only one you haven't been spending much time with lately."

"Now, you wait a minute!" Tamarra pointed. How dare Maeyl question her walk and relationship with God? Although, if she was being honest with herself, she had to admit that lately she hadn't prayed like she used to pray. She hadn't even read her Bible on a regular basis. She'd allowed so much to clutter her mind, to distract her from the things of God . . . from God Himself. Slowly but surely she was straying. If she wanted to be brutally honest, heck, she'd become a Sunday-only Christian, the one thing her mother had once indirectly tried to accuse her of being.

"No, you wait a minute," Maeyl shot back. "I've been waiting long enough, but the wait is over." He paused for a moment, closed his eyes, and took a deep breath. "And so are we." He opened his eyes after saying those words, almost as if he didn't want to look at Tamarra's face while saying them. "The wedding is off. I'll reimburse you for any expenses you've incurred. I'll chalk mine as a loss—a great loss."

Tamarra froze. She was in shock. She hadn't expected this. She didn't know what she had expected, but it sure wasn't to be dumped on the side of Family Café . . . next to the dumpsters, like trash. She couldn't think straight as she massaged her temples with her index fingers. Her head felt like it was going to explode, like there were backed-up tears filling her head like a water balloon that was going to burst at any time. She was in pain.

Maeyl knew that his words had caused the pain, and he couldn't stand there and watch it. "Good-bye, Tamarra." He walked away with tear-filled eyes from the woman he truly loved.

Tamarra just stood there, tears finally dropping one after the other. Her head was spinning round and round. She had to lean up against the building to balance herself. Her breath shortened. She tried to take in deep breaths and count, but her head wouldn't even allow her to come up with the numbers. She couldn't speak; she couldn't breathe. Everything turned into a blur; then everything went black.

Chapter Twenty-eight

"Am I being punked or something? What do you mean you're getting married?" Lynox let off a nervous laugh. Deborah didn't laugh. She just sat stone-faced on the bench next to Lynox. "Oh my goodness, you're serious, aren't you? You asked me to meet you in the middle of Easton Town Square on a cold night just to tell me that?" He stood. "You could have told me that mess over the phone."

"Wait, Lynox. Please don't leave. Sit back down, please," Deborah requested. He hesitated, but did as she asked. "I just felt the need to tell you in person. You know?"

"Actually, no, I don't know." He chuckled. "I don't . . . I don't understand, Deborah. Who? Why? When? I mean, just yesterday it seemed we were out at a restaurant and . . ." Lynox's words trailed off as it suddenly hit him. "It's that guy, that Elton guy, isn't it?" Deborah looked down. Lynox stood again. "You don't see this guy for five years, then he's back in town and you two are engaged? Well, that explains why you were so short with me on the phone the one or two times I was able to get you on the line." Lynox washed his hands down his face. "Wow. This is a joke, and the joke's on me."

"Lynox, you're not a joke. You're a wonderful man. I really did like you. I'm even willing to go as far as to say that I could have seen a future with you." Deborah wasn't saying that just to make Lynox feel good. It was truly how she felt.

"Then what happened? I mean, how can you just change your mind about us because Kobe Bryant blows back in town? The dude's a joke; he's a player. He's ego trippin' and you're feeding right into it."

Now Deborah stood. "Look, I know you might be hurt, but that doesn't mean you need to say things that are hurtful to me."

Lynox sighed. "You're right. I apologize. It's just that I know his type. I can see right through that cat. It's not about you. It's not about him having you. It's about him knowing that he can have you. You're no better than one of the groupies that probably waits outside of his hotel room door after—"

Lynox couldn't even finish his insult—not after the stinging on his right cheek from Deborah's slap. Deborah stood there with a trembling lip and a balled fist as if she wanted to slug him again. There was no regret, no repenting.

"Okay, I deserved that," Lynox said, rolling his tongue on the inside of his jaw. "I was out of line. Way out of line. I was trying to hurt you because I'm hurt." This much honesty in a man was not a trait Deborah was used to over the past few years.

Deborah could see the pity in Lynox's eyes. "I didn't mean to hurt you, Lynox, but I have to do what is going to make me happy."

"And how do you know he's going to make you happy? There have been years between you two. People change."

"You're right. I've changed. Both Elton and I have changed. We're older and wiser. We realize we made some mistakes, but we're going to give it a try again."

"You sound like you're reading a script, like you've rehearsed this or something."

Actually, Deborah had rehearsed it. In her head. A thousand times. She'd rehearsed these words not only to say to Lynox, but to say to herself, because that's who she was having the hardest time convincing that marrying Elton was the right thing to do. Lynox calling her out was starting to upset her. No one likes to face the truth. Deborah didn't like facing the truth.

"I'm sorry you feel as though this is staged. I'm sorry you're hurt. I didn't want to do this." Deborah looked down at her twiddling thumbs.

"Then don't," Lynox said to her as if it were just as easy as that to call off her engagement with Elton. "Just hold off on this idea of marriage. Give me a chance to show you that it's not about some baller bouncing into town and proposing, but instead, it's about a gentleman strolling into your life and sweeping you off your feet." Lynox closed in the space between him and Deborah then placed his hands on each of her cold cheeks, forcing her to look him in his eyes. "Let me be that gentleman."

Deborah was touched. She was moved. But she was engaged. She couldn't think about what might have been with Lynox. She had to focus on what would be with Elton. "I'm sorry, Lynox. Take care of yourself." She walked off quickly before Lynox said one more thing out of a romance novel that would have her sinning again.

After making it to her car, she started it up and turned on the heat. Her car had only been sitting fifteen minutes, so it wasn't completely cold air coming out. She watched Lynox walking past her in the aisle in front of her. He didn't see her watching him in the night, mainly because his head was down. She hated the fact that she'd gotten his hopes up about them, only to bring them down, kick them down, but she couldn't help but feel that God was giving her another chance with Elton. It was a chance to make things right, to right the wrong they had done. Even when she'd lain with Elton the other night, it didn't feel like a sin. It felt good being one with him, and now, soon, they'd be one as man and wife, and that would blot out the sin of them fornicating. Wouldn't it? That was Deborah's train of thought anyway.

When Elton had first contacted her, Deborah thought of the possibility that Satan might be up to his old tricks. Then she realized that she couldn't go giving the devil credit for something God might have had in the works. Maybe God had brought Elton back into her life just in the nick of time before she got too serious with Lynox. Maybe her feelings for Lynox hadn't been real at all. Maybe she'd been subconsciously using Lynox to keep from ever having to deal with her true feelings about Elton in the first place.

She sniffed.

Who was the dawg now?

Chapter Twenty-nine

Deciding to pull herself out of bed and go out to the game and dinner with Blake felt like the hardest thing in the world for Paige to do. Lugging her body out of bed felt like lugging mounds and pounds of bags of wet sand. It was bags, all right . . . baggage. It was baggage that Paige had mistakenly thought would disappear after she said "I do" to Blake. She couldn't have been more wrong.

She wasn't the person everyone thought she was, the person she thought everyone wanted her to be. The confidence, the being-happy-in-the-skin-she-was-in, sassy big girl was this person she'd created. It was like her alter ego. At home, when she was alone, she was a sad-sap, size-sixteen-wearing big girl who really wore a size eighteen, but would trade anything in the world to be a size ten. She'd even work a size twelve like she was a runway model if she could.

There had been so many times she'd fantasized about being a nice, healthy weight, wearing swimsuits without cover-ups and not being ashamed to go to the gym in micro workout pants. Fantasizing had been what she'd done for as long as she could remember. It was something that, when she was a chunky little girl, could make all her dreams come true—in her mind. In her fantasies, she could be the same size as all the other girls in her class and not get teased when the teacher called her up to the chalkboard to work out a problem. In her mind, she was the hottest little number on the block, the one who all the boys wanted to take to the school dances. In her mind, she was the most successful and beautiful woman on the planet. She was every man's choice for a wife, but wounded them all by shooting down their efforts to make her a wifey.

All this had been in her mind, in her fantasies, but whenever reality would knock her upside the head, she'd snap out of it. Behind closed doors, she reverted back to the person she really was. The person nobody wanted. The person she didn't even want to be.

It became apparent that Paige had allowed her fantasy world to get mixed up with the real world; unfortunately, often times she couldn't determine which was which. This was why she'd been through so many men. For so many years, she had allowed her mind to fantasize about romantic encounters with men, but the real thing never quite transpired the way she had imagined it. She'd pursue a man, or at least her alter ego would; then, just like that, and before they could really get to know each other, she'd drop him like a hot potato.

Dinner and movie? Yes. A long, drawn-out, romantic affair? No. That was all just a part of her fantasy. She'd often lie in bed for hours fantasizing about how she wanted her relationship with a man to play out. Sometimes while watching television, her mind would even wander off to *Fantasy Island*. She was so loved, so wanted by a man in her head, but then she'd snap out of it. She'd get up to go to the bathroom or something and see herself in the mirror. Her round face. Her chin and a half. Her chubby arms and disappearing shoulder blades that were being smothered in excess skin. Yeah right! What man would want a woman like her? Only in her dreams.

So, she convinced herself that no man would really want to spend the rest of his life with her. She told herself that it was only a matter of time before he started talking about her and teasing her like the kids at school did. Well, before he could get her, she would get him.

This is the true reason why almost no man had gotten a second date with her. She'd already taken the liberty to point out all of his flaws; to point out all of the reasons why she couldn't spend the rest of her life with him. She was bound and determined to be the dumper and not the "dumpee." She'd been dumped on enough in life. As a young girl, she had often felt like even her own mother didn't want to be bothered with her because she wasn't the ideal daughter, a daughter her mother could put in pageants and talent shows. Well, as an adult, it was time that the tables turned. This attitude had allowed her to feel like she had such control, such authority. She had loved boasting so much about it during her worldly talks with Norman.

Most of her conversations with Norman had been enhanced to some degree . . . well, enhanced a great deal. Most of what she shared with him came from her fantasies and not reality. But even if Norman had to say so himself, it certainly made for good conversation. She was a diva to the tenth degree in his book, which, deep down inside, was one of the reasons he had never tried to get at her. He knew her record and wasn't about to allow her to damage his playa ego.

Little did he know that Paige's stories were intended to hide the truth. She told him she broke off relationships because the men were too much like her father, but the real reason was fear. She was afraid that the men just wanted to use her because they thought she was some overweight woman with low self-esteem who they could walk all over. This was why she made it a point to try to convince herself and the entire world that she was comfortable in the skin she was in.

But all that was in the past now. She'd let Blake into her real world, and now he was her world. He was her husband. There was no dumping him like a hot potato. She had to make this work, which was why she'd decided to get up out of bed and get herself together.

Paige chose a nice-fitting pair of slacks and the sexiest shirt in her closet that still allowed her to be holy. After wallowing in misery a few more seconds after Blake had gone into the bathroom to get dressed, she decided that she was no quitter. She was not going to give up. If she wanted her marriage to work, then she had to act like it. She had to show Blake what she wanted out of this marriage by giving him what she wanted: attention, intimacy . . . and lots of it.

By the time they got ready to hit the road, they knew they would have missed the first half of the game. Paige had wanted her husband's eyes on her anyway. She hadn't wanted to take the chance of his eyes wandering off to the sideline to get a glimpse of those cheerleaders. So, she convinced Blake the two should just skip the game and do dinner.

Blake agreed, taking Paige to an expensive steak house in a neighboring town. Afterward, the two went down to the Riverfront Park in downtown Columbus and watched the moonlight dance on the nearly frozen water.

"You cold?" Blake asked his wife as he stood behind her and wrapped his arms around her.

"Not anymore." She smiled as she closed her eyes and thanked God for bringing this fantasy to life. She'd dreamed many times of doing something as romantic as this with the man she loved, who loved her back, and now it had come to pass. Just to think, two hours ago her flesh had been on the verge of a willingness to call it quits. Paige rested her head on Blake's arm that was wrapped around her shoulder. She then placed soft kisses on his manly hand. She kissed him up his arm until her body had completely turned around and was now facing his. She looked him in his eyes with the most sensual look ever. "Let's get out of here. I'm ready to go home and go to bed."

Blake raised his arms, stretched, and yawned loudly. "Yeah, you're right. I am pretty beat."

Paige was waiting for him to start laughing, to show that he was only joking around . . . that he could read between the lines of the words she'd just spoken. But he never did. He was as serious as a heart attack as he led the way back to their car through the chilly end-of-February weather. Spring was right around the corner to warm things up, but Paige couldn't wait until spring to warm things up in her marriage.

Later that evening, back at home, Paige cried silently as she watched Blake's chest rise up and down as he slept. She shook her head in disbelief. Even after she slipped out of her Donna Karan pants and blouse and into a gorgeous nightie and robe set she'd picked up from Fashion Bug, Blake still managed to just roll over and go to sleep. Right about now, Paige would have settled for feeling like the only woman in the world period. Now she didn't even feel like a woman.

Angrily snatching the covers off, she got out of bed. Mumbling angry words to herself about her husband, she took off the nightie set and threw on some jeans and a T-shirt. She hurriedly put on some tennis shoes. She didn't even put on a bra or socks. She just wanted to hurry up and get out of that house, out of the place that was suffocating her . . . that was making her feel less than a woman. She needed someone to talk to, but the past few times she'd talked to Tamarra, she felt as though Tamarra couldn't relate.

Lately, the only person who could relate to her was Norman. It would be midnight soon. She knew he would be getting home from work shortly. Maybe she would go to his house, spend the night there. And she wouldn't feel bad about it, either. Right now she needed to feel as though a man wanted her and needed her. She'd given her husband the opportunity and he hadn't taken it. Perhaps Norman would.

Paige shook the thought of infidelity from her mind. What was she thinking? She didn't know what to do. She just felt hopeless and useless, unwanted. So, even when she got into her car, she had no idea where she was headed . . . or if she even wanted to come back.

Chapter Thirty

When Tamarra woke up, she was lying in a hospital bed in the emergency room. At first thought, she had no idea where she was. It didn't take long for everything to register once she looked around the room.

She grabbed her throbbing head and felt a knot. "What the—"

"I see you're awake," a nurse said as she entered the room with a little cart, prepared to take Tamarra's vitals. Noticing Tamarra rubbing her head, she added, "Yeah, you took a nice little fall there when you passed out. Good thing your friend found you. As a matter of fact, your friend is waiting in the lobby."

Tamarra's heart started to race. Her friend? The last person she remembered talking to, the last person she remembered seeing was Maeyl. He was waiting for her? He hadn't given up on her. Once again, he was there for her just like always, but this time, she wasn't going to let that man get away. She was going to pray, fast, and seek God in order to change her heart about Maeyl's circumstance of having a child and a baby's momma. No, she wasn't going to feel uncomfortable sharing birthday parties and attending events that Sasha would more than likely be at as well. She would be the one who was Maeyl's wife. She would be the one he would come home to, so that's all that would matter. Now, more than ever, she realized that she needed Maeyl; she really needed him. No man was ever going to be there and love her the way Maeyl did—ever.

"You're smiling. Must mean you're feeling better," the nurse concluded as she took Tamarra's blood pressure.

Tamarra hadn't even realized a huge grin was spread across her face. "As a matter of fact, I am feeling better."

"Good, because in spite of what people know and believe, panic attacks can be very, very dangerous. Mix that with passing out and landing on hard concrete pavement, you have nobody but The Man Upstairs to thank for you even being alive," the nurse told her. "Well, The Man Upstairs and your friend, of course." She winked.

"Yeah, God and my friend." Tamarra imagined how frightened Maeyl might have been when he went to walk away from her, only for her to go crashing down. Like she had just a minute ago, he must have seen their lives flash before his face, and now couldn't wait to reconcile with her . . . just like always. He'd realize she was sorry for feeling the way she did about him and his relationship with Sakaya, and he'd forgive her, just like always. And they'd get married as planned. And she'd make him macaroni and cheese every night for dinner. They'd be so happy, just the two of them. She shook her head. *Just the three of us*, she reminded herself. Just that quickly, she'd already erased the child from the scenario.

The nurse finished taking her blood pressure then proceeded to take her temperature, check her IV, and take her pulse. The entire time, Tamarra just lay back, smiling. Never mind that this nurse was poking and prodding; no complaints or murmuring came from Tamarra. She was just glad to be among the living. She was just glad to know that Maeyl, her friend—her best friend—her soon-to-be fiancé again, and then soon-to-be husband, was there for her.

"Everything's lookin' good," the nurse concluded and then headed for the door. "I think the doctor wants to keep you overnight. I'm not sure. But in the meantime, can I do anything for you or get you anything?" she asked Tamarra.

"Yes. Can you send my friend in, and do you mind turning the television up?" Tamarra got comfy in the bed, pulling the covers over her chest and propping her pillow.

"The volume is right there on the arm of your bed." The nurse pointed. "And I'll be happy to let your friend know that he can come see you now."

"Thank you," Tamarra replied as she turned up the volume of the television.

She flicked from one channel to the next as she waited for Maeyl to come in. It was later than she thought, as the eleven o'clock news was on. She listened to how a man had gunned down his girlfriend then shot himself. Next they showed a police chase that resulted in the suspect being shot and killed. Right after that they showed where a homeless man had been beaten and left for dead.

"They should call it the eleven o'clock bad news," Tamarra said, deciding to turn the channel. Turning only landed her on another news station. This report was one about a female they had just found dead. They suspected that suicide was the cause. Tamarra shook her head and said a prayer for the deceased. She recalled the times she felt her life was so bad that she would be better off dead.

Just when Tamarra was about to turn the channel yet again, they showed a picture of the victim that looked to be taken from a driver's license. Darting up in the bed, Tamarra couldn't believe her eyes. Was the deceased female they were showing . . . was it really . . . ? Maybe it was just an uncanny resemblance. But then they put the name under the photo and Tamarra thought she was going to absolutely lose her mind.

At the same time that Tamarra's fear was confirmed, when she knew who the dead victim was, she saw a male figure appear in the doorway. Covering his face was a huge bouquet of flowers. When he lowered the flowers he was smiling, but Tamarra was screaming in shock at what she'd just witnessed on the news.

"Oh my God, Tamarra, honey. I'm sorry. I didn't mean to startle you," he said, setting down the flowers and trying to comfort her.

There was no comforting her as she cried out hysterically. Nurses came instinctively to see what was going on. All they could see was the back of her visitor while Tamarra clutched him tightly, staring at the news, crying her eyes out and trembling. It was obvious it wasn't a panic attack, but that something had truly upset her.

"Is everything okay?" one of the nurses asked.

"I think so," her visitor replied. "I think I might have just startled her is all. We haven't seen each other in years." He began patting Tamarra's back and rubbing her.

The nurses stood in the room a few more moments just to see to it that everything was okay. Once Tamarra had calmed down, she wasn't able to speak, but she could nod when the nurses questioned whether she was up to having a visitor. After giving her some water, they left Tamarra and her visitor alone.

Tamarra looked up into his eyes and still couldn't speak. She was too distraught, too confused.

"Come here now, sweetie." He pulled Tamarra against him and let her cry on his shoulder for at least ten minutes. No words were spoken, just the sounds of Tamarra sniffing. Even when she stopped crying, she just stayed there, another ten minutes, in his arms.

Tamarra didn't know why he was there, but after what she'd just witnessed on the news, she was glad he was. She even told him so. "I'm so glad you are here." Those were the only words she spoke for quite some time while she just allowed him to hold her.

She needed someone there for her like never before, and was glad that God had made it so that someone had been there for her—even if it was Edward, her ex-husband.

Chapter Thirty-one

"You are the best," Elton said as he lay next to Deborah, breathing heavily. "I knew there was something else I missed about you." He looked over at her and winked.

"So, is that the only reason why you came back to the States?" she asked, trying to hide her pleasure if his answer was in the affirmative. It had been a while since she'd been with a man sexually. In all actuality, Elton had been the last man she'd been with. After that incident, sex had become a scary thing. Well, not sex itself; just the result of the act. Obviously making love was like riding a bike: once a person learns how to do it, they never forget. Guess the same goes for sinning as well.

"No way. There's nothing more I'd rather be doing than playing basketball back over in Chile." He looked to Deborah then touched her cheek. "But if all this had to happen with my knee in order to get me back to Malvonia, Ohio so that I could reunite with you again, then it was all worth it." He leaned over and kissed her softly on the lips.

It was Elton's kisses after he and Deborah made love that seemed to push any guilt to the back of her mind. He made her feel like the woman she used to be: loved, vulnerable, not always looking for the worst in a man, but just carefree and happy-go-lucky. Surely God would understand her backsliding in one area just a little bit. Surely God wanted her to be happy. Besides, she wouldn't be sinning for too long, as she and Elton planned on eloping to somewhere like Vegas to get married. Neither of them wanted a great big wedding for show. They just wanted to do what they should have done years ago—make things right.

"Well, I'm sorry about your knee, but I'm not sorry you came back," Deborah told him.

Cutting his eyes away from Deborah, he proceeded to get out of bed. "Speaking of this knee . . ." He cleared his throat. "The doctors here say it's not as bad as the doctors over there in Chile thought. As a matter of fact, my rehab doctor says my knee is almost as good as new."

"Praise God!" Deborah shouted. "He's still in the healing business, that's for sure." Deborah noticed that Elton wasn't joining in on her praise party. "Elton, your knee, that's great news."

"It is, Little Debbie, which is why I talked with my agent, who spoke with my coach the other day. The coach wants me back, babe. They want me back playing for the team." Now here came Elton's excitement. "Isn't that great? It really will be just like old times, only this time when I go overseas, I won't be leaving my girlfriend behind. I'll be taking you with me, Little Debbie."

Deborah tried to crack a smile, but it was just as forced as a big girl trying on a pair of jeans in the juniors department. "Elton . . . I . . . I can't move to another country. What about church and work?"

"There are plenty of worship temples over in Chile, and you can type on that computer in any country. I mean, with the Internet, e-mail, mail delivery services, phone . . . come on. You could work out of a bathroom stall if need be."

Deborah shook her head. "I don't know, Elton. This is all just happening—"

"Did you or did you not say you wanted to be my wife?" Elton reminded her as he sat back down on the bed. "If you've changed your mind, I'll understand." He attempted to stand, but Deborah grabbed his hand and pulled him back.

"No, Elton. I haven't changed my mind. I want to be Mrs. Elton Culiver more than anything else in my life right now. I know that's what God wants for me. It's what I want. I . . . I don't think He would have brought you back here unless this is exactly what was supposed to happen. I think God had meant for us to get married and move to Chile as husband and wife over five years ago when you first went . . . without me." Deborah looked down, but Elton instantly lifted her chin so that she was facing him again.

"And I'm not leaving you again, Little Debbie—at least I don't want to. But basketball is my calling. It allows me to live the lifestyle I live. It's what's going to allow me to maintain that lifestyle and provide you with only the best."

Deborah wasn't sure how Elton was living. Since returning to Ohio, he'd been staying in the beautiful home he had custom built for his mother. It had more than enough extra guest rooms, but she imagined his place over in Chile was to die for. Elton himself always looked like a million bucks. She was sure his home life reflected his person. She imagined maids and butlers—and nannies when the time came for them to have children. She lived a good life now, but she knew God had even more for her, and it would be provided through her husband, Elton.

"And I'm not going to let you leave me, Elton," Deborah said. "Chile, here I come!" she yelped with excitement as the two embraced.

"Oh, Deborah, once again you've made me the happiest man in the world." Elton released Deborah then stood up and headed to the bathroom.

"Wait. When are we leaving? I need at least a month to close down shop here."

"I was thinking we'd leave as soon as possible, possibly next week. I can pay people to get you moved, to get your house on the market, and whatever else you need to do."

"Next week? But what about getting married? I thought you wanted to go to Vegas or something and—"

"I do . . . and we will. But first there are a couple of things I need to get in order before we do all that." Elton entered the bathroom.

"A couple of things like what?" Deborah sniffed.

"You know, just the regular things an athlete like myself needs to take care of." He shrugged and added nonchalantly, "The prenup." He went to close the door, but right before it closed, he opened it again and stated, "And get my divorce finalized." Then he closed the door.

Chapter Thirty-two

The two male hospital workers rolled Paige's stiff body down the corridor and into the assigned room. It was cold in the room, very cold. Cold enough to keep a dead body from decomposing.

It had been more than an hour since the police had found Paige's unresponsive body on the side of the road. When the police first arrived on the scene of the accident, where they found Paige's car practically wrapped around a tree, they were very suspicious. It was apparent that the vehicle had somehow veered off the road right into the tree. From what they could determine in the late night hours, there were no skid marks or anything, which meant the driver hadn't even thought about pumping the brakes. It was as if the tree was the target: final destination. As if the driver had purposely hit the tree.

The ambulance got Paige to the hospital within a half hour of the accident, where doctors immediately worked on her, drawing blood and whatnot. After doing all they could do, she was now in the hands of the two gentlemen.

As the two men entered the room with Paige in tow, they anchored the bed to the floor by putting the brakes on each wheel. They then left the room, giving the woman one last look. She looked so peaceful. Though neither man spoke on it, from the way in which the severity of the accident was de-

scribed to them, they couldn't believe her body hadn't suffered more than just a couple of bumps and bruises.

"Excuse me," one of the gentlemen said to Blake, who was
entering as they were exiting.

"They said it was okay for me to come see my wife," Blake
told them. It was difficult for him not to get emotional in
front of the men.

"She's right in there." The other man pointed as the two
left through the same route they'd come.

Closing his eyes and then taking a deep breath, Blake
whispered a prayer. "Lord, I come to your throne of grace as
humble as I know how to be right now. Forgive me for all of
my sins and for all the times I have fallen short of your glory. More importantly, Father, forgive me for not making the
things first in my life that should be first, starting with you, oh
Lord. Secondly, my wife." Trying to keep from crying, Blake
continued. "I love her so much. She means the world to me,
and this is what I should have been telling her. As her lord on
earth, the way you are her Lord in heaven, you are more than
a provider; I should have been more than a provider to her.
She needed more from me, God, and I didn't give it to her.
So, I'm seeking forgiveness, Lord, and that you'll make me a
changed a man. In Jesus' name, amen."

"Amen," he heard the soft voice repeat after him.

He opened his eyes and looked over at his wife. He'd passed
the scene of the accident on the way to the hospital and didn't
know what to expect when he saw her. The car was a total loss.
He was just happy that his wife wasn't.

"Hey, sweetie," Blake said as he walked toward Paige. He
looked her up and down. "How are you feeling? You don't
look so bad."

She looked down at her arms that just had a couple of bruises on them. "Yeah, I know, praise God. Jesus must have definitely taken the wheel," she joked using the lyrics of the song by Carrie Underwood, former *American Idol* winner.

"Jesus had the wheel all along," Blake stated. He stroked his fingers through Paige's hair. He'd never realized how soft it was. He thought that perhaps he hadn't been stroking it enough to find out. "So, what did the doctors say?"

"Well, nothing yet, but hopefully someone will be in to tell me something, because one minute I'm driving down the street, and the next minute I'm in here. I can't remember anything in between."

"When the nurse called me, I thought it was some joke. The last I remembered, you were laying next to me in bed. So, when I looked over and saw that you weren't there, I nearly lost my mind. Couldn't think straight trying to get here."

Paige looked down and chuckled. "Well, does that explain your mismatched shoes?"

Blake looked down at his feet and burst out laughing. "Oh, wow. I hadn't even noticed." He stopped laughing then turned his attention back to his wife. "All I could think about was you." He swallowed hard, as if swallowing back emotions. "I . . . I didn't know what to expect when I walked into this hospital room. I didn't know how bad . . ." His words trailed off. He couldn't finish; he was so overcome with emotion. "I love you, Paige. I really do. If I'd lost you, I might have . . . I don't know what I would have done. Probably kill myself."

"Blake Dickenson! I rebuke that in the name of Jesus!" Paige declared. "No god-fearing husband of mine will talk like that."

"I'm serious, honey. That's how much I love you," Blake

told her, grabbing her hand. "And I'm sure if anything ever happened to me, you'd probably feel the same way. Wouldn't you?" Blake tightened his grip on her hand, almost to the point where it was painful. "By the way, what were you doing out driving in the middle of the night? Where were you going?"

Paige broke down and told Blake exactly how she'd been feeling since their wedding. What she didn't tell him was that she was possibly on her way to Norman's house before the crash. She couldn't help but wonder if the accident had been God's way of keeping her from making one of the biggest mistakes of her life. *But, Lord, couldn't you have just let me run out of gas?* she thought, but then she realized she probably would have called Norman to come to her aid, and the two still would have ended up together.

"How is our miracle patient?" the doctor said as she entered the room.

"I'm fine, Doctor," Paige said, a little uneasy as she wriggled her hand from Blake's grip. He'd been gripping her wrist the entire time she spoke.

"You do know that you coming out of such an accident alive was nothing short of a miracle. You must have God on your side," the doctor continued.

"We do." Blake spoke for Paige with a smile. "I was just telling my wife, Doctor, that I don't know what I would have done if I had lost her."

"Well, you don't have to worry about that." She looked down at the chart she carried in her hand. "Mr. Dickenson, your wife is going to be just fine." She shot Paige a discerning look. "For now."

"Wha-what do you mean?" Paige asked her, getting a little nervous.

"Well, looks like you blacked out, the result of very low blood sugar. If we don't get this diabetes under control—"

"Diabetes!" both Blake and Paige said in unison.

"But I'm not even diabetic," Paige replied.

"According to your blood work and the tests we ran, you are," the doctor confirmed. "Ironically, the accident saved your life. Had you been home in bed asleep and your sugar level dropped as low as it did, you might not have woken up."

"Jesus!" Paige said as her eyes watered.

"When was the last time you'd seen your family doctor for a checkup?" the doctor asked Paige.

"Uh, I don't know. Never, that I can remember. All I pretty much have is my gynecologist. I mean, I never get sick, so I really don't have a family doctor that I see on a regular basis."

"Hmm, that's a problem I run into quite often. We grown-ups only go to the doctor when we get sick. Just think about how much sickness we could prevent if we'd at least just go for an annual checkup. I mean, we don't wait until all the oil leaves from our cars and the check engine light comes on before we give our cars an oil change, do we? So, we should at least take care of our bodies to that same degree; get it checked out before the warning lights start flashing."

"I hear you, Doctor," Paige said, "but what do I do now?" There was fear evident on Paige's face. "How do I know I won't be driving around again and end up in another accident? And maybe that time I won't be so lucky. Even worse, what if I hit and kill someone? A pedestrian walking across the street? Somebody's child?" Paige shuddered at the thought as a tear dropped.

"The first thing we're going to do is change your diet, your eating habits," the doctor informed Paige, while Blake rested his hand on her shoulder to calm her down. "Unfortunately, I am going to have to put you on insulin."

"The shots? In my stomach. Oh God, I can't do it!" Paige buried her face into her husband's stomach.

"You are going to have to do it. It's a matter of life and death: *your* life and death. But I'm telling you, Mrs. Dickenson, if you change the things you eat, then you can get yourself to the point where you won't even need those shots. I've seen it done."

"You can do it, honey." Blake kissed Paige on top of her head. "You're just going to have to make the sacrifice."

"Not to downplay anything," the doctor chimed in, "but when we are talking about extending your days here on earth, giving up donuts and fried chicken isn't really a sacrifice."

"I'd have to agree with the doctor, honey," Blake said to Paige. "Lord knows I'm not getting up on a soap box or anything, but what Jesus did . . . now, that was a sacrifice. God's not asking you to do that. All He's asking you to do is to treat your body—His body, really—like the temple it is."

The doctor nodded. "Not that you are a very big woman, Mrs. Dickenson, but you are a bit overweight."

"I know." Paige sniffled. "And gluttony is a sin. I gotta come out of sin. Sin truly is death." She looked up at Blake. "And I want to live, Doctor. I want to live." Wiping her eyes dry, Paige composed herself, then with determination and her head held high, she said, "So, tell me, Doc, what do I have to do to live?"

Chapter Thirty-three

"Are you okay? Do you need more water?" Edward asked his ex-wife.

"No, I'm fine," Tamarra told him as she finally allowed herself to fall from his arms and lay back on the bed. She rubbed her hands through her hair. "Oh my God, I must be a sight."

"Oh, stop it. You know you look good in any state. To this day, you're still the only woman I know who can wake up in the morning and look better than some women do smack in the middle of the day."

"Such flattering words coming from my ex," Tamarra said. "Guess I didn't look good enough, or else—"

"Hey, hey now, we're not going to go there. It's all about you right now, and why I found you laid out on the ground over there outside of Family Café."

Edward was right, Tamarra thought. They'd been divorced for two years now. She was over it—really over it. No need stirring up and rekindling past hurts. She was healed and delivered from that situation, and that's how she wanted things to stay.

"I, uh, I've been having these panic attack episodes lately is all," Tamarra said, downplaying it. "It's nothing."

"Well, it sure looked like something to me. You were out cold when I found you. That's why I called 911."

"I was out cold, because evidently when I passed out, my head hit the cement and it knocked me unconscious. Thank God you showed up when you did, or I don't know what might have happened. I might have ended up like Sister Lorain. God only kno—" Tamarra thought for a minute. "As a matter of fact, what in the world were you doing there, on the side of Family Café's building?"

"Well, you know I've been the accountant for Family Café for years now. I was there to go over a couple of things regarding their finances. You know I work special hours, for their convenience, around closing time, so I can get their undivided attention."

Actually, Tamarra had forgotten all about the fact that Edward was the accountant for the business. When she and Edward were married, they always got to eat free when they would go to the restaurant together. And she also remembered that whenever he was there for official business, to go over the books in the back with the owners, he always used the service entrance on the side of the building.

Edward never really cared for the food at Family Café, not even the famous chili. Tamarra, on the other hand, enjoyed the family-owned restaurant. So, after the divorce, Edward never really patronized the place anymore, but still maintained his business relationship as the accountant there. Tamarra realized that's probably how Zelda knew where she lived: she'd looked at some old paperwork with her and Edward's address on it.

"I didn't expect to find my ex-wife lying flat out on the side of the building," Edward told her.

"And I didn't expect to find my ex-husband standing in my hospital doorway." She looked over at the bouquet of flowers he'd set on the table. "With my favorite, a spring bouquet."

"Oh, yes," Edward said, turning his attention toward the flowers. "I almost forgot. Those are for you."

"You don't say." Tamarra smiled. "Thank you, Ed."

He cleared his throat at the sound of his ex-wife referring to him by the name she'd always called him. No one else called him by that name. Eddie, maybe, but not Ed. "Uh, no problem. And, I, uh, didn't mean to catch you so off guard or anything by being here. I mean, I knew I'd get a reaction out of you, but whoa!" He chuckled, referring to the way Tamarra was reacting when he entered the room. "I'm so sorry."

"Oh, no need to apologize." She shooed her hand. "It wasn't that. I mean, of course I was shocked to see you standing there, of all people. But it wasn't just that."

"I know. You were scared as well. I don't blame you. I was scared. I had no idea what was going on. But I'm glad you're going to be okay."

"Yeah, me too." Tamarra lowered her head. There was silence.

"Well, I guess I better get going." He looked down at his watch. "Although it's way too late for me to go over Family Café's books now," he joked. "Anyway, take care of yourself, you hear me?"

Tamarra nodded and smiled.

"Good-bye, Tamarra."

And Edward was gone, leaving nothing behind but the flowers. No stirred-up feelings or emotions; no regrets or temptations; no bitterness or anger that he was probably headed off to the arms of the woman he'd cheated on her with and their love child. Tamarra thought that maybe everything was just too fresh, Edward's being there, and maybe it all needed some time to register. But she gave it a couple more minutes, and still nothing. She really had been delivered from the anger, bitterness, and regret toward Edward, his infidelity, and his child. There really was love after divorce, and for Tamarra, it went by the name of Maeyl.

"Maeyl," slipped through Tamarra's lips in a whisper. "Where are you? I need you." Tamarra knew she would need him more than ever to cope with the reality of what she'd witnessed on the news. Thank God Edward had been there during the initial shock to take her mind off things, but now Edward was gone. She needed Maeyl.

Tamarra flicked to a couple more channels to see if there was any more coverage about the suspected suicide, but she saw nothing. She had to see it again: the face, the name. Just one more time to make sure she hadn't been seeing things, to make sure she hadn't been dreaming—having a nightmare was more like it. She surfed through the channels again: nothing. Tamarra knew she wouldn't be able to think straight until she found out more details. But who could she call?

She picked up the hospital phone and dialed Paige's number only to receive no answer, either at home or on her cell. That was peculiar. Then again, Paige was a married woman. Perhaps she and Blake had finally started to minister to one another in the bedroom. Next she tried Maeyl. She didn't get an answer on either his home phone or his cell. Now, that was peculiar . . . period. Where in the world could Maeyl have been this late?

A worried look covered Tamarra's face as her mind suggested all types of scenarios as to where Maeyl could be. But then she relaxed as her lips spread into a smile thinking that maybe, just maybe, he was on his way to see her.

Chapter Thirty-four

Deborah lay there in the bed as if someone had just slapped her across the face . . . twice. She was stunned. Had she really heard Elton say what she thought she'd just heard: he was getting a divorce? Even worse, he was married? Elton was a married man?

"Oh my God!" Deborah jumped up out of the bed. "I've been . . . I've been sleeping with a married man? Not only have I been fornicating, but I've been aiding this man in committing adultery too? Oh, Lord, forgive me." Deborah fell to her knees next to the bed as she prayed in tongues, her prayer language.

She cried freely as she repented for everything. She should have never lain with Elton in the first place. Hadn't she learned her lesson already? God had forgiven her, and now here she was putting herself in a position to relive the nightmare all over again. "I'm so sorry," she cried for the next few minutes.

Her tears seemed to drop at the pace of the shower water Elton was running, only when his shower stopped, her tears didn't. When he exited the bathroom, he found Deborah still kneeling next to the bed.

"Little Debbie, what's wrong?" Elton asked in a worried tone as he dried himself off and slipped on some boxers he'd grabbed from the top drawer of Deborah's dresser. Yes, she'd given him the infamous single drawer at her place—that and a wee little bit of closet space. Oh yeah, and a spot for his toothbrush in the bathroom.

She couldn't believe this man, after the atomic bomb he'd so casually dropped on her, asking her what was wrong.

"What do you think is wrong?" Deborah shot.

"Baby, I don't know. What happened? What did I do? What did I say?" Elton sat on the floor next to her as he coaxed her to speak by rubbing his hand up and down her back.

Why did his hand have to feel so good, so comforting on Deborah's back while she was so angry at him? Huh? Why?

"Elton, am I going crazy, or did you just mention something about having to finalize a divorce? Your divorce?"

"Yeah, honey, but that's nothing. It's been over between Lonna and me for over a year now." Elton's nonchalant tone was like nails down a chalkboard to Deborah's ears.

"Then don't you think you should have made sure it was officially over before you came back into my life and got me to sleep with you?"

"It is official"—he tapped on his chest—"in my heart. And that's all that matters. I haven't been mentally connected to Lonna since I can remember, and we haven't been physically connected for even longer than that. And to top it all off, we've never been spiritually connected. Not like you and me, Little Debbie." He rubbed his hand down her cheek. "Please don't hate me. I'm sorry. Yes, I should have told you, but honestly, all I could think about was you. Lonna was the last person on my mind. You were the only woman on my mind. You've been the only woman on my mind since I can remember." He continued caressing her cheek. "I never should have married Lonna. I wronged her by doing so. I've never loved her, never been in love with her. Not the way I loved you."

Deborah didn't know a romance author alive who could even create a leading male character as smooth, as kind, as loving, and as convincing as Elton. But Elton was real, a real man before her. He wasn't some made-up person on paper. And maybe no author could create anything like him, but God had, and He'd created him for her. This was her Boaz, her prodigal fiancé, all in one. God couldn't count it against her for wanting to be with him. They were practically already one anyway. They were soul mates. And as far as her sleeping with a married man, she didn't know. She hadn't known she'd been giving herself to another woman's husband. God couldn't hold that against her . . . could He? How she saw it, if God hadn't wanted it to go down, then He should have warned her.

"I love you too, Elton, and I'm going to stick by your side through the divorce."

"Thank you, baby. I'm going to need the support." Now it was as if the roles had flip-flopped and Elton was the one who needed comforting. "Lonna's been fighting it. Won't agree on the offer my attorney has presented. Gold digger. This entire marriage was a trap just for her to get what she wanted: to get up out of Malvonia, live in the lap of luxury over in a country where she could be someone else, anybody but the chicken head everybody here knew her as."

A lump formed in Deborah's stomach. "Are you talking about Lonna-Lonna? Sang-in-the-New-Day-church-choir Lonna?" She asked hesitantly because she wasn't sure she really wanted to know the answer.

"Yeah, that Lonna," Elton said, full of shame.

Deborah shook her head in disbelief. "Lonna Mason?"

"Well, it's Lonna Culiver right now, but not for long," Elton assured her.

Deborah was still in a daze. "The Lonna-who-was-supposed-to-sing-in-our-wedding Lonna?"

Elton went to touch Deborah's arms, but she pushed him away and stood up. "But, when . . . how . . . ? I don't get it."

"Listen, Little Debbie—" Elton started as he stood.

"Don't you Little Debbie me, Elton. I can't believe what I'm hearing." Deborah put her hands on her forehead in pure disbelief. She walked back and forth, but then halted in her tracks. "Is that why she just up and left without even telling Pastor or her own mama that she was leaving? Sister Mason was worried sick for three days straight. Fasted and prayed and even shut in at the church until she finally got a voice message from Lonna telling her that she was okay, that she'd fallen in love, gotten swept off her feet, and was getting married." She looked into Elton's eyes. "It was with you? You were the man who swept her off her feet?" Deborah started doing the math in her head. When Lonna went missing, it was shortly after Deborah had paid a visit to the clinic.

"It wasn't what you think," Elton told Deborah.

"What I'm thinking is that while I was laid up in an abortion clinic, ending our child's life, you were starting a new life with Lonna." Deborah's lips trembled as she waited on Elton to confirm what she'd just said.

After a pause and deep breath, Elton did confirm her suspicions—and a lot more. "You don't understand, Deborah. I . . . I wasn't ready to raise kids, especially not two. And you were willing to get it done . . . and she wouldn't . . . and I didn't know what else to do. I had to do the right thing and marry her, to raise our son together. But in the long run, having two parents who don't love each other did Junior more harm than good."

Now Deborah's head was spinning. The knot in her stomach was doing a climb up her intestines and into her throat. Was Elton saying what she thought he was, that while he'd convinced her to have an abortion, he'd allowed another woman to have his son? A woman who, from the sounds of it, was pregnant at the same time she was? A woman who was supposed to sing at their wedding, but instead, had been sleeping with him on the side? This couldn't be happening. This was all a nightmare, and she was going to wake up. Soon, hopefully.

"You . . . you have a son?" Deborah managed to ask as she held her stomach—her empty womb.

"Yes. Elton Junior."

"How . . . how old is he?" Deborah swallowed hard, but the lump wouldn't go back down.

Elton hesitated, as if he knew what his answer would mean to Deborah. "He'll be five on his next birthday."

That's all Deborah needed to hear. She brushed past Elton, racing to the bathroom. She'd barely gotten the toilet seat lifted when all the contents of her stomach made an escape to the toilet bowl.

"Deborah, you okay?" Elton asked as he bent over her, holding her locks so that they wouldn't fall into the commode.

Deborah couldn't answer, not because she was getting sick, but because she just simply didn't even know what to say . . . what to think. A couple of minutes went by before she stopped puking, but she still remained in her position over the porcelain bowl. Now tears were pouring into it: big tears and lots of them. All that pain she'd been delivered from seemed to be coming back; only now it felt seven times worse.

Elton just stood there, holding her hair, allowing her to get it all out, allowing every tear that needed to fall to do just that. After a few minutes, Deborah went from her knees to her bottom. She wrapped her arms around her legs and just rocked while shaking her head in disbelief. Finally, Elton stood up and got her a cup of water.

"Here, drink this," he told her.

She pushed it away, making him spill some down his hand. "I don't want anything from you," she told him without looking him in the eyes. "Not even this ring." She snatched it off and threw it. Neither was too concerned about its landing.

"Come on. Get up off the floor and let's talk about it."

Elton pulled Deborah up. She resisted at first, but knew she couldn't hide out in the bathroom forever; although she wished she could. She wished she could crawl inside the toilet bowl and be flushed away with its contents.

Elton filled the cup with water again and then handed it to Deborah.

This time she took the cup, swishing the water around in her mouth then spitting it out in the sink. After all the water was gone, she just went ahead and brushed her teeth, hoping to get the bad taste out of her mouth. Afterward, the bad taste of the throw-up was gone, but still, there was a bad taste in her mouth that she knew would take more than toothpaste to eliminate.

Elton stood behind her over the sink. Something in him was afraid to leave her in the bathroom alone. She looked as though she didn't even want to be here on earth anymore. He needed to stay by her side until he was certain her mind was right. "You ready to talk to me?" he asked once she'd dried her mouth on her towel. She didn't answer, but she headed toward the door, so Elton took that as a yes.

"Why don't you lie down and rest while we talk," Elton suggested, pointing at the bed.

She shook her head in the negative. "I'd rather stand."

After taking a deep breath, Elton told Deborah what he knew she wanted to hear. "First off, you have to know that I had never, ever cheated on you before in our relationship. Lonna was the first and the only."

Well, so far his words weren't any comfort to Deborah.

"I can't even really remember how it happened." He shrugged in an effort to downplay it. "I think she came by my place because she wanted me to hear the song she wanted to sing in our wedding. She began to serenade me. One thing led to another, and . . . " His words trailed off until he could catch up with them. "Ugh," he said in frustration at just the mere thought of the huge mistake he'd made. "You and I had just agreed to stop having sex and live a celibate life until we got married. Her timing was just all bad, all wrong."

"So, it was her fault?" Deborah halfheartedly chuckled.

"No, I'm not saying that. I take full blame. I'd made a commitment to you."

"I was your fiancée!" Deborah shouted as she brushed tears away.

"I know, baby, I know." Elton walked toward Deborah, but she backed away and went and sat on the bed. "We ended up getting together a couple more times, but I broke it off the day before I left to go to Chile. It was just sex with her, and I was committed to you."

"So, let me guess: you two had breakup sex?"

Elton nodded in shame.

"Wow, you are some piece of work."

"I'm sorry, Litt—"

"Just keep going."

"Well, she got pregnant that last time we were together. I didn't know, though. I didn't find out until I came back to the States. She'd been leaving messages with my mom that she needed to speak to me about something urgent. Moms just thought it had something to do with her singing in the wedding or something. That she was bailing on us. Well, once I got home, before I came over to see you, I called her, and that's when she told me she was pregnant. I couldn't even think straight after that. She was due any day pretty much."

"I guess that explains why she up and quit the choir months before she ran off. She didn't want anyone to know she was pregnant," Deborah concluded.

"When I got off the phone, I just began to holler out to God," Elton continued. "Moms came in the room, and I had to tell her what was going on. She just prayed and prayed, then listened and listened, until she got a word from God. The word was that I needed to do the right thing by both you and Lonna. I needed to marry her and raise our child together and break things off with you."

"Your mother never did really like me that much," Deborah shot.

"Oh, come on. You know Moms loved you," Elton told her. "She just loves God more and wanted me to do the right thing in His eyes. She didn't want her grandchild to be born out of wedlock."

"So, you were actually coming to break up with me that day I told you I was pregnant?"

"Yes, but before I could, you told me that you were pregnant too. It was like a nightmare. That couldn't have been happening to me. I couldn't marry two women, and I didn't want a child born out of wedlock, and with Lonna being due practically any day, she wouldn't hear of an abortion, adoption, or anything. So, the only thing I could think of was to get you to terminate . . . to end the—"

Deborah helped him out. "It's called abortion. You let her keep your baby while you forced me to kill mine?" she spat as she cried.

"Wait a minute now. Forced you? I didn't have a gun to your head, Deborah. You agreed. It was your body. You didn't have to do anything you didn't want to do."

Elton's words stung with truth. The stinging hurt Deborah's heart. "You're right," she told him. "I could have kept my baby. I should have kept my baby. Oh God, what did I do?"

Elton went and sat beside her to comfort her. "I'm sorry. I didn't mean it like that. I didn't mean to make you feel bad. It was my fault too. Getting rid of the baby was the last thing on your mind. I planted the seed and watered it down until you were drowning in it. I'm sorry. I'm so sorry. I should have stopped you. I shouldn't have left town knowing what you had to do, what you had to go through. And believe it or not, I couldn't live with myself. I felt awful. I didn't know what to say or what to do. I knew I couldn't face you, though. I couldn't talk to you. I wanted to tell you the truth about Lonna, but after what you'd gone through, I knew I couldn't. So instead, I just started a new life with the mother of my child."

He became very intense and serious as he grabbed Deborah's arms and forced her to look in his eyes. "But you have to know that that's all she ever was to me. I never loved her like I loved you. I was never in love with her, Deborah. You stayed on my heart, stayed on my mind to the point where it was no longer fair to her. And believe it or not, I told her I wanted a divorce even before I injured my leg, before I came back to Malvonia, before I saw you again. I love you, Deborah. I want you to be my future, so please, I'm begging you, woman of God, don't let the past destroy our future. Forgive me, forgive me just as Christ instructed. Forgive me just like God has forgiven you."

Deborah broke down into Elton's arms as his words first penetrated her ears and then her heart. "I forgive you, Elton. Oh God, I forgive you." How could she not? He'd reminded her of Christ's instructions on forgiving, and how God had even forgiven her. Who was she to deserve forgiveness and not Elton?

Deborah threw her arms around Elton and he kissed her passionately. Just as Elton gently pushed Deborah back onto the bed, the phone rang.

"Let it ring," Elton said, barely coming up for air from the kiss.

"Okay," Deborah moaned as she closed her eyes and returned his kisses. Then the phone rang again, and again. Deborah opened her eyes and managed to look at the clock. "It's after midnight. It must be important for someone to be calling this late. Let me just answer it." Without Elton giving his say-so, Deborah slid from underneath him and answered the phone. "Hello."

"I don't know why," the caller spat out, "but the Lord woke me up out of my sleep and told me to call you. What in the world is going on over there, child?"

"Mother Doreen?" Deborah said, sitting up and grabbing something to cover herself with as if her elder, mentor, and counselor could see her through the phone. "Uh, I, uh, nothing. Uh, what's going on?"

"Unh-uh. That was my question to you. Now you're stuttering and you're stammering, which means you're lying or you're about to lie. It's late, and I don't have time to play with you, child, so talk to me, because evidently you ain't been talking to God, or He wouldn't have woke me up to get to you."

Deborah was speechless. She didn't know what to do or what to say.

"Hmm, got nothing to say for yourself now, do you?" Mother Doreen surmised. "Then that means only one thing: either the cat's got your tongue"—she paused—"or the devil does. So, which is it?"

Chapter Thirty-five

For the past couple of days, Paige had been so consumed with reading up on her diagnosis, learning the do's and don'ts of having the disease, that she didn't have room in her mind to even think twice about Norman, or any other man, for that matter—any other man except for her husband.

After almost losing his wife, Blake was shaken up. He realized how awful he would have felt if Paige's car accident had been fatal. He thought about all the times he could have spent with her instead of work. He was still a hard worker and still worked longer hours than most, but for the past week, he had made it a point to be home every night by at least seven o'clock, so that he and Paige could have dinner together.

After spending two days in the hospital, Paige was a little disappointed on the morning of her release because Blake had been an hour late picking her up. She'd waited down in the hospital lobby in a wheelchair, feeling ridiculous. The hospital was a full house with that swine flu in full force attacking people, so they needed her room.

He just couldn't stand not to go into work, Paige had thought while she sat in the hospital fighting back tears of anger. He'd called her and told her that he'd gone into work early that morning to tie up some loose ends and was running a little late. It wasn't until he showed up in a limousine with three dozen flowers and a box of sugar free chocolates that her anger subsided.

"I'm going to start treating you like the queen you are," Blake had declared when he showed up at the hospital and kissed Paige on the lips—a long kiss—not caring who was watching.

Paige was beside herself even more as they rode home in the back of the limo and Blake told her he'd taken the next couple days off from work to cater to her. And that's just what he did. He waited on her hand and foot. Well, actually, he paid Flo, their new maid, to wait on her hand and foot.

"Tomorrow is not promised. I've worked hard all my life; now it's time to start putting all those hard-earned dollars to use," Blake had told Paige.

Between the limo, the maid, and the brand new Lexus Blake had waiting in the driveway the day she came home from the hospital, Paige's self-esteem was immediately catapulted. That and the fact that her husband gave up what she thought he loved most—work—to spend time with her. The same effort he'd spent trying to close big deals, he now spent on handling his home affairs. He'd accomplished a great deal in only two days.

The day after she got out of the hospital, Blake assisted Paige in going through the refrigerator and every cupboard. They trashed anything that didn't fit into Paige's new diet: the sweet snacks, the sugar-loaded cereals, the regular soda pop, the frozen dinners, and more. After that they went grocery shopping together, purchasing all the things that were on Paige's "can eat" list.

"When all this is done and over with," Paige declared, "I'm going to be the poster child for how to beat diabetes. And I'm

going to have the Lord and a testimony to prove it," Paige had
said as they loaded up the car with bags of groceries.

"Amen to that!" Blake had proclaimed.

Paige's testimony would not only be about how, with God's
healing power and her doing her part, she got the victory over
diabetes, but how God had also used the disease as a wakeup
call to both her and her husband.

Now it was Sunday morning and Blake was escorting Paige
to church. That was something he hadn't done in a month of
Sundays. Paige was full of joy and praises to God, and Blake
was too.

"It certainly is good to see you this Sunday morning." Pastor
greeted Blake after service as several members of the congregation made their way to the pulpit in order to tell Pastor what a
fine job the Holy Spirit had done in ministering through the
head of the house. "First Brother Elton returns, and now you.
I think I've got all one hundred sheep accounted for." Pastor
laughed.

"I might have strayed from the church a little bit, Pastor, but
you best believe I never strayed away from God." Blake looked
over at Paige, who was standing next to him arm in arm. "He's
worthy to be praised. Worthy, worthy, worthy." Blake almost
broke out in a shout just thinking about what God had done
for him and Paige: how God had brought his wife out of both
a car accident and diabetic blackout; how God had begun the
works of mending their marriage that had slowly but surely
been in the beginning stages of falling apart. "Worthy is the
blood of the lamb. Holy is our God. Holy! Holy! Holy!"

Before anyone knew it, Blake had let go of Paige's arm, and
his feet started moving and stomping quickly. "Hallelujah," he
shouted as his feet continued to stomp as if he were smashing
the heads of the beast that had come to kill, steal, and destroy.

"That's right, son. Praise Him!" Pastor declared.

Paige's eyes filled with tears as she watched her man give God some praise. When a few other brothers made their way up and began to shout with Blake, it was like church was taking place all over again. To see all these men of God not ashamed to show love to the Father was awesome.

It was when Brother Maeyl practically leaped from the sound booth and joined them that Deborah realized Tamarra hadn't been in church. With so much going on in her life these past few days, she hadn't talked to Tamarra. She'd seen on the caller ID where her best friend had called her a couple of times while she was busy with Blake or something. One thing Paige had learned during marriage counseling was how valuable time with a spouse was. The last thing a spouse wanted was for his or her mate to be yapping on the phone when they were spending time together. So, Paige had made it a point these last few days to give her man one hundred percent of her attention. She'd meant to return Tamarra's calls, but she'd never gotten around to it. And now with Tamarra not being in church, she knew that whatever it was that was going on with Tamarra deserved more than a call back. It deserved a drive-by.

"You two aren't sneaking off to the Golden Corral, are you?" Blake asked Paige, full of skepticism as they still stood up at the front altar. By this time, the praise party was over and Pastor was still greeting folks.

"No, sweetie, I promise," Paige assured him. "I just want to do a drive-by to see if everything is okay with Sister Tamarra." Paige turned and tapped Maeyl on the shoulder. He had been standing next to her, talking to one of the other brothers. "Brother Maeyl, do you think you could give my husband a ride home? I want to drop by and check on your fiancée. All is well, right?" Paige shot Maeyl a look that a teacher would give a child who'd forgotten to do their homework.

"Uh, well . . ." Maeyl stammered. Paige had put him on the spot. He hadn't talked to Tamarra since the day outside of Family Café—since the day he'd broken off their engagement—but he didn't want to put their business on blast, nor did he want to be the one to tell Paige what was going on. He'd allow Tamarra to share that information with her best friend when she was ready.

He had an idea why Tamarra hadn't been in church. Perhaps over the past few days word had gotten back to her, and she didn't want to come to church and face the situation: the situation with him and Sakaya. The situation with him and—

"Sister Sasha, God bless you, woman of God," a bystander said as Sasha approached Paige, Blake, and Maeyl. She nodded, smiled, then walked up next to Maeyl.

"Honey, we're ready to go," Sasha practically whispered in Maeyl's ear. "Sakaya's getting restless." She looked down at her little girl, who was holding her hand. "You know how kids can get when church gets over."

Did she call him honey? Paige was thinking. She shook her head. She had to have been hearing things. She looked down and noticed the slight little tug Sasha was giving the bottom of Maeyl's suit coat. It was discreet, but Paige saw it.

"Give me a second; then I'll walk you two to your car," Maeyl told Sasha.

"But, Daddy, aren't you coming back home with us? Aren't you going to sleep at our house again?" Sakaya whined.

Sasha cleared her throat—loudly. "Come on, sweetie. Let's go thank Sister Helen for teaching you such wonderful things in youth children's church before we go." Sasha dang near dragged the little girl away before she could say anything else.

Maeyl stood there silently, staring down at the floor.

"Well, are you just going to stand next to that elephant and say nothing?" Paige spat after a few seconds.

"Elephant?" Maeyl had a confused look on his face.

Paige threw her hands on her hips—hips that she swore had already shrunk down an inch. "Yeah, the elephant. You know, the old English idiom also known as the obvious truth. Or in this case, Sasha!" Paige had gotten a little loud.

"Honey, calm down." Blake gently grabbed her arm.

"I think I am calm. More calm than I should be after seeing my best friend's fiancé—"

"Babe," Blake gritted as Paige now drew folks' attention. His grip on her arm was no longer so gentle.

"Ouch!" She looked down at the grip her husband had on her arm. It hurt. She didn't know how to feel about that. Perhaps Blake didn't realize he was hurting her. Surely he hadn't meant to squeeze her arm so tightly. So hard.

"Look, Brother Maeyl, if you don't mind, can you give me a ride home while Paige goes to see about Tamarra?" Blake smiled. He released Paige's arm as he charmingly walked over to Maeyl and put his hand on his shoulder, patting it gently.

"Uh, sure, yeah, that's not a problem. Let me just walk Sakaya and—" He looked at Paige then nervously back at Blake. "Let me just do something first. Meet me at my car in a couple minutes," he told Blake before walking away.

Blake turned his attention back toward his wife. "See, honey, everything is going to be fine. I'll talk with Maeyl on the way home to get his side of the story of what's going on. Just relax, okay?" He rubbed Paige's arms up and down while she still caressed the spot on her arm he'd practically crushed. He then planted a loving kiss on her forehead before walking away, but not before saying, "And don't you go sneaking off trying to go out to that buffet you and Tamarra love so much." He tapped his watch. "I'm gonna time you. Don't be more than an hour." He winked, but he wasn't joking. Paige could tell. There was someone else who could tell as well.

"Everything okay, Sister Paige?" a female voice asked Paige out of nowhere.

Paige turned to see Sister Nita slipping on her gloves, probably headed somewhere in the church to start cleaning. As the head of the Janitorial Ministry, Sister Nita saw to it that the church was spotless.

"Oh yeah, Sister Nita, I'm fine." Paige smiled.

"Is your arm?" Sister Nita asked knowingly.

Paige didn't like what Sister Nita was trying to insinuate. "Yes, all of me is okay, thank you very much."

"All right. Well, I was just checking." Nita paused as if she were waiting to take direction from someone. "You know if you ever needed anyone to talk to, I'm—"

"I think there is a clog in the women's bathroom that is calling your name, Sister Nita. Why don't you run off and go see about it."

Nita could take the hint. She smiled and nodded. "God bless you, Sister Paige. Enjoy the rest of your day."

Paige was immediately convicted for the way she'd just spoken to Sister Nita, but she hadn't appreciated one bit the way the woman had approached her. Paige looked around in what one might consider a paranoid way. She wondered what Sister

Nita had seen to make her approach her like that in the first place. She wondered if anyone else had seen the same thing. Obviously Sister Nita had jumped to the wrong conclusion, but Paige didn't have time to stand there and worry about it. She had to run to see what was going on with her best friend. She had to run from her own thoughts—thoughts that she knew mirrored Nita's to some degree.

Chapter Thirty-six

Tamarra had just finished packing and was carrying her suitcase down the steps when the doorbell rang.

"Ugh." She sighed and looked at her living room clock. It was after one o'clock, later than she had thought it was. Later than what she wanted it to be. "A drive-by," she said under her breath.

She'd planned to be on the road by now, gone before anyone from New Day came to see about her. She didn't know how many people had witnessed or heard about her collapsing outside of Family Café. She knew at least one had, because Pastor had called her up at the hospital the next morning after her fall with plans to come visit her. Tamarra convinced Pastor it wasn't necessary, and instead, they just prayed together over the phone. Pastor hadn't yet shared Tamarra's hospitalization with the church family. Pastor wanted to get all the details first before calling up folks and just telling them anything blindly. Tamarra had promised her pastor she'd call and give all the updates on her health and what was going on with her. And she planned to . . . once she returned.

Tamarra told Pastor she didn't want to worry her church family and have folks calling and coming by; instead she wanted rest. Pastor agreed. But Tamarra wasn't a fool. She knew someone who'd been up at Family Café and watched her get

hauled off on a stretcher had told someone. And that someone was probably the someone at her door now.

After creeping over to the door and looking out of the peep-
hole, Tamarra was somewhat relieved to see her best friend,
but she was also somewhat perturbed. She had a right mind
to let her stand out there, to leave her hanging the way she'd
left her hanging by not answering or returning her calls. Paige
hadn't answered her calls when Tamarra needed someone
to talk to, when she had the courage to tell someone everything—absolutely everything—for real this time. Neither her
nor Maeyl had been there. For that, Tamarra was bitter, but
still, not so bitter where she'd leave her best friend outside her
door knocking.

"Well, well, well, you've finally found the time to see if I
was over here breathing or not," Tamarra spat as she opened
the door.

"Tamarra, I'm sorry." Paige immediately apologized. "It's
just that you have no idea what these last few days have been
like for me. I—"

"What they've been like for you!" Tamarra shouted. "Tuh."
She walked away, letting go of the screen door that she'd been
holding open. It almost slammed in Paige's face. Luckily,
Paige caught the door with her hand and invited herself in,
following behind Tamarra.

"Tamarra, I . . ." Paige's words trailed off when she spotted
Tamarra's suitcase. "You're leaving?" Paige asked. "Where . . .
where are you going?"

"To Maryland," Tamarra answered, short.

"But Maryland? For . . . for how long?" Without giving
Tamarra time to answer, Paige continued in a panicked tone.
She was afraid she was about to lose her best friend. "Are you

sure this is what you want to do? Leave the state? I mean, I can understand you wanting to leave the church. I don't blame you, because I know how hard it would be for you to sit up in there Sunday after Sunday and see Maeyl and Sasha together. But you shouldn't–"

"Wait a minute. Hold up." Tamarra put her hand up to yield Paige's words. She grabbed her stomach with her other hand. It took her a couple of seconds to find her breath. Paige's words had knocked the wind out of her. "Maeyl and Sasha?"

"Yeah, girl, I realized that's what you've been calling me for, trying to tell me, when I saw them in church today." Paige mocked Sasha. She walked over to Tamarra and tugged at the bottom of her jacket the way Sasha had tugged on Maeyl's suit jacket. "Honey, we're ready to go." Paige rolled her eyes while sticking her tongue out in disgust. "Made me sick. And then like some ol' Stepford Husband, Maeyl walks her to her car. But what blew my mind was the little girl." Now Paige began to mock the words Sakaya had spoken. "Daddy, aren't you coming back home with us? Aren't you going to sleep at our house again?" Paige shook her head. "Come to think of it, I'm glad you weren't in church today. I probably would have had to pull you off that floozy the same way my husband dang near had to . . ."

Tamarra didn't know what Paige was talking about. Maeyl? Sasha? Tamarra was clueless about the entire Maeyl and Sasha thing. Paige's words had trailed off once Tamarra realized that everything she was saying was all new to Tamarra's ears . . . to her heart. Paige could tell by the blank expression on Tamarra's face.

"Oh my. . . . That's not why you were calling me, huh?"

Paige figured out. Tamarra didn't answer. She just stood there in shock, trembling. She was angry. She was hurt. Paige could see those emotions as well as a zillion others taking turns expressing themselves on her face. "Oh, sweetie," Paige said and walked over to comfort her friend. "I'm so sorry. I didn't know. I just assumed . . ."

"Wow," Tamarra said, staring straight on. "Wow. He calls our wedding off one day, and then he's right in her bed the next. I can't believe . . . I'm . . . I don't know what to say."

"Come and sit down." Paige led a stunned Tamarra over to the couch. "I'm sorry you had to find out this way about Maeyl and his baby's momma."

"That's why he did it. That's probably the real reason why he broke the engagement off, using me and my feelings for his daughter as an excuse. All the while it was because he was knocking boots with Sasha. Probably been sleeping with her since the day she so conveniently strolled back into his life. Once again, joke's on Tamarra." She smacked her hands upside her forehead . . . hard . . . harder.

"Stop it!" Paige said while grabbing her friend's hands. "Stop it right now." She held Tamarra's hands and prayed. "In the name of Jesus, Lord, we come to you—"

"You stop it!" Tamarra spat back. "I ain't thinking about praying. Praying has gotten me nowhere."

"The devil is a lie."

"And so are men. Liars, cheats, cheats and liars."

"I know how you must feel—"

"No, you don't," Tamarra snapped as she stood up. "No one does, nobody but God knows, and yet He just keeps piling it on." She looked upward. "'Here you go, Tamarra. You can take it. You can bear it. Here you go. Here's a little more poop to add to the pile.' Well, God, I can't take . . . any . . . more." Tamarra lost control of her breathing, so she quickly did her inhaling and exhaling exercise until she regained some semblance of control. The last thing she needed was to have another panic attack when she was supposed to be getting on the road. Speaking of the road . . .

"I gotta go." She headed for her suitcase.

"Wait. I can't let you leave like this, in this condition." Paige stood up and walked over toward her friend.

"I've gotta go. My folks are expecting me."

Paige stood erect and placed her hands on her hips. "Like I said, I can't let you leave like this. Now, sit down and calm down for a minute." Tamarra shot Paige a look as if to say if she didn't move out of her way, she was going to go through her. Paige countered with, "Look, God might have given me all this extra weight and big bones for a time such as this. Don't make me use it on you, girlie."

Tamarra could see that Paige meant business. She released the suitcase, stared at her friend momentarily, and just broke down and sobbed.

"Now, now," Paige said, hugging Tamarra. "It's going to be all right." The two friends stayed in their embrace while Tamarra shed every tear that felt the need to release itself. "You know as well as I do that God will put on us no more than we can bear. I mean, this whole diabetes thing, the diabetic coma, blackout, or whatever the doctors called it, I can handle it. And you can han—"

"Wait. What are you talking about?" Tamarra made an early exit from her own pity party to see about Paige. "Diabetes? Coma?"

"Yes, that's what's been going on with me the past few days.

Girl, one minute I was driving my car down the road, and the next minute I woke up in the hospital. Come to find I'd blacked out. My blood sugar had dropped. It was the scariest thing ever," Paige reminisced.

"My God, Paige. You should have called me."

"It had to register with myself first. And then Blake." A smile lit up Paige's face. "He's been consuming all my time. He's been more attentive than ever, just taking care of me and treating me like a queen. I was going to call you. I meant to call you. Then I figured I'd just see you at church and talk to you then." She took a quick breather. "God is good. He saved me from an accident that, if you could have seen my car, there is no way I should have lived. Yeah, I might have been diagnosed with a disease, but my God is a healer. All I have to do is walk in the healing; do the things I'm supposed to do as a healthy, healed woman of God. I'm starting with changing my diet."

"Well, I'm glad to see you're dealing with all of this just fine."

"Girl, I ain't dealing with nothing. God is dealing with me. I think He's using diabetes as a wakeup call for me. For me and Blake. Life is too short and too precious."

Tamarra thought for a minute. "Yes. Yes, it is." Her eyes watered.

"Best friend, what's going on with you? I mean, obviously you haven't been trying to get a hold of me the past couple of days to tell me about Maeyl and Sasha, because it was clear a minute ago that you didn't even know about them."

"You're right; I didn't. I mean, yes, we broke off the engagement, but no, I had no idea it was so that he could be with her."

"And I'm so sorry I wasn't there for you," Paige apologized. "But I'm here now."

Tamarra looked into her friend's eyes. "I'm glad you're here now." And she was glad Paige was there, but she wished she'd been there a few days ago, when she was lying in the hospital bed watching the news. When she'd had the guts, the nerve, and the courage to share exactly what she was going through. Even right now, she still could hardly believe what she'd seen on the news that day in the hospital. Suicide? She couldn't believe the girl was dead. She couldn't believe she had killed herself. She'd just talked to her only days before. Why hadn't she seen a sign? Maybe there was a sign but she hadn't wanted to see it. After all, she hadn't even wanted to see her. But after receiving the phone call from her distraught mother, Tamarra knew what she'd watched on television was true. And now here she was preparing for a six-hour drive to Maryland to go to the funeral.

"So, talk to me now, then," Paige insisted.

"I . . . I . . . it's nothing. It was just about Maeyl's and my wedding being off."

Paige studied Tamarra's face for a minute. "No, that's not why you were blowing my phone up. There's more."

Do I tell her? Do I not tell her? Tamarra swallowed hard. "Oh yeah, there was one other thing." Tamarra inhaled. "I kind of passed out at Family Café and it landed me in the hospital too." Tamarra exhaled. *Coward.* She couldn't tell Paige what she really wanted to tell her, about the girl . . . about the suicide.

"What happened?" Paige asked with concern.

"Just a little panic attack. It happened after my conversation with Maeyl. But I'm okay. Everything is good."

"What hospital were you at?"

"Mount Caramel East."

"Me too," Paige proclaimed. "Heck, we were probably there at the same time. I'm just glad that we are both okay." She looked at the suitcase. "But that still doesn't explain why you're all packed and leaving."

Tamarra looked over at her suitcase. "Oh yeah . . ." She stalled. "I, uh, I have to go back home. Things aren't good back at home. My family needs me."

Paige shot Tamarra a peculiar look. "It doesn't have anything to do with that brother of yours, does it?"

Tamarra didn't want to straight-out lie. "Just some stuff going on back at home." So she lied by omission. "I'll tell you about it when I get back." *Maybe.*

"When are you coming back? How long do you plan on staying gone?"

"Just a couple of days." Finally, the truth. She planned on coming back home the day after the funeral. She knew she wouldn't be able to bear being around her parents much longer than that because deep inside, she knew they blamed her. She could tell by the words her mother had spoken when she called her after learning of the death: "Did you hear? She's dead. My baby is dead. All she wanted to do was come there to be close to you. To come there to be with you."

Tamarra read between the lines and knew that in so many words, her mother was blaming her. Tamarra blamed herself. Something inside of her just couldn't stop thinking about whether things would have been different if she'd just accepted the girl, welcomed her with open arms into her life. But she couldn't. There had been just too much pain there and more wounds to open up. Even now that the girl was gone, the pain was still there. Tamarra had a gut feeling that the moment she arrived back in Maryland, the stitches that had barely held the wounds closed were about to burst wide open.

Chapter Thirty-seven

"Lynox, is that you?" At first, Deborah wasn't going to speak when she saw Lynox standing in line in front of her at the food court in the mall. She really didn't know what to say. She hadn't spoken to him since the day she broke things off with him. She decided to go ahead and acknowledge him, though, before he spotted her, because if he spotted her first, then he'd know that she had been deliberately avoiding him. The thing was, she didn't know why she was avoiding him. She didn't owe him anything. . . . Did she?

Lynox turned around upon hearing his name bellow from a familiar female voice. "Well, if it isn't Miss Lucas, soon to be Mrs. . . . Mrs . . . " he stated, snapping his fingers as if trying to recall Elton's last name.

"Culiver." She filled in the blank.

"So, how have you been?"

"Actually, I've been good. Blessed."

"That's good to hear." There was a pregnant pause. "Oh, by the way, I found a literary agent. Signed the contract last week."

"That's wonderful. Congratulations."

There were a few seconds of dry silence before Lynox said, "It's been a while, you know, since we've last talked."

"Yes, and much to my surprise, if I don't say."

"Excuse me?" Lynox wondered.

"Ummm, I don't know. I guess I just didn't expect you to give up so easily." She was only half joking. It was true that Lynox put the "P" in the word "persistent," and here this time around he'd let her go without a fight. Perhaps this was even more confirmation that she was meant to be with Elton. The fact that God was keeping Lynox, a.k.a. Mr. Temptation, far from her had to be a sign among the many others Deborah thought God was showing her. Yep, God had done everything in His holy power to keep Lynox's eyes, his mouth, and that voice of his far from her; that was, until now.

Lynox put his hands up in defeat. "Oh, the last thing I'd ever do is step on another brother's toes. When you said you were getting married, hey, you became hands off, both in the flesh, and certainly in my spirit. Shoooooooot, if I do end up in hell, it ain't gonna be because I was with another man's wife."

Deborah let her head drop in shame, knowing she'd been with another woman's husband. It was true that at first she had no idea Elton was a married man, so maybe God wouldn't hold that against her. But even after finding out he was married, she and Elton had finished what they'd started the other night when she got off the phone with Mother Doreen. Surely God would hold that against her. Why couldn't she see that ever since Elton had walked back into her life, she'd been slowly but surely going down the list of commandments as if in a race with time to break them all?

Lynox looked down at Deborah's vacant ring finger. "So, uh, have you two set a date? The wedding is still on, isn't it?" That last question was wishful thinking on Lynox's part.

Deborah followed Lynox's eyes down to her finger. She

hadn't been able to find the ring since snatching it off and throwing it. "Oh yeah. We're getting married just as soon as he gets his d—" Deborah cut off her own self. She was about to say "divorce." That was too much information to share with Lynox. Her sins were nobody's business but God's. "As soon as he gets . . . done, uh, having my ring sized. It's just beautiful, but it was a little too big," Deborah lied, still making her way down that engraved stone of commandments.

"Hmm, I see."

"Yep, and we're going to start our life together, or should I say finish our lives together, over in Chile. Everything is working out as planned."

"Whose plan?" Lynox questioned.

"Why, both of our plans, of course. Well, actually, it wasn't planned at all. Not really. It just all seems to be happening in divine order."

"Hmm, I see," Lynox repeated.

What did, "Hmm, I see" mean? Deborah wondered. Did it mean he wasn't buying it? She tried to read Lynox's face to see if he believed her. His mind really didn't even seem to be on her reply. She could tell by the expression on his face that his mind had already traveled toward its next inquiry.

"Are you sure you're doing the right thing?" Lynox just came out and asked, catching Deborah off guard to say the least.

"Puh—Pardon me?" She half smiled while tilting her head from left to right.

"Are you sure you are doing the right thing? Running off and marrying this man after a few weeks' whirlwind romance? I mean, I know it worked for Khloe and Lamar Odom, but come on, Deborah."

"Do I sense a little jealousy on your part?" Deborah asked,

somewhat offended that he was doubting her and Elton's relationship, one that he knew nothing about other than the
little bit she'd told him. That little bit wasn't enough for him
to judge their intentions.

"No, just concern," Lynox stated. He then moved closer in
to Deborah as if he was about to tell her something that he
didn't want people around them to hear. "God placed you in
my spirit, and He's never done that before, placed a woman
in my spirit so securely that she felt like she was a part of me.
No, I'm not up in church every Sunday. Heck, I'm not even
a member of the one I drop in on every blue moon. I don't
know the Bible like the back of my hand. As a matter of fact,
I have very few scriptures under my belt. I don't pay regular
tithes, and I can't speak in tongues. But what I can do is listen
to God and obey Him." Lynox looked Deborah dead in her
eyes. "Can you? Can you hear God telling you to do this? Is
this God's plan, or was it Elton's plan that you fell right into
like he probably knew you would?"

"How dare you insult my intelligence like I'm just some
high school girl being wooed by the school jock?"

"If it walks like a duck, and if it quacks like a duck . . ."
Lynox stated. He could see where his last comment had upset Deborah, as he watched her eyebrows furrow and her jaw
tighten. "Look, I'm sorry. It's not my intention to stand here
and insult you or your . . . fiancé." Lynox could hardly say the
word. "I just can't imagine God telling me one thing and then
telling you another about the same situation. One of us isn't
hearing Him clearly. And I guess since you're a saved, sancti-
fied, Holy Ghost–filled saint, then you're hearing Him a lot
more clearly than I am. So, forgive me if I offended you in any
way, okay?"

Deborah didn't know what to say. She didn't know what to think. Lynox had definitely given her some food for thought. Only thing is, she didn't want to think about it. Her mind had already been made up prior to running into Lynox.

When Deborah didn't respond because her mind was like a tornado of thoughts, Lynox took it as a sign that she wasn't ready to forgive him just yet. "Look, I wish you and Elton nothing but the best. Just be careful. I know Elton is suave and charming on the outside, but what about his insides? What about his heart? He left you once; what if he does it again? What if he's just playing you like a game of basketball? No pun intended."

Still, Deborah remained silent. She didn't want to entertain Lynox's perception about Elton.

"Excuse me, sir," the woman behind Deborah said to Lynox. "She's ready to take your order."

Both Deborah and Lynox had been in their own little world, forgetting that others were around. That's just how intense the conversation had been. Lynox turned to see that it was his turn in line. He then turned back to Deborah. "You go ahead. I've lost my appetite." He looked at Deborah for a moment and then gave her a hug.

She sniffed, inhaling Lynox's smell. It was so strong, so sincere. It scared her that a part of her didn't want him to let her go. What was up with that? She should have only had those types of feelings for her husband-to-be. Could it be that Lynox was . . . ? She cut off her own thoughts that she hoped had only been sparked by the words Lynox had spoken to her, not incited by her very own heart.

After a few seconds, Lynox released Deborah. "When you

get a chance, check out Jeremiah 17:9-10. It's one of the few scriptures I have under my belt." He winked. Then Lynox walked away from Deborah . . . forever.

Chapter Thirty-eight

Paige pulled up in her driveway after seeing Tamarra off to Maryland. It had been a little more than an hour and a half since she'd left Blake at the church to go see about her friend. Since the days of pigging out at The Golden Corral buffet were pretty much over, Paige contemplated what she would make for Sunday dinner. As she turned off her vehicle and exited, she rubbed her hands together, thinking it'd be even better if Blake had taken the liberty to cook for her. He had been at her beck and call lately. With the maid being off on Sundays, it wouldn't have surprised her if Blake had whipped up something special just for the two of them.

She fiddled around with her key ring until she came upon her house key. She stuck the key inside the lock, but before she could even turn the key, the door flung open.

"Where have you been?" Blake shouted. "It's been an hour and a half. I was worried sick about you." He pulled her tightly up against him then just as quickly pushed her away. "Where else did you go? Who were you with?"

Paige was a little caught off guard by Blake's reaction. Okay, a lot caught off guard. She knew he'd been doting over her the past few days, worried about her health and well-being, but now it was like he was taking it to the extreme. Paige paused for a minute, not replying to Blake. She had to see if he was for real.

"I tried your cell phone but didn't get an answer," he said seriously enough that Paige determined that he was definitely for real. "I couldn't find Tamarra's number, but I even called Norman up at your job, just to see if maybe you stopped by to check on things or something."

"You called Norman? Blake, but you knew where I was. You didn't have to go calling around town looking for me like I'm your runaway child or something." Paige's tone was pretty neutral, but she was a little agitated inside.

"I knew where you said you were going, but I'd asked you not to be any longer than an hour. After an hour went by, I called you and you didn't answer the phone."

Paige shook her head as if she could shake away the entire scene. She removed her purse from her shoulder and went to set it down on the countertop. After two steps, Blake grabbed her arm.

"So, why didn't you answer your phone?" Blake questioned. Paige looked down at her arm, then back up at her husband. She did this twice. The third time, she tightened her lips and shot daggers at Blake with her eyes. He released her.

Was Paige going crazy, or had this man put his hands on her in a not-so-gentle way twice already today? The same man who, for the first months of their marriage, she couldn't get to put his hands on her in any kind of way? Red flags were starting to go up. The spirit within Paige was starting to become vexed by whatever spirit it was that was calling itself taking over her husband.

"I left my cell phone in the car," Paige told Blake boldly, as if she were daring him to put his hands on her again.

"Well, you're lucky you came home when you did, because in about five more minutes I was on my way over there."

"Then it sounds to me like you are the lucky one." Paige puffed up her chest and threw her hands on her hips.

"Look, honey, no need to get defensive. It's just that I told you to be no longer than an hour, and when you were . . . I don't know . . . My mind just—" Blake took a deep breath. "Just don't let it happen again, okay, sweetheart?" Blake kissed Paige on the forehead. "What's for dinner?"

Paige couldn't believe the way Blake was turning it on and off. He'd changed since her car accident and diagnosis. He'd changed for what she thought was the better, but what she thought was the better seemed to be bringing out the worst in him. It was almost scary, and one thing Paige was not about to do was live in fear.

"Baby, sit down for a minute," Paige said to Blake. "Let's talk."

"Yeah, you're right. I'm thinking the same thing you are thinking." Blake walked over to the kitchen drawer and pulled out a notepad and pen. "We should write out a meal plan for dinner. We should plan our weekly meals in advance. That will help with your—"

"No, Blake, honey, we need to talk about us."

Blake set the pad and pen on the counter then walked over to the table and sat down. "What is it?"

Not knowing what else to do but get right to the point, Paige said, "Boo, it's you. You're changing."

"Wait. I'm confused. Isn't that what you wanted? I mean, I realize that I was neglecting you before the accident, and it took both the accident and your diabetes to get me to realize that I never want to take my time with you for granted ever again. I want to make sure I'm doing everything possible to keep you happy, to keep you here with me. To keep you healthy. And as your husband, I'm going to make sure I take good care of you. Just work with me, Paige. I can do this. Trust me. I took care of my father for years; I can take care of you. I won't do you like my mother did my father. I promise you I won't just . . . just . . ."

Paige's eyes had already filled with tears when she realized what was going on in Blake's head. Why, all of a sudden, he'd been acting so possessive and watchful. As he sat there rambling on, Paige could picture him as a three-year-old boy wondering why his mommy just picked up and walked away. She could see him missing out on school activities and playing with friends while he took care of his father. She could see the fear in his eyes of having to relive the nightmare all over again as an adult.

"I'm not your mother, Blake," Paige told him as the tears released themselves from his eyes. "And you're not that little boy who got left behind by the only woman he loved at the time. When I leave, you don't have to worry about whether I'm coming back."

Blake wiped away the tears caused by the pain of his past. He couldn't even look in his wife's eyes. Past memories were about to turn him into some kind of monster. Just the fear of losing Paige, of her never coming back to be with him, had triggered a reaction. It had triggered emotions he didn't even know he had inside of him.

"And I'm not your father either, Blake," Paige continued. "You don't have to wait on me hand and foot. I can take care of myself. I mean, I definitely need your support. I want your support. Baby, I love your support, but I have to be strong and walk in my own healing. God is a supernatural healer indeed, but at the end of the day, He expects me to change some things in the natural world and not just spiritual in order to take care of my body. And that's where you come in. I need you to stay on top of me, to hold me accountable." Paige grabbed Blake's hands and caressed them. "But I need you to do it lovingly."

Blake nodded.

"You put your hands on me today in a way that made me feel uncomfortable, first at the church, and then just a few minutes ago." Paige shook her head. "I'm not having that. You put me on a clock as to how much time I can spend with my friends." She shook her head again. "Nuh-uh. I'm not having that either. I've never been in an abusive relationship, but that doesn't mean I don't know what one looks like."

"Baby, I would never—"

"I know you would never, because I would never allow it. See, babe, I might be thick, and for years I might have even pretended to be okay with that, but I wasn't. And no one, not even you, knew that about me. I feigned a confidence that deep down inside I didn't really have. In other words, I faked it until I made it. And it took me almost losing my life because of this thickness to open my eyes. I don't want to die. I see why the comedian Mo'Nique lost all that weight. God has stuff for that woman to do on earth, and she wants to do it. She wants to be able to take her child to the amusement park and fit on the rides. I feel her. And just because she lost the weight probably doesn't mean that she really wasn't happy with herself. I'm just speaking for me. But guess what? Thick, skinny, or medium build, I know I'm a child of the King and undeserving of any type of abuse, be it physical, sexual, mental, spiritual, and whatever other type of abuse there is."

"You're right, honey, and it will never happen again. I'm

so sorry. I just . . . the fear of losing you the way I lost my mother—and my father, for that matter. It just triggered something in me. But I promise, it will never happen again."

"I know it won't, because we're going to go to Pastor for counseling. We're nipping that demon in the bud before he has a chance to fully rear his ugly head. Obviously there is something inside of you that you need to be delivered from and Blake, as long as that spirit dwells in you, there is always a chance that things could get worse. I love you, God knows I do, but it's not a chance I'm willing to take. Not when I know the same God, who by His stripes I am healed. You are healed too. So, I guess this counseling thing will be like what the doctor referred to as an oil change—preventative maintenance."

Blake stared into Paige's eyes. She was worried about what his thoughts would be about counseling, but then a smile spread across his lips.

"Baby," Blake said, "You da bomb-diggity."

"I know," she said, leaning over and kissing him on the lips. "So, I'll call Pastor and see when we can start our counseling sessions." She got up to go get the phone.

"No, wait. Don't." Blake grabbed her wrist. Not wanting her to think he was being aggressive, he let it go. "It's just that . . . why don't you call Pastor afterward?"

"After dinner?" Paige questioned.

Blake stood up with a sensual look in his eyes and said, "No, after dessert."

Paige's lips formed into a huge smile. "I'll get the whipped cream." She winked before the husband and wife enjoyed one another like never before.

Chapter Thirty-nine

When Tamarra pulled up to her parents' house, she couldn't believe all the cars that were parked in the driveway and in front of the house. She could never recall her parents having many friends. She couldn't recall them having any friends at all. As a young girl, she realized why after a while. Having friends around meant there was a chance the family secret could get out. Friends were sometimes nosy, meddlesome. Or sometimes a person could just get so close to another person that they'd be inclined to tell them all their secrets. Tamarra's parents didn't want to take that chance. So now, where in the world had they mustered up so many caring friends?

Tamarra turned off the car and sat for a moment. She had to get it together. She'd cried practically the entire way there. Her emotions were mixed with those of a pregnant woman and one going through menopause: they were unpredictable and all over the place. As if what she was about to face weren't enough, she had the bright idea to stop by Maeyl's apartment before hitting the expressway to Maryland.

When he had answered the door, what she really wanted to do was slap him across the face for being the man who made a fool out of her big-time for the second time in her life.

"I'm sorry," were the words he'd mouthed, knowing that Paige had run straight over to her house to tell her about him and Sasha. "I know Paige probably told you—"

"No, I want to hear it from you. I want to hear it from you, Maeyl," Tamarra had insisted.

"Can you step inside?" he offered, opening the door wide and stepping aside.

She shook her head. "That won't be necessary. All I need is to hear you say it, and then I'm on my way."

Maeyl swallowed and then told Tamarra what she'd come to hear. "Sasha and I are going to . . . we're, uh, going to try and, you know, raise Sakaya the right way. We're going to try to raise her as a, you know, couple." Maeyl coughed.

"Man up, would ya? Just say that you and Sasha are back together. Wow, after only what? Not even a full day after breaking off our engagement. And I really thought this was because of my feelings toward your little girl, while all along it was because you wanted to get back with your baby's momma."

"Now, wait a minute. That's not true. I didn't plan to go to Sasha's house that night, but after leaving the hospital, after seeing you in the arms of your ex-husband, you telling him how glad you were that he was there, I just felt . . ." Maeyl couldn't even describe the way he felt.

Tamarra was taken aback by this new revelation. "You mean you came to the hospital to see me?"

"Yeah, but when I got there, your ex was there. I recognized him from the few times he'd shown up at New Day with you back in the day. I waited outside the room for the right time to enter, but that time never came. And as I drove away from the hospital, I just kept seeing you in his arms, him being the one to comfort you, and the words I heard you speak to him. You were telling him how glad you were that he was there. I couldn't understand why you'd call him up there for support and not me. Then I realized that maybe you didn't feel the way about me like I thought you had. After all, you've just been so distant, like there is something you aren't sharing with me. I feel that if you love and trust me as much as you say you do, then there should be nothing you can't tell me. And I knew it wasn't the distraction of planning a wedding, because it wasn't like we were having this really big wedding or anything. Then on top of all that, your relationship with Sakaya. I just . . ."

"Edward keeps the books for Family Café. He just happened to be there when I passed out. I didn't call him to come see about me. It was you I wanted there," Tamarra wanted to say, but she didn't. She knew it was useless. On top of that, she was tired and defeated. Besides, Maeyl might not have been right about her and her ex, but he was right about so many other things.

Even so, there was still one thing she wanted to know. The woman in her needed to know. "Did you sleep with her?" she asked Maeyl. "Did you leave the hospital, run into Sasha's arms, and have sex with her?"

"Tamarra, does it really matter?"

She let out a nervous little laugh. "You're right. It doesn't matter, does it?" She touched his cheek. It was almost comical, because when she lifted her hand, he flinched as if she were going to deck him. But all she did was rub his face. She just wanted to look into his eyes and touch him one last time, because she knew that unless in passing, she'd never be that close to him again. She'd never be at his place again, and she certainly was never going to step foot in New Day again. She wouldn't be able to bear watching Sasha live the life with Maeyl that Tamarra had so badly wanted. Tamarra removed the engagement ring from her finger and gave it back to Maeyl. "Good-bye, Maeyl." Tamarra smiled, got in her car, and headed toward her parents' house.

Now here she sat parked in front of her parents' house, hesitating to go in, though she knew she had to. So, she got out of the car and walked up to the door. She raised her hand to knock, all the while her stomach doing cartwheels in anticipation of what awaited her on the other side.

"You must be Tamarra," an older woman said after she opened the door.

Tamarra peered over the woman's shoulders. "Yes, I am."

"Sister Evans has been expecting you. And, ooohhh, girl, you look just like your mother. My, my, my." She let Tamarra in the house, closing the door behind them. "She's, uh, your mother is in the kitchen. She's been keeping busy. I been telling her she needs to slow down and grieve properly; that way she ain't actin' a fool at the funeral tomorrow morning. You know what I'm saying?"

Tamarra just nodded as she followed the woman to the kitchen. She passed several people and assumed they were church friends. After all, this woman had referred to her mother as Sister Evans.

"By the way," the woman said before they entered the kitchen, "I'm Elder Butler, a member of Saints Alive, the church your mother attends here and there. She's been trying to get your father to come visit, figuring if he liked it and started coming, she could come more often. He never would come, though. Looks like he's got no choice now."

She opened the swinging kitchen door for Tamarra to see the back of her mother busy over at the refrigerator. She could tell that her mother had lost weight since the last time she'd seen her, and her hair was thinned out. She was wearing it in a salt-and-pepper bun, pulled tightly to the back of her head. But still, Tamarra could tell her hair wasn't as thick as it used to be.

"Sister Evans, look who's here," Elder Butler said with enthusiasm as though she were introducing Jesus himself.

"Huh? What?" Tamarra's mother said, slowly turning around. She looked as though she'd lost her breath when she laid eyes on her daughter. "Tamarra, honey, is that you?" She pulled her glasses down from the top of her head and squinted through them.

Tamarra gasped upon seeing her mother. She looked old. Well, she was an older woman, but she looked really old. Almost made a lie out of the cliché "Black don't crack." Tamarra couldn't believe the bags under her mother's eyes. Worry lines etched the outer corner of her eyes, eyes that were so sad. Crow's footprints sat at the corners of her mouth.

"Ma?" Tamarra said, not knowing what to do next. She and her mother had never been the touchy-feely type with one another, but considering the circumstances, Tamarra didn't know what else to do but go and embrace her mother. After all, she sure didn't know what to say to her.

Mrs. Evans opened her arms to receive her daughter's embrace. Tamarra was surprised at how good it felt being held by her mother. She closed her eyes. Her mind wandered back to her being a little girl. She pictured herself hugging a younger version of her mother, her mother kissing her on top of her head, and telling her she loved her. The two baked cookies and drank lemonade while they sat at the kitchen table talking about stuff—nothing in particular, just stuff. Stuff a mother would talk to her little girl about.

"Well, I'm going to leave the two of you alone," the women heard Elder Butler say before they heard the swishing of the swinging door.

It was Elder Butler's voice that brought Tamarra's thoughts back to reality. Now feeling a little awkward for some reason, Tamarra pulled away from her mother. "So, how are you doing, Ma?"

"As well as can be expected, I suppose," she said, closing the refrigerator door, forgetting what she'd been looking for in the first place. "I . . . I can't believe my baby is gone."

Tamarra cringed to hear her mother refer to the deceased girl as her baby. Try as she might, she couldn't recall a time her mother had ever referred to her as her baby.

"Raygene was so smart, so beautiful. I . . . I just wish you would have . . . at least gotten to know her." Mrs. Evans looked up at Tamarra with pleading eyes. "She really wanted to have a relationship with you, Tam—"

"Look, Mom," Tamarra said as she walked over to the kitchenette table and sat down. "I . . . I really don't want to get into all that. Not now. I just want to pay my respects and—"

"Pay your respects?" Mrs. Evans was on the verge of becoming indignant. "You act like she's just some old friend you went to elementary school with or something. Whether you like it or not, Raygene was your—"

"Mom!" Tamarra shouted. "Please, don't do this to me right now."

"If not now, then when?" Mrs. Evans asked. "I mean, she's gone now, for Pete's sake. What damage can claiming her now do?"

"Ma, you just don't understand."

"Oh, I understand just fine. You've been living a life as

if her father didn't even exist, so surely you've been living as though she didn't exist either." Mrs. Evans looked at her daughter with disdain and said those awful words any man or woman of God hates to hear: "And you call yourself a Christian."

She continued, "Well, I don't know what they teaching you at the church you attend in Ohio, but here in Maryland they teach love. They teach forgiveness. And poor Raygene never did nothing to you, so there wasn't nothing you needed to forgive her for. All you had to do was love her, and you couldn't even do that." Mrs. Evans shook her head.

Tamarra stood and said, "The nerve of you, woman. Who are you, of all people, to stand here and criticize me? All you had to do was love me, and you couldn't do that. Oh, but you loved her. You loved that . . . that monster's child." Tamarra didn't know where such evil words were coming from, but she couldn't stop them. "You raised her and took care of her and protected her far better than you ever did me. How do you think that made me feel? Huh, Mother, how?"

Now Mrs. Evans stood. "So, is that what this was about? You being jealous of Raygene? You jealous that I raised her? Well, what did you expect me to do? Someone had to take care of the girl." Mrs. Evans tightened her lips and stared right into Tamarra's eyes. "Her own mother sure didn't want to."

Tamarra got right up in her mother's face. "Can you blame her? Who wants to take care of a child that belongs to a rapist? Even worse, a child that was conceived through rape?"

"But it wasn't the child's fault. It wasn't Raygene's fault, Tamarra. Can't you see that? And all she ever wanted to do was have a relationship with her mother. That's all she ever dreamed of, talked about, ever since the day I told her that you were really her mother and not her aunt. That's why she came to Ohio. She wanted to be close to you. She figured if she was there, right in the same town with you, then you two would be drawn together. And then her dream would come true. That's all she wanted, Tamarra, was to be close to you . . . her mother." Tears trickled from Mrs. Evans' eyes.

"Stop it!" Tamarra yelled. "Stop it. Don't you dare put this on me. Once again, you're blaming me. Well, how about, for once, you place the blame on the person who it really belongs to? Raymond. All of this is his fault. If he'd never raped me, then I never would have gotten pregnant!" Tamarra shouted.

"Hold your voice down," Mrs. Evans ordered through gritted teeth. She looked to make sure no one was entering the kitchen.

Tamarra followed her mother's eyes to the kitchen door. "Oh, so you ain't told the good folks over at Saints Alive that your son raped your daughter, and that when your daughter told you about the rape, all you and Daddy did was a fake a divorce and live in separate houses so that my brother and I wouldn't be in the same house. So that he couldn't creep into my bedroom anymore. Then when your son got old enough and moved out on his own, you two suddenly reconciled. And did you tell them that not only did he rape me, but he got me pregnant? That I was just this young girl having a baby, a baby that tore the insides of me up so that I could never have another baby again? The only child I would ever carry in my womb was the one that belonged to that monster, my brother."

"But she wasn't a monster," Mrs. Evans spat back. "She was a baby: your baby! All the more reason why you should have taken care of her, showed her love so that she'd grow up knowing that she was loved. That's all she wanted was love . . . just like you. She didn't ask to be conceived the way that she was, but you insisted on singlehandedly punishing her for the way she came into this world by acting like she didn't exist. Acting like you're the only one in the world who deserves God's love." Mrs. Evans paused for a moment before continuing. "Well, God did love Raygene. She was His daughter, not some scar of Satan like you'd like to see her as, and one day you'll realize that you made a mistake when it came to that girl. Sure, I made many mistakes regarding the situation, mistakes that I can't take back, but the one mistake I didn't make was having the heart and decency to raise Raygene when her own mother wouldn't."

"Then you shouldn't have made me keep her," was Tamarra's comeback. Sure, she felt convicted by her mother's words, but her flesh still felt the need to justify her actions.

"Then you shouldn't have hidden your pregnancy for so long," her mother retaliated. "You were already three months by the time we found out. Besides, I know a woman of God like yourself is not suggesting we should have allowed you to get an abortion."

Of course, now Tamarra would never consider engaging in the act of abortion, but back then, as a young girl pregnant by her own brother, who's to say? "You ain't been saved but a month of Sundays, so don't you dare try to use God as a reason why you made me go through with that pregnancy. You and Daddy probably figured you'd been hiding everything else; surely you could get away with hiding my pregnancy too. Well, I guess you were right."

"No, we were wrong, because what we failed to realize is that we couldn't hide the child. She was here and there was nothing we could do about it, but you as her mother should have wanted—"

"I didn't want her. I didn't want her then and I didn't want her when she showed up on my doorstep. I'm glad she's gone. I'm glad she's dea—" Before Tamarra could even finish her words, a stinging slap came her way by means of her mother's open hand. The smack was so hard, striking part of Tamarra's face and her mouth, that it knocked Tamarra to the ground. Her mother may have been frail and old looking, but she had a punch like Ali in his prime.

"What's going on in here? I could hear you two all the way from the back bedroom," Tamarra's father roared as he entered the kitchen. Behind the swinging door were onlookers who looked too afraid to enter the ring.

Mrs. Evans stood trembling with her hands covering her face. Tamarra lay on the floor tasting the blood that was oozing from her bottom lip. Not knowing which woman to comfort first, Mr. Evans shuffled back and forth for a moment, then ran to the aid of his . . .

Chapter Forty

"Ah-ha! I caught you. I knew if I called your tail from a blocked number you'd pick up," Mother Doreen spat from the other end of the phone. "You been dipping and dodging me, so since I couldn't get a hold of you, I got a hold of Pastor."

Deborah sighed into the receiver. She knew what that meant. If Mother Doreen had spoken to Pastor, then surely by now she knew Deborah's plans to marry Elton.

"I hate to say it, but child, you've strayed. You've strayed from the Lord." Mother Doreen spoke sadly, sounding disappointed.

"Mother Doreen, that's not true. As a matter of fact, that's the furthest thing from the truth. I haven't missed a Sunday in church since I returned from my sabbatical."

Mother Doreen burst out laughing. It started off low; then it got louder and louder. It was as if someone were tickling her and she couldn't control the laughter. Deborah became frustrated.

"What's so funny?" Deborah asked.

"You." Mother Doreen continued to laugh for a few more seconds before she was able to calm down. "Whew, child. That was too funny. You almost sounded like a . . . sounded like a . . ."

"A what?" Deborah spat in anticipation.

"A Sunday-only Christian," Mother Doreen said seriously, not a chuckle remaining in her voice. "Talking about you ain't missed a Sunday in church. So what? The devil ain't either. He's sitting up in church every time the doors are open, so what does that say about you?"

"Well, I . . ." Deborah didn't have an answer.

"Exactly. Do you think just because you show up in church every Sunday makes you close to God? Humph. How many Bible studies you been to? I mean really been to, not just going so Pastor can see your face and think you are a dedicated Christian. How many times have you really gone to get deeper into God's Word? How many times have you cracked your Bible open in your own home in the last month?"

Now that Deborah thought about it, she couldn't remember the last time she'd cracked open a Bible outside of the church walls. Not in the last couple months anyway. She used to read the Word daily before ever even thinking about reading or editing an author's work. Heck, she didn't even know where her house Bible was. The one she used at church was in her Bible bag by the door, but she couldn't think off the top of her head where she'd last had her house Bible, or when she'd last read it.

"And I've talked to that little girl, what's her name, Sister Unique. The girl says she's been running the Singles' Ministry without you. Guess you got better things to do on Friday nights these days. Thank God Sister Lorain will be off her sabbatical next week."

Deborah had some reasoning for that one. "Technically, I'm not single anymore, so why should I have to be bothered by the Singles' Ministry?"

"Bothered by it? Is that what you call doing God's Kingdom work?" Mother Doreen was offended. "A bother?"

"I didn't mean it like that," Deborah explained.

"And what do you mean, you ain't single? The last I checked a person was single until they said 'I do.' So, since you got the mindset that you ain't single, then I hope you ain't doing things that people who think they ain't single do: you know, that thing that is reserved for married couples."

Deborah was silent. She figured no reply was better than a lie.

"In the name of Jesus!" Mother Doreen belted out. "Oh, child, you've strayed. You've strayed far from God. Oh, what must the Bridegroom be thinking? When you wed Christ, you promise to love, honor, and obey, not love, honor, and stray."

Deborah was so convicted that she felt a pain in her stomach, in her heart. She snorted back tears.

"Look, daughter," Mother Doreen lovingly said, "I'm going to pray for you. I'm going to fast and pray that God puts up a supernatural barrier of protection around you. I don't know all what's going on with you, but I do know that the Elton I knew was a good man. That don't mean he's supposed to be *your* good man. But it sounds like to me you've made up your mind. So, I'm going to pray, pray for you both, that God blesses you both and watches over you in Jesus' name."

"Thank you," was all Deborah could get out between the tears.

"So, uh, make sure you get international calling on that cell phone of yours and stay in touch. But I've got to go. I've got some praying to do. I love you, child."

"I love you too," Deborah said before they ended the call. She held the phone in her hands as her shoulders started to heave. She cried harder than she'd ever cried before. She didn't even know why she was crying. She concluded that it must have been the Holy Spirit within her crying out. She'd grieved Him. She'd grieved Him bad.

"You know we're going to miss you here at New Day," Pastor said to Deborah as they stood in the church foyer after service. You've been such a blessing to us here, especially with the Singles' Ministry."

"Ahem!" Unique walked up on the tail end of Pastor's statement and cleared her throat. In other words, she begged to differ.

"I know, I know, Sister Unique." Deborah smiled. "I kind of left you hanging there, and I'm so sorry."

"Oh, no worries." Unique swatted the air with her hand. "We didn't even have a meeting this month, because with Sister Tamarra being away on a family emergency, I had to be in charge of a catering affair for her that day."

"How's working with Sister Tamarra going anyway?" Pastor asked.

"Wonderful," Unique replied.

"That's good to hear," Pastor stated.

"Actually, better than wonderful," Unique assured Pastor. "Well, I need to go get my little angels from Children's Church." Unique gave Sister Deborah a hug. "I appreciate the help you did give me, though, and I'm going to miss you. But thank God Sister Lorain is back from her sabbatical. She and I can pick up where we left off."

"You most certainly can," Deborah said as Unique walked off, Deborah not knowing the half of where Unique and Lorain had left off. "Well, Pastor, I guess this is it." Deborah smiled and shrugged her shoulders.

"I guess it is." Pastor's arms were extended wide. "You know New Day will always be home for you. No matter what. No matter what situation or condition you are in, know you can always walk through those doors anytime." Pastor gave Deborah a knowing look that sent chills through her body.

"Yes, Pastor, I know." She nodded, hardly able to even look her pastor in the eyes.

"Give Elton my love," Pastor said, patting Deborah on the shoulder. "I'm sorry he couldn't join you today, but I know he's doing a lot of last minute things to make sure you guys are ready to leave the country in the morning."

"Yes, but he sends his love to you, Pastor. And I love you too." Deborah battled with the moisture forming in her eyes.

"Oh, go on and get out of here before I lock you in my office and make you miss your flight."

"Okay, Pastor. Good-bye."

"Good-bye. I'll pray for you. I'll be praying for you both," Pastor said, holding back tears. It always hurt Pastor to see a member of the New Day flock about to make one of the biggest mistakes of her life, knowing all that could be done was to cover them in prayer.

"Thank you, Pastor. I'm going to need it," Deborah said as she walked away and exited New Day, preparing herself for the days ahead.

Chapter Forty-one

"So, how was it filling in for my position while I was out this past week?" Paige asked Norman after returning to work. She hadn't seen or talked to Norman in the last week or so. Actually, she hadn't even thought twice about him, let alone having her head filled with nonsense fantasies about the two of them. That part of her life was over. Although it took some crazy turn of events, she now felt as though she really was living out a fantasy indeed: a real live fairy tale with her husband. No longer living in La-La Land, she'd made every fantasy she'd ever had with a man a reality, and with her own husband.

Paige realized that over the years, she might have been putting on a façade for the rest of the world about how she felt in her skin, but she couldn't fool God. He'd shaken up her world; that was for sure. Paige wasn't ashamed to admit that she blamed God for her diabetes, but in a good way. Had God not given Satan authority to curse her with the disease, a weapon formed against her, then she might have never come to terms with reality. God put her in a position that forced her to make the changes that allowed her to truly begin to love herself. When God's word said that no weapon formed against her would prosper, that included diabetes. It would not prosper in her life; oh, but how life itself would prosper.

She had a glow about her now, a shine that the world could see. She just had no idea that Norman would be blinded by the shine.

"Actually, I kind of liked being the man in authority," Norman replied. He looked at her almost seductively. "Now I know how you felt being the woman in authority. And although it was nice filling in for you, I like it better when you're in charge." He winked then continued to look her up and down. "Have you lost weight?"

"Oh, uh, yeah," Paige answered, a little thrown off by how strong Norman was coming on, but flattered by his compliment nonetheless. "Having diabetes has actually turned out to be a blessing. I'm losing weight. I feel good."

"You look good." Norman licked his lips as though he'd just eaten a piece of fried chicken.

Paige's eyes zoomed in on Norman's lips: his tongue slowly brushing across his top lip. She almost cringed. A couple of weeks ago she might have envisioned him looking like LL Cool J doing that, but today, she was disgusted. She shook the image from her head, bound and determined to stay on track, not to allow her mind to stray or be the cause of Norman's mind straying to a forbidden place when it came to her.

"My health is good too. To maintain my health in the spirit realm, I continue to confess what God's Word says about my health on a daily basis, such as the scripture Jeremiah 30:17." She thought that throwing God into the conversation would serve as a crucifix to a vampire. But she was wrong.

"Umph, umph, umph! Well, to God be the glory," he said.

Still bound and determined to stay on point, she said, "Yeah, and uh, there are also physical things I do along with reading and confessing and living by God's Word. Now that it's March and spring is practically creeping in, Blake and I have been walking every evening when he comes home from work." Maybe mentioning Blake's name would remind Norman that she was another man's wife.

"I try to tell women all the time that there is nothing like a good workout with a man." Norman winked.

Oh, goodness, Paige thought. Had she brought the beast back out in Norman? Had just a couple of weeks with harmless flirting cancelled out all she'd accomplished in changing Norman's worldly conversations and actions with her?

"Exercise is good." Paige still kept her thoughts and her mind on the path of righteousness. "Paul writes in 1 Timothy 4:8: *For bodily exercise profiteth little* . . . Well, my prayer is that I make the most out of that little. I mean, God, indeed, has a part to play in our health, but our part in keeping our temple healthy is just as important."

"I hear you. And I see you too."

It was obvious to Paige that Norman just wasn't getting it. Perhaps she would have to start back at square one and do what she'd done originally: invite Norman to New Day so that he could witness the God in her firsthand and back off. Then again, this time, why not just nip it in the bud herself?

"Look, Norman, I really appreciate you being there for me when Blake wasn't. You are a good friend—but that's all. I'm sorry if I led you to think otherwise, or that I looked at you in any other way. Right now, my focus is my husband and my disease."

It was funny to Paige, the expression that crossed Norman's face. She assumed it had something to do with the word "disease."

"Disease?" Norman said, looking Paige up and down, but

this time with a hint of disgust, as if Paige had just told him she had an STD or something.

"Yes, Norman, what I have is a disease in my body. Diabetes is a disease." Paige went on to school Norman a little bit about diabetes and how it was forcing both her and Blake to make a change in their lifestyle.

"I . . . I didn't know diabetes was so serious," Norman said.

"You could have died. You still could if you don't take care of yourself."

"You're absolutely right," Paige confirmed. She then went on to give him a little bit more information regarding the disease. By the time she finished the conversation, Norman and Paige had said a prayer regarding her health, and he'd promised to visit New Day on the upcoming Sunday to make sure he was still in God's good graces, so as not to be struck with a plague. Paige decided she'd wait until after he visited New Day to correct his thinking. For now, whatever it took to get him back up in church and prevent him from straying from God, so be it.

As Paige left the ticket booth, she laughed inside. Once again, her diabetes, instead of being used as a weapon against her, had allowed her to prosper in her situation with Norman. "God sure is good," Paige said out loud to herself, "all the time!"

Chapter Forty-two

Tamarra felt as though she'd been sitting out in the shivering cold all of her life and that a warm blanket had finally been thrown over her. That's the warmth and the comfort she'd longed to have felt. That is the warmth and comfort she felt as her father embraced her as if he were protecting her from a wild animal. That was the warmth and comfort she realized her only child had wanted from her.

Knees not as strong and as healthy as they once had been, Mr. Evans had managed to lower himself to the floor and wrap his arms around his wounded daughter. He knew that she was wounded not only on the outside, but on the inside too. He knew of those wounds she'd carried around for years, and he felt partially to blame. He hadn't protected her as a father should have when she was a little girl. He had done what parts of society might have considered the right thing then, when it came to the sexual abuse against his own daughter by his own son. He'd kept what went on in their house in their house, but he was going to protect her now.

Tamarra, for once, felt that her father had finally—finally—come to her rescue. Not only was he protecting her from the swinging fist of his wife, but from the swinging fist of life. That huge, powerful, invisible fist had been swinging at her since she could remember, knocking her down, and just when she'd gotten up and dusted herself off again, here came that fist to knock her down yet again. This love, this comfort, this sense of security and protection she was receiving from her father was a sort of healing balm. It was mending all her wounds.

For years Tamarra thought her father didn't love her. Didn't want her. He'd left her in order to be with and protect his other child. For Tamarra, that felt like a cycle she'd experienced with every man in her life. Her ex-husband left her and went off to be a family with his child. Maeyl had just recently done the same thing. It was a cycle, a curse that was being broken at that very moment in the name of Jesus.

Mr. Evans pulled himself away from Tamarra and held her at arm's length, the two of them sitting on the floor. He stared at her for what seemed like forever as tears rolled down his face. He shook his head in awe at what a beautiful daughter he had. He allowed his imagination to wander back to him, sitting there holding his crying daughter and comforting her the day she told him and his wife about what her brother had done to her. But he hadn't. Instead, he'd just walked away, went off to his bedroom to think of a quick fix to the situation without his son having to go to jail and without too much shame and embarrassment coming to the family. An hour later, he came up with the entire charade of him and his wife faking a divorce. At the time, it had felt like the right decision; of course, at the time, they hadn't known Tamarra was pregnant. The goal was to just separate brother and sister.

Upon finding out a couple months later that Tamarra was pregnant, he knew it had been the wrong decision. His actions had separated him from his daughter, and although they eventually ended up moving back into the same home together, their relationship remained severed.

But on this day, this very moment, before he met his maker, he was going to do what he should have done a long time ago. After looking Tamarra in her eyes for a few more seconds, he pulled her tight again in a bear hug. Just quiet enough for her ears to hear, but loud enough to penetrate her heart, he said the words, "I'm sorry. Daddy loves you. Please forgive me."

Tamarra had no idea that simply having her father hold her, telling her he was sorry and that he loved her, could play such a huge role toward her complete healing from the abuse she suffered as a child at the hands of her brother. And healing from the hurt she felt for the role she believed her mother and father had played in it. Strangely enough, Tamarra didn't even have to think on it, pray about it, or anything after her father had apologized. She immediately accepted by saying, "I forgive you, Daddy, and I love you too."

Before she knew it, her mother had joined them on the floor as well. There were apologies coming left and right. By the time they had gotten up from the floor, they'd each apologized to each other a dozen times at least, but the greatest thing was that they'd each said "I forgive you" at least a dozen times as well.

It was genuine, so genuine that not one of them cared about the fact that on the other side of the kitchen door a room full of people had just overheard the Evans family's deepest and darkest secret. Shockingly, they were glad the secret was out, that it had been overheard. It was as if all of them had been holding their breath for years, and now they were able to exhale . . . one big breath, all together.

As the three got up off the kitchen floor, they could hear intercessory praying going on on the other side of the door. They could hear praise-shouting and folks speaking in tongues. When they entered the room, the anointing was so high that Mrs. Evans received the Holy Ghost for the first time in her life.

It was the ringing of the telephone that brought a sudden silence to the room. The ring just seemed louder than usual. When Mrs. Evans walked over and answered it, it was obvious it was a collect call as she stared upon the onlookers and stated, "Yes, I'll accept the call."

Before her mother could even speak another word into the phone receiver, Tamarra, Spirit-led, walked over to the phone and removed it from her mother's hand.

"He-hello," she spoke into the phone.

"Tammy, is that you?" the voice on the other end of the line asked.

"Yes, Raymond, it's me. It's your baby sister," she replied. "I'm sorry about Raygene." Tamarra burst out crying. "I'm sorry about your daughter." She then swallowed hard and without shame said, "I'm sorry about our little girl."

Mr. Evans and a couple of visitors had to run over to Mrs. Evans' aid as she dang near passed out and lost consciousness, but not before hearing her daughter speak into the phone receiver, "I forgive you . . . brother." She regretted not making the right choice that day Raygene came to her house, so that she could have possibly heard those very same words directed at herself: "I forgive you . . . mother."

The next morning, repenting, rejoicing and restoration was the atmosphere at Raygene's funeral. It was so very unfortunate that it had taken Raygene's death to bring about true and complete healing to the Evans family. They no longer had to walk on eggshells and live a lie. Not only had they lived a lie regarding Tamarra's rape by her brother, but they'd hidden the fact that she'd had a baby as a result of the rape. Mrs. Evans had raised the child as her granddaughter, but her son's daughter, not Tamarra's. Tamarra had wanted nothing to do with Raygene, so that was one secret Tamarra hadn't resented her parents for keeping. Come to find out, it had been a secret they'd resented her for keeping.

All of that was in the past now. God showed up and showed out. For Tamarra, it was proof that when God says He will move the heavens and the earth for His will to be done, He ain't playing.

Now it was two days after the funeral, and Tamarra was driving back to Ohio. She'd decided that upon arriving back in Ohio, she was going to meet with her pastor and officially, decent and in order, withdraw her membership from New Day Temple of Faith. She was also going to share with her pastor her truths . . . all of them. The pastor had been there for her so much and for so many years that she just felt her leader deserved to know the person she really was.

After that, on the following Sunday, she planned to start her journey of finding a new place to worship. It wasn't that there was anything wrong with New Day, the church she'd been a member of going on eleven years. It was just that for Tamarra, it was literally a new day for her. She wanted to enter into a new season, new beginnings, and a fresh start. With the help of God Himself and the strength of Jesus Christ, that's just what she was going to do. To God be the glory!

Chapter Forty-three

Deborah and Elton had been on their plane to Chile for over an hour. Elton sat next to her in their first class seats, fast asleep. Deborah couldn't sleep if she wanted to. She had far too much on her mind. She shifted in her seat and then decided to close her eyes and force herself to sleep. Her eyes might as well have been open, as she was fully alert, too focused on all the thoughts fluttering through her mind. She suddenly opened her eyes and looked down at her carry-on bag. She could see the burgundy edge of her Bible and the golden edges of the pages. Her Bible seemed to be calling her name. She picked it up and opened it to a random page, no particular chapter or scripture.

"Hmm, Jeremiah 17:9-10," she said to herself. That scripture rang a bell for some reason, so she read it softly to herself: *"The human heart is most deceitful and desperately wicked. Who really knows how bad it is? But I know! I, the LORD, search all hearts and examine secret motives. I give all people their due rewards, according to what their actions deserve."*

Why had she turned to this particular passage? Was God trying to tell her something? She looked over at Elton, who, at that moment, let out a loud, disgusting snore. Deborah cringed. She always did hate that. Oh well, seemed as though she'd have to get used to it.

Deborah read the scripture again and again. She just couldn't seem to move past that scripture. Closing her Bible, Deborah looked over at a sleeping Elton once again. He looked so peaceful, so kind, gentle, and loving. He had the innocence of a child—at least on the outside anyway. For some reason, she couldn't get that scripture out of her head. Then it hit her: Lynox had given her that scripture to read, but she hadn't. And now God Himself had all but pulled out her Bible for her and turned directly to the scripture. She was convinced; God was definitely trying to tell her something. Perhaps He was trying to tell her what was in Elton's heart, if he was sincere in everything he'd told her since returning to Malvonia.

She then looked down at her engagement ring that Elton had given back to her the day before after finding it. She'd been sitting at her computer holding her stomach that was doing cartwheels. She'd been so full of doubt about leaving the country and starting a new life with Elton. Then he had come in the house with that beautiful ring fit for the bride of a rock star, and he'd proposed again, down on one knee. She couldn't give up the dream, could she?

Besides that, Deborah had gone too far to turn back now. She looked out of the airplane window, thousands of feet up in the sky. Literally, she'd gone too far to turn back now. She wasn't going to be humiliated again by going back to Malvonia without Elton as her husband. She looked down at her stomach and rubbed it. And she certainly wasn't going back as an unwed mother . . . again. She had to do it this time no matter what. She had to stay with Elton and see to it that the two of them became husband and wife, no matter if Elton was married or not. No matter how long it took for his divorce to be final. No matter what his intentions with her truly were. She was carrying his baby. Once again, he didn't know it yet, but if his heart reflected his outside, he would be able to do nothing but rejoice. That's what Deborah prayed for, anyway, as she closed her eyes in an attempt to fall off into a deep, restful sleep, knowing that the next time she opened them, she'd be on new soil, starting her new life, eventually with her new husband . . . and her new baby.

Readers' Group Guide Questions

1) Do you think there are other women like Tamarra: women who get involved with men with children, but are secretly jealous of the children?

2) Would you categorize Lynox as persistent, or as a stalker?

3) In your opinion, did Blake play any role in Paige's infidelity?

4) Do you think Deborah and Lynox's cyber-relationship was unholy?

5) Even though Deborah and Lynox had initially met in person, they used the Internet to get to know each other on a more intimate level. Do you classify this in the arena of cybersex? How do you feel about cyber-relationships? Have you or anyone you know met someone over the Internet and had a successful relationship?

6) Deborah wouldn't allow Lynox to talk negatively about Helen, even though she and the woman weren't the best of friends. What does that say about her spiritual maturity? Do you cut people off when they try to run someone

else in the ground, even if you aren't the best of friends with the person, or do you just listen?

7) Do you believe it's possible for a man to suffer the same way the mother does as a result of his child being aborted?

8) Deborah felt that by marrying Elton, she was going back in time to wipe her slate clean. Do you agree with her mindset, or do you feel that her slate was already cleaned by the blood of Jesus when He died on the cross?

9) Paige wasn't really happy with the skin she was in, which led to depression and mind games. Do you think God uses diseases such as diabetes to get someone's attention, to make them change for the better, like it did for Paige? Or do you believe things like diseases are works of Satan? Explain.

10) Do you feel that Deborah made the right decision when it came to Lynox and Elton? Why or why not?

11) Will Maeyl truly be happy in his relationship with Sasha? Why or why not?

12) Do you feel as though Mother Doreen made the right decision by not trying to talk Deborah out of her decision, but instead deciding to just pray for her? Why or why not?

13) Are there any New Day Divas characters that you feel are washed up, that their storyline is no longer interesting?

About the Author

E.N. Joy is the author of *Me, Myself and Him*, which was her debut work in the Christian Fiction genre. Formerly a secular author writing under the names Joylynn M. Jossel and JOY, when she decided to fully dedicate her life to Christ, that meant she had to fully dedicate her work as well. She made a conscious decision that whatever she penned from that point on had to glorify God and His Kingdom.

The New Day Divas series was incited by her publisher, Carl Weber, but birthed by the Holy Spirit. God used Mr. Weber to pitch the idea to E.N. Joy, to sort of plant the seed in her spirit, over which she prayed. Eventually the seed was watered and grew into a phenomenal five-book series that she is sure will touch readers across the world.

"My goal and prayer with the New Day Divas series is to put an end to the Church Fiction versus Christian Fiction dilemma," E.N. Joy states, "and find a divine medium that pleases both God and the readers."

With book one, *She Who Finds a Husband*, launching the series, and then book two, *Been There, Prayed That*, readers agreed that this project is one that definitely glorifies God in

About The Author

every aspect, but still manages to display in a godly manner that there are "Church Folks" (church fiction) and then there are "Christian Folks" (Christian fiction) and come Sunday morning, they all end up in the same place.

E. N. Joy currently resides in Reynoldsburg, Ohio, where she is continuing work on the New Day Divas series, as well as working on the Sinners series, which includes the anthologies *Even Sinners Have Souls*, *Even Sinners Have Souls TOO*, and *Even Sinners STILL Have Souls*.

You can visit the author at www.enjoywrites.com or e-mail her at enjoywrites@aol.com to share with her any feedback from the story, as well as any subject matters you might want to see addressed in future New Day Divas books.

Trying to Stay Saved

New Day Divas Series Book Four

Lorain is back from her sabbatical, and although God didn't reveal to her all that she wanted Him to regarding her past, she refuses to just let things be. When all the pieces of the puzzle begin to come together, just how many lives will be damaged, and how many will be restored?

The survivor of one of the most horrific experiences a person could ever endure, it appeared as though Sister Nita, as leader of New Day's Janitorial Ministry, was hiding behind a mop and a broom. When her spirit discerns a cover up amongst a couple at New Day Temple of Faith, will she turn a blind eye and mind her own business, or will she finally begin to operate in her true calling?

Mother Doreen knows who she is and whose she is; a child of the King on assignment doing Kingdom work. When the plot thickens to a story she thought God had closed the book on, will she forget who she is and what she was called to do?

The New Day Divas series, known as the soap opera in print, is full of chance, coincidence and fate. But more importantly, it's full of faith.

ORDER FORM
URBAN BOOKS, LLC
78 E. Industry Ct
Deer Park, NY 11729

Name: (please print):_____

Address: _____

City/State: _____

Zip: _____

QTY	TITLES	PRICE
	A Man's Worth	$14.95
	Abundant Rain	$14.95
	Battle Of Jericho	$14.95
	By The Grace Of God	$14.95
	Dance Into Destiny	$14.95
	Divorcing The Devil	$14.95
	Forsaken	$14.95
	Grace And Mercy	$14.95
	Guilty & Not Guilty Of Love	$14.95
	His Woman, His Wife His Widow	$14.95
	Illusions	$14.95
	The LoveChild	$14.95

Shipping and handling - add $3.50 for 1st book, then $1.75 for each additional book.
Please send a check payable to:
Urban Books, LLC
Please allow 4 - 6 weeks for delivery

ORDER FORM
URBAN BOOKS, LLC
78 E. Industry Ct
Deer Park, NY 11729

Name:(please print):_____

Address: _____

City/State: _____

Zip: _____

QTY	TITLES	PRICE
	16 ½ On The Block	$14.95
	16 On The Block	$14.95
	Betrayal	$14.95
	Both Sides Of The Fence	$14.95
	Cheesecake And Teardrops	$14.95
	Denim Diaries	$14.95
	Happily Ever Now	$14.95
	Hell Has No Fury	$14.95
	If It Isn't love	$14.95
	Last Breath	$14.95
	Loving Dasia	$14.95
	Say It Ain't So	$14.95

Shipping and handling - add $3.50 for 1st book, then $1.75 for each additional book.
Please send a check payable to:
Urban Books, LLC
Please allow 4 - 6 weeks for delivery

ORDER FORM
United Brothers, LLC
PO Box 3045
Farmingdale, NY 11735

Name:(please print):_____

Address: _____

City/State: _____

Zip: _____

QTY	TITLES	PRICE
	The Cartel	$14.95
	The Cartel#2	$14.95
	The Dopeman's Wife	$14.95
	The Prada Plan	$14.95
	Gunz And Roses	$14.95
	Snow White	$14.95
	A Pimp's Life	$14.95
	Hush	$14.95
	Little Black Girl Lost 1	$14.95
	Little Black Girl Lost 2	$14.95
	Little Black Girl Lost 3	$14.95
	Little Black Girl Lost 4	$14.95

Shipping and handling - add $3.50 for 1st book, then $1.75 for each additional book.

Please send a check payable to:

United Brothers, LLC

Please allow 4 - 6 weeks for delivery

ORDER FORM
URBAN BOOKS, LLC
78 E. Industry Ct
Deer Park, NY 11729

Name: (please print): _____

Address: _____

City/State: _____

Zip: _____

QTY	TITLES	PRICE

Shipping and handling - add $3.50 for 1st book, then $1.75 for each additional book.
Please send a check payable to:
Urban Books, LLC
Please allow 4 - 6 weeks for delivery

Notes

Notes